D0312443

THE NOVEL

VAL EMMICH
WITH THE CREATORS OF THE HIT SHOW
STEVEN LEVENSON,
BENJ PASEK & JUSTIN PAUL

POPPY
LITTLE, BROWN AND COMPANY
New York Boston

Poppy
Hachette Book Group
1290 Avenue of the Americas, New York, NY 10104
Visit us at LBYR.com

Originally published in hardcover and ebook by Little, Brown and Company in October 2018
Media Tie-In Edition: August 2021

Poppy is an imprint of Little, Brown and Company. The Poppy name and logo are trademarks of Hachette Book Group, Inc.

The publisher is not responsible for websites (or their content) that are not owned by the publisher.

Library of Congress Cataloging-in-Publication Data
Names: Emmich, Val, author. | Levenson, Steven, 1984– author. | Pasek, Benj, author. | Paul, Justin, author.
Title: Dear Evan Hansen : the novel / Val Emmich with Steven Levenson, Benj Pasek & Justin Paul.
Description: First edition. | New York ; Boston : Little, Brown and Company, 2018. | "Poppy." | Summary: Evan goes from being a nobody to everyone's hero and a social media superstar after a chance encounter with Connor just before his suicide leads others to believe Evan was his only friend.
Identifiers: LCCN 2018023821| ISBN 9780316420235 (hardcover) | ISBN 9780316420228 (ebook) | ISBN 9780316420464 (library edition ebook)
Subjects: CYAC: Popularity—Fiction. | High schools—Fiction. | Schools—Fiction. | Social media—Fiction. | Suicide—Fiction.
Classification: LCC PZ7.1.E475 De 2018 | DDC [Fic]—dc23
LC record available at https://lccn.loc.gov/2018023821

ISBNs: 978-0-316-31659-0 (media tie-in), 978-0-316-42022-8 (ebook)

Printed in the United States of America

LSC-C

Printing 1, 2021

DEAR EVAN HANSEN

THE NOVEL

I made my exit.

Better to burn out, right, than to fade away? Kurt Cobain
said that in his letter. I watched a video about all the famous
ones. Ernest Hemingway. Robin Williams. Virginia Woolf.
Hunter S. Thompson. Sylvia Plath. David Foster Wallace. Van
Gogh. I'm not comparing myself—trust me. Those people
actually made an impact. I did nothing. I couldn't even write
a note.

Burning is the right way to paint it. You feel yourself getting
so hot, day after day. Hotter and hotter. It gets to be too much.
Even for stars. At some point they fizzle out or explode. Cease
to be. But if you're looking up at the sky, you don't see it that
way. You think all those stars are still there. Some aren't. Some
are already gone. Long gone. I guess, now, so am I.

My name. That was the last thing I wrote. On another kid's
cast. Not quite a goodbye note. But hey, I made my little mark.
On a broken limb. Seems about right. Poetic if you think about
it. And thinking is just about all I can do now.

PART ONE

CHAPTER 1

Dear Evan Hansen,

That's how all my letters begin. First the *Dear* part, because that's just what you write at the top of any letter. That's standard. Next comes the name of the person you're writing to. In this case, it's me. I'm writing to myself. So, yeah, *Evan Hansen.*

Evan is actually my middle name. My mom wanted me to be Evan and my dad wanted me to be Mark, which is his name. My dad won the battle, according to my birth certificate, but my mom won the war. She has never called me anything other than Evan. As a result, neither has my dad. (Spoiler alert: My parents are no longer together.)

I'm only Mark on my driver's license (which I never use), or when I'm filling out job applications, or when it's the first day of school, like today. My new teachers will call out "Mark" during attendance, and I will have to ask each one to please call me by my middle name. Naturally, this will have to be done when everyone else has vacated the room.

There are a million and ten things from the subatomic to the cosmic that can rattle my nerves on a daily basis, and one of those things is my initials. M.E.H. Like the word: *meh. Meh* is basically a shoulder shrug, and that pretty much sums up the reaction I get from society at large. As opposed to the surprise of *oh.* Or the wow of *ah.* Or the hesitation of *uh.* Or the confusion of *huh. Meh* is pure indifference. Take it or leave it. Doesn't matter. No one cares. Mark Evan Hansen? *Meh.*

But I'd rather think of myself as *eh,* which is more like seeking approval, waiting for confirmation. Like, *How about that Evan Hansen,* eh?

My mom says I'm a true Pisces. The symbol for a Pisces is two fish tied together trying to swim in opposite directions. She's into all that astrology crap. I installed an app on her phone that displays her daily horoscope. Now she'll leave me handwritten messages around the house, saying things like: *Step outside your comfort zone.* Or she'll cram the day's message into our conversations: *Take on a new challenge. A business venture with a friend looks promising.* It's all nonsense if you ask me, but I guess, for my mom, her horoscopes give her some hope and guidance, which is what my letters are supposed to give me.

Speaking of which. After the greeting comes the actual meat of the letter: the body. My first line is always the same.

Today is going to be an amazing day, and here's why.

Positive outlook yields positive experience. That's the basic concept behind this letter-writing assignment. I tried to get out of it at first. I told Dr. Sherman, "I don't think a letter to myself is going to help much. I wouldn't even know what to write."

He perked up, leaning forward in his leather chair instead of casually sitting back as he usually did. "You don't have to know. That's the point of the exercise. To explore. For example, you could start with something like, 'Today is going to be an amazing day, and here's why.' Then go from there."

Sometimes I feel like therapy is total bullshit, and other times I think the real problem is that I can never get myself to fully buy in.

Anyway, I ended up taking his advice—verbatim. (One less thing to think about.) Because the rest of the letter is tricky. The first line was just an opening statement, and now I have to support that statement in my own words. I have to prove *why* today is going to be an amazing day when all evidence suggests otherwise. Every day that came before today was definitely not amazing, so why would I think today would be any different?

Truth? I don't. So, it's time to power up my imagination, make sure that every single molecule of creativity is wide awake and pitching in. (It takes a molecular village to write an *amazing* pep talk.)

Because today all you have to do is just be
yourself. But also confident. That's important.
And interesting. Easy to talk to. Approachable.
And don't hide, either. Reveal yourself to others.
Not in a pervy way, don't disrobe. Just be you—
the true you. Be yourself. Be true to yourself.

The true me. What does that even mean? It sounds like
one of those faux-philosophical lines you'd hear in a black-
and-white cologne commercial. But okay, whatever, let's not
judge. As Dr. Sherman would say, we're here to explore.

Exploring: I have to assume this "true" me is better at life.
Better at people. And less timid, too. For example, I bet he
never would've passed up the chance to introduce himself to
Zoe Murphy at the jazz band concert last year. He wouldn't
have spent all that time deciding which word best captured his
feelings about her performance but also didn't make him come
off like a stalker—*good, great, spectacular, luminescent, enchant-
ing, solid*—and then, after finally settling on *very good*, end up
not speaking to her at all because he was too worried his hands
were sweaty. What difference did it make that his hands were
sweaty? It's not like she would've demanded to shake his hand.
If anything, it was probably *her* hands that were sweaty after
all that guitar playing. Besides, my hands only got sweaty after
I thought about them getting sweaty, so if anything I *made*
them get sweaty, and obviously this "true" Evan would never
do something so profoundly sad.

Great, I'm doing it again, willing my hands to get sweaty.

Now I have to wipe down my keyboard with my blanket. And I just typed out *csxldmrr xsmit ssdegv*. And now my arm is sweating, too. The sweat will end up sitting under my cast, no air getting in, and soon my cast will take on that smell, the kind of smell I don't want anyone at school to catch even the slightest whiff of, especially on the first day of my senior year.

Damn you, fake Evan Hansen. You really are exhausting.

Deep breath.

I reach into my bedside drawer. I already took my Lexapro this morning, but Dr. Sherman says it's fine to take an Ativan, too, if things get really overwhelming. I swallow the Ativan down, relief on the way.

That's the problem with writing these letters. I start off on a direct route, but I always end up taking detours, wandering into the sketchy neighborhoods of my brain where nothing good ever happens.

"So you just decided not to eat last night?"

It's my mom, standing over me, holding the twenty-dollar bill I didn't use.

I shut my laptop and shove it under my pillow. "I wasn't hungry."

"Come on, honey. You need to be able to order dinner for yourself if I'm at work. You can do it all online now. You don't even have to talk to anyone."

But see, that's not true, actually. You have to talk to the delivery person when they come to the door. You have to stand there while they make change and they always pretend like they don't have enough singles, so you're forced to decide on the spot whether to tip less than you planned or more, and if you tip less, you know they'll curse you under their breath as they walk away, so you just tip them extra and you end up poor.

"Sorry," I say.

"Don't be sorry. It's just, this is what you're supposed to be working on with Dr. Sherman. Talking to people. Engaging. Not avoiding."

Didn't I just write that exact thing in my letter? About revealing myself? Not hiding? I know all this already. I don't need her to keep repeating it. It's like the sweaty-hands thing; the more you acknowledge the problem, the worse it gets.

Now she's circling my bed, arms crossed, scanning the room like it's somehow different from when she was last in here, like there's a new answer to the great Evan conundrum waiting on my dresser or hanging on my wall that she can finally find if she looks hard enough. Believe me, considering how much time I spend in this room, if the answer were in here, I would have spotted it already.

I slide my legs off the bed and pull on my sneakers.

"Speaking of Dr. Sherman," she says. "I made you an appointment with him for this afternoon."

"Today? Why? I'm seeing him next week."

"I know," she says, staring down at the twenty in her hands. "But I thought maybe you could use something a little sooner."

Because I chose to skip dinner one night? I should have just pocketed the money so she wouldn't have known, but that would be like stealing from her, and karma's a bitch.

Maybe it's more than just the unused twenty. Maybe I'm giving off an extra-worrisome vibe that I'm unaware of. I stand up and check myself in the mirror. I try to see what she sees. Everything looks to be in order. Shirt buttons are lined up. Hair has been tamed. I even took a shower last night. I haven't been taking as many showers lately because it's such a pain to have to cover my cast, first with the plastic wrap, then the shopping bag and duct tape. It's not like I get dirty anyway. Ever since breaking my arm, I basically just sequester myself in my room all day. Besides, nobody at school will be paying attention to how I look.

There's something else happening in the mirror that I'm only noticing now. I'm biting my nails. I've been biting them this whole time. Okay, the truth is I've been dreading this day for weeks. After the safe isolation of summer, returning to school always feels like sensory overload. Watching friends reunite with their bro hugs and high-pitched screeches. The cliques forming in corners as if all parties had been notified in advance where to meet. Bent-over laughter at what must have been the funniest joke ever told. I can navigate my way through all that because it's familiar to me by now. It's the stuff I can't predict that concerns me. I barely had a handle on the way things were last year, and now there will be so much newness to absorb. New wardrobes, tech, vehicles. New hair styles, colors, lengths. New piercings and tattoos. New couples. Whole new sexual orientations and gender identities. New classes, students, teachers. So much change. And everyone just marches on like nothing's different, but for me, every new year feels like starting from zero.

My mom is also visible in my mirror, the tassel of her personalized key chain dangling from her pocket. (Over the years, I've elevated many crummy gifts—mugs, pens, phone cases—by simply slapping *Mom* or *Heidi* on there somewhere). Poking around my room in her scrubs, she looks more like a forensic scientist than a nurse. A very tired forensic scientist. She was always "the young mom," because she had me right after college, but I'm not sure the title still applies. Lately there's this permanent fatigue in her eyes that seems less to do with how much sleep she manages to squeeze in each night and more to do with her finally starting to look her age.

"What happened to all your pins?" she says.

I turn and face the map on the wall. When I started working at Ellison State Park this summer, I got into the idea of trying to hike all the best trails in the country: Precipice Trail in Maine, Angel's Landing in Utah, Kalalau Trail in Hawaii, Harding Icefield in Alaska. I had them all marked on my map with different colored pins. But after how the summer ended, I decided to take them all down—except one.

"I thought I'd focus on one at a time," I say. "The first one I'm hoping to do is West Maroon Trail."

"And that's in Colorado?" my mom asks.

She can see it on the map, but still, she needs confirmation. I give it to her. "Yes."

The breath she takes is painfully showy. Her shoulders practically lift up and touch her ears before they drop down even lower than they hung before. Colorado is where my dad lives. *Dad* is a word you have to be careful about using in our house, and the same goes for any word that makes you think of my dad, like *Mark* or, in this case, *Colorado.*

Mom turns away from the map and presents me with a face that is meant to be brave and carefree but looks exactly not those things. She's wounded but still standing. That makes two of us. "I'll pick you up right after school," she says. "Have you been writing those letters Dr. Sherman wants you to do? The pep talks? You really have to keep up with those, Evan."

I used to write a letter every single day, but over the summer I slacked off. I'm pretty sure Dr. Sherman told my mom, which is why she's been nagging me about them lately. "I was just working on one," I tell her, relieved to not have to lie.

"Good. Dr. Sherman is going to want to see it."

"I know. I'll finish it at school."

"Those letters are important, honey. They help you build your confidence. Especially on the first day of school."

Ah, yes. Another clue for why she thought today in particular warranted a visit to Dr. Sherman.

"I don't want another year of you sitting home alone on your computer every Friday night. You just have to find a way to put yourself out there."

I'm trying. It's not like I'm not trying.

She spots something on my desk. "Hey, I know." She pulls a Sharpie from the cup. "Why don't you go around today and ask the other kids to sign your cast? That would be the perfect icebreaker, wouldn't it?"

13

I can't think of anything worse. That's like panhandling for friends. Maybe I should find an emaciated puppy to sit on the corner with me, really dial up the sympathy.

It's too late. She's in my face. "Evan."

"Mom, I can't."

She presents the Sharpie. "Seize the day. Today is the day to seize the day."

This sounds like a horoscope. "You don't have to add 'today.' 'Seize the day' already means 'seize today.'"

"Whatever. You're the wordsmith. I'm just saying, go get 'em, eh?"

Without meeting her eyes, I sigh and take the Sharpie. "Eh."

She heads for the door, and just when I think I'm in the clear, she turns with an uneasy smile. "I'm proud of you already."

"Oh. Good."

Her smile sags a bit, and she walks off.

What am I supposed to say? She tells me she's proud, but her eyes tell a different story. She ponders me like I'm a stain on the tub she can't wipe clean no matter what product she uses. Proud of me? I don't see how that's possible. So, let's just keep lying to each other.

It's not like I totally mind the sessions with Dr. Sherman. Sure, our conversations are scheduled, inorganic, and typically one-sided, but there's some comfort in sitting down and talking with another human being. You know, besides my mom, who's so busy with work and classes that she's hardly ever around and who never quite hears what I'm saying even when she's listening (and is also my mom). I call my dad every once in a while, on the few occasions where I have news worth sharing. But he's pretty busy. The problem with talking to Dr. Sherman, though, is I'm bad at it. I sit there, struggling to squeeze out even the simplest monosyllabic answers. I assume that's why he suggested I write these letters to myself. He told me it might be a better way of extracting my feelings and could also help me learn to be a little easier on myself, but I'm pretty sure it makes things easier for him, too.

I open my computer and read what I've written so far.

Dear Evan Hansen,

Sometimes these letters do the opposite of what they're intended to do. They're supposed to keep my glass half full, but they also remind me that I'm not like everyone else. No one else at my school has an assignment from their therapist. No one else even has a therapist, probably. They don't snack on Ativan. They don't shift and fidget when people come too close to them, or talk to them, or even look at them. And they definitely don't make their mother's eyes well up with tears when they're just sitting there not doing anything.

I don't need reminding. I know I'm not right. Believe me, I know.

Today is going to be an amazing day.

Maybe—if I just stay here in my bedroom, then it might actually come true.

Just be yourself.

Yeah. Sure. Okay.

CHAPTER 2

I'm finished at my locker, but I'm still standing here, pretending to look for something. There's too much time before the bell rings, and if I shut my locker now, I'll be forced to hang around. I'm awful at hanging around. Hanging around requires confidence and the right clothing and a bold but casual stance.

Robbie Oxman (aka Rox) is a master hanger-arounder, always whipping his hair out of his face and keeping his legs shoulder-distance apart. He even knows what to do with his hands: four fingers inside his jean pockets and thumbs through his belt loops. Brilliant.

I want to do what Dr. Sherman and my mother keep asking me to do—*engage*—but it's not in my DNA. When I walked onto the bus this morning, everyone was either talking to their friends or staring down at their phones. What am I supposed to do? Fact: I once did a search for "how to make friends" and I clicked on one of the videos that came up and I swear I didn't realize until the very end that I was watching a car commercial.

That's why I prefer to keep my back to everything. Unfortunately, I have to head to class now.

I shut my locker and command my body to rotate exactly 180 degrees. I keep my head low enough to avoid eye contact but high enough to see where I'm going. Kayla Mitchell is showing off her Invisalign to Freddie Lin. (I could ask one of them to sign my cast, but no offense, I don't need signatures from kids who register as low as I do on the relevance meter.) I pass by The Twins (not actually related; they just dress alike) and the Russian Spy. (At least I don't have a nickname—that I know of.) Vanessa Wilton is talking on the phone, probably to her agent. (She's been in local commercials.) Up ahead, two jocks are literally wrestling on the ground. And there's Rox outside Mr. Bailey's class. He's got one thumb in his belt loop and the other hand on Kristen Caballero's waist. Last I heard, Kristen was with Mike Miller, but he graduated last year. On to the next, I see. They're making out now. It's very wet. Don't stare.

I make a pit stop at the water fountain. I've already forgotten the plan: *Let people see you.* How am I supposed to do that? Carry around sparklers? Hand out free condoms? I'm just not the seize-the-day type.

Over the running water, I hear a voice. I think the voice could possibly be talking to me. I stop drinking. There is indeed a person standing next to me. Her name is Alana Beck.

"How was your summer?" she says.

Alana sat in front of me in precalc last year, but we never spoke. Are we speaking now? I'm not convinced. "My summer?"

"Mine was productive," Alana says. "I did three internships and ninety hours of community service. I know, wow."

"Yeah. That's, wow. That's—"

"Even though I was so busy, I still made some great friends. Or, well, acquaintances, more like. There was this girl named Clarissa, or Ca-rissa—I couldn't hear her that well. And then Bryan with a y. And my adviser at National Black Women's Leadership Training Council, Miss P. And also..."

The only time I heard Alana's voice last year was when she was asking or answering questions, which she'd do incessantly. Mr. Swathchild would ignore her hand at first until he realized it was the only hand up and he had no choice but to call on her—again. She's got a bravado I'll never have, not to mention a very committed smile, but in another way Alana Beck and I have a lot in common. Even with her class participation and her gigantic backpack always slamming into people, she goes around this school the same way I do: unnoticed.

Seize the day, Mom says. Fine, here goes. I lift my cast up. "Do you maybe want to—"

"Oh my god," Alana says. "What happened to your arm?"

I unzip my backpack and dig around for my Sharpie. "I broke it. I was—"

"Oh, really? My grandma broke her hip getting into the bathtub in July. That was the beginning of the end, the doctors said. Because then she died."

"Oh . . . that's terrible."

"I know, right?" she says, her smile never wavering. "Happy first day!"

She turns and her backpack knocks the Sharpie out of my hand. I bend down to pick it up, and when I'm upright again, Alana is gone and Jared Kleinman is in her place.

"Is it weird to be the first person in history to break their arm from jerking off too much, or do you consider that an honor?" Jared says much too loudly. "Paint me the picture. You're in your bedroom. Lights off. Smooth jazz in the background. You've got Zoe Murphy's Instagram up on your weird, off-brand phone."

Jared and I have a history. His mother sells real estate. She's the one who found my mom and me a new place to live after my dad left. For a few years there, the Kleinmans would have us at their swim club in the summertime, and we'd go to their house for dinner, once for Rosh Hashanah. I even went to Jared's bar mitzvah. "Do you want to know what really happened?" I ask.

"Not really," Jared says.

Something's driving me to say it, to share it with someone, maybe just to set the record straight. No, I was not stalking Zoe Murphy's Instagram. Not on this particular occasion. "What happened is, I was climbing a tree and I fell."

"You fell out of a tree? What are you, like, an acorn?"

"You know how I was working as an apprentice park ranger this summer?"

"No. Why would I know that?"

19

"Well, anyway, I'm sort of a tree expert now. Not to brag. But I saw this incredible forty-foot-tall oak tree and I started climbing it and then I just..."

"Fell?" Jared says.

"Yeah, except it's a funny story, because there was this solid ten minutes after I fell when I was just lying there on the ground, waiting for someone to come get me. 'Any second now,' I kept saying to myself. 'Any second now, here they come.'"

"Did they?"

"No. Nobody came. That's what's so funny."

"Jesus Christ."

He looks embarrassed *for* me. But hey, I'm in on the joke. I know how pathetic it sounds that I waited there on the ground for someone to come and help me. I'm trying to have a laugh at my own inadequacy, but as usual, my delivery is way off. There's a lot going on in my head right now. Grandmothers are passing away and I've got dark spots on my shirt from the fountain spraying everywhere, and I still haven't made it to first period, where I'll have to answer to "Mark" for at least forty-five minutes.

This is what I get for trying to have a conversation with Jared Kleinman, who once laughed during a lesson on the Holocaust. He swore he was laughing at something unrelated to the horrific black-and-white photos that the rest of us were gasping at, and I believe him, I guess, but still, I'm pretty sure the guy doesn't have a conscience.

Jared hasn't walked away yet, so I ask a question that I stole straight from Alana Beck's mouth. "How was your summer?"

"Well, my bunk dominated in capture the flag and I got to second-base-below-the-bra with this girl from Israel who's going to, like, be in the army. So, yeah, does that answer your question?"

"Actually." The Sharpie is still in my hand. I don't know why I'm even bothering with this cast-signing thing, but here I go anyway. "Do you want to sign my cast?"

He laughs. He laughs right in my face. "Why are you asking me?"

"I don't know. Because we're friends?"

"We're *family* friends," Jared says. "That's a whole different thing and you know it."

Is it? I've played video games on Jared's basement couch. I even changed out of my bathing suit in front of him. He's the one who informed me that it's not normal to wear your underwear under your bathing suit. Fine, we don't hang out like that anymore, and we only ever spent time together with our families around, but those memories still count for something, right? A family friend is still a friend, technically.

"Tell your mom to tell my mom I was nice to you or else my parents won't pay for my car insurance," Jared says, and walks away.

Jared is a dick, but he's my dick—I mean, no, that's not what I mean, not like that. I just mean that he's not the worst ever. He acts like he's the shit, but he's not totally convincing. His tortoiseshell glasses and beach-bum shirts don't quite fit him right, and the oversize headphones he keeps around his neck aren't even plugged in. That being said, his whole look is far better than I could pull off.

I make it to class just as the bell rings and find a seat. (I prefer to be in the row closest to the door at the back of the room, out of sight and near the exit.) As I'm getting situated, I feel a slight sense of accomplishment. No names yet on my cast, but I've already interacted with more people than I did the entire first month of school last year. How's that for seizing the day?

Who knows? Maybe this will be an amazing day after all.

CHAPTER 3

Nope. Not amazing.

First period was fine, meaning nothing terrible happened. Same for my next few classes. All name corrections from Mark to Evan were successful. I was feeling decent, even positive.

But then, lunch.

I've never loved lunch. There's not enough structure. Everyone's free to go where they please, and where they please is nowhere near me. I tend to claim a spot at a forgotten corner table with the other randoms, force-feeding myself the SunButter and jelly sandwich I've packed in my bag every day for a decade. (What I eat is the only thing about lunch I can control.) But sitting in the corner now feels like hiding, and I promised myself I wouldn't hide. Not today.

I spot Jared carrying his tray through the food line. He

usually sits by himself and codes on his laptop. I wait for him at the cash register. He's thrilled to see me.

"You again?" Jared says.

My instinct is to let him walk away, but for once I tell my instinct to fuck off. "I was thinking maybe I could sit with you today?"

Jared looks about ready to vomit. Before he can officially deny me, he disappears behind a dark shroud. Passing between us is the mysterious creature known as Connor Murphy. Connor cuts through our conversation, head low, unaware of his surroundings. Jared and I watch him go.

"Love the new hair length," Jared mumbles to me. "Very school-shooter chic."

I cringe.

Connor halts, his heavy boots landing with a thud. His eyes—what little I can see of them through his overgrown hair—are two steely blue death rays. He definitely heard Jared. I guess he's not as oblivious as he seems.

Connor isn't moving, isn't speaking, just staring. Everything about this kid makes me shiver. He's permafrost. Maybe that's why he's wearing all those thick layers even though it's still technically summer.

Jared may be brazen but he's not stupid. "I was kidding," he tells Connor. "It was a joke."

"Yeah, no, it was funny," Connor says. "I'm laughing. Can't you tell?"

Jared isn't looking so cocky anymore.

"Am I not laughing hard enough for you?" Connor says.

Jared begins to laugh nervously, which makes me laugh nervously. I can't help it.

"You're such a freak," Jared says to Connor, darting away. I should be following Jared, but I can't move my legs.

Connor steps to me. "What the fuck are you laughing at?"

I don't know. I do stupid things when I'm nervous, which means I'm constantly doing stupid things.

"Stop fucking laughing at me," Connor says.

"I'm not," I say, which is true. I'm no longer laughing. I'm officially petrified.

"You think I'm a freak?"

"No. I don't—"

"I'm not the freak."

"I didn't—"

"You're the fucking freak."

A bomb blast.

I'm on the ground. Connor is standing above.

Not a real bomb. Connor's two arms, weighed down by all those black bracelets, slammed my chest and knocked me off my feet.

Before he storms off, I see that he looks as shaken as I feel.

I sit up and lift my hands off the floor, the dust from so many sneakers clinging to my moist palms.

People walk by, stepping around me, some offering unhelpful commentary, but it doesn't matter. I can't hear them. I can't move, either. I don't want to. Why should I? It's like when I fell from that tree in Ellison Park. I just lay there. I should have stayed under that tree forever. Just like I should have stayed home today. What's wrong with hiding? At least it's safe. Why do I keep doing this to myself?

"Are you all right?"

I look up. Shock. Double shock. One shock because it's the second girl who's spoken to me today. Two shocks because it's Zoe Murphy. Yes, the one and only.

"I'm fine," I say.

"I'm sorry about my brother," she says. "He's a psychopath."

"Yeah. No. We were just messing around."

She nods the way my mother might when she's dealing with a delusional patient (i.e., me). "So," Zoe says, "is it comfortable down there on the floor or...?"

Oh yeah, I'm on the floor. Why am I still on the floor? I stand up and wipe my hands on my pants.

"Evan, right?" Zoe says.

"Evan?"

"That's your name?"

"Oh. Yeah. Evan. It's Evan. Sorry."

"Why are you sorry?" Zoe says.

"Well, just because you said Evan, and then I repeated it. Which is so annoying when people do that."

"Oh." She puts out her hand. "Well, I'm Zoe."

I wave my hand, instead of shaking hers, because of all the dust stuck to my sweaty palm, and I immediately regret doing it. I've somehow made this exchange even more awkward than it already was. "No, I know."

"You know?" Zoe says.

"No, I mean, I know you. I know who you are. I've seen you play guitar in jazz band. I love jazz band. I love jazz. Not all jazz. But definitely jazz band jazz. That's so weird. I'm sorry."

"You apologize a lot."

"I'm sorry."

Damn.

She lets out a laugh.

I don't know why I'm so nervous, other than the fact that I'm always nervous and I just got thrown to the ground by a burnout who happens to be related to Zoe by blood. But why does Zoe in particular do this to me? It's not like she's this gorgeous, popular girl or anything. She's just normal. Not normal as in boring. Normal as in real.

I guess it's because I've waited for this moment, the chance to talk to her, for so long. It goes back to the first time I ever saw her perform. I knew she was a year below me. I had seen her around school plenty of times. But I didn't *really* see her until that one concert. If you asked anyone else who was in the audience that day—and there weren't many of us—what they thought of the guitarist's performance, they probably would have said, "Who?" The horn players were the stars, followed by the super tall bass player and the look-at-me drummer. Zoe, meanwhile, was way off to the side. She didn't have a solo or anything. She didn't stand out in any overt way. Maybe it's *because* she was in the background that I connected so strongly to her. To me, there was no one else onstage, just this one spotlight shining down on her. I can't explain why it happened that way, but it did.

I've watched her perform many times since. I've studied her. I know her guitar is eggshell blue. Her strap has lightning bolts on it and the cuffs of her jeans are covered in stars scribbled in pen. She taps her right foot when she plays and keeps her eyes shut tight, and this sort of half smile forms on her face.

"Do I have something on my nose?" Zoe says.

"No. Why?"

"You're staring at me."

"Oh. I'm sorry."

I said it again.

Zoe nods. "My lunch is getting cold."

Something tells me she's done this a million times before, arrived to clean up one of her brother's messes. Now that she's confirmed that I'm okay, she can go about her day. But I don't want to be just another mess to her.

"Wait," I say.

She turns back. "What?"

Reveal yourself, Evan. Say something. Anything. Tell her you like Miles Davis or Django Reinhardt, one of those famous jazz guys. Ask her if she likes them, too. Tell her about that documentary you streamed recently about EDM and how you tried to make your own EDM song afterward, and the song was atrocious, obviously, because you have no musical talent. Just give her something to hold on to, a piece of yourself that she can carry with her. Ask her to sign your cast. Do not shy away. Do not be *meh*. Do not do what you know full well you're about to do.

I look down at the floor. "Nothing," I say.

She lingers a moment, and then her toes seem to wave goodbye inside her worn-in Converse as she turns and walks away. I watch her go, step by step.

When I finally get around to eating lunch, I find that the spill I took not only flattened my already-thin ego but also my loyal SunButter and jelly sandwich.

• • •

My mom texts me when I'm in the computer lab, asking me to call her. I'm thankful for the interruption. I've been staring at a blank screen for twenty minutes now.

I'm trying to finish this letter for Dr. Sherman. When I started seeing him back in April, I'd write a letter every morning before school. It became part of my daily routine. Every week, I'd show Dr. Sherman my letters, and although I didn't always believe in what I'd written, I felt a sense of accomplishment just seeing him hold that stack of papers in his hands. That was me, right there. My work. My writing. But after a while, Dr. Sherman stopped asking to see my letters, and pretty soon I stopped writing them, too. It's not like the letters were really working. They weren't actually changing my mind.

Summer brought a new routine, and writing those letters just wasn't part of it. Dr. Sherman sensed that I had been skipping my assignments. Now he's asking to see my letters again, and if I don't finish this one, I'll have nothing to show him later today. I've been through that before—shown up without a letter when he was expecting one. One time I arrived at a session empty-handed (I'd forgotten my letter at home), and I'll never forget the look Dr. Sherman gave me. He tried to keep his face neutral, but he couldn't fool me. After all these years, I'm a wizard at detecting even the slightest hint of disappointment in others, and any amount at all is unbearable.

I'll have to show Dr. Sherman something, and all I have so far is *Dear Evan Hansen*. I erased all the stuff from this morning. All that crap about being true to myself. I just wrote it because I thought it sounded good.

Of course it sounded good. Fantasies always sound good, but they're no help when reality comes and shoves you to the ground. When it trips up your tongue and traps the right words in your head. When it leaves you to eat lunch by yourself.

There was one silver lining to the day, though. Zoe Murphy not only talked to me, but she knew who I was. She. Knew. My. Name. As with black holes or stereograms, my brain cannot compute this. As hopeful as I feel after our brief interaction, I worry that I squandered the moment and that there may never be another.

I call my mom. After a few rings, I'm ready to hang up, but then she answers.

"Honey, hi," she says. "Listen, I know I was supposed to pick you up for your appointment, but I'm stuck at the hospital. Erica called in with the flu, and I'm the only other nurse's aide on today, so I volunteered to pick up her shift. It's just, they announced more budget cuts this morning, so anything I can do to show that I'm part of the team, you know?"

Sure, I know. She's always part of the team. The thing is,

she's supposed to be part of *my* team. My mom is more like a coach who gives impressive pregame speeches, and then when the whistle blows and it's time for me to step onto the field, she's nowhere to be found.

"It's fine," I say. "I'll take the bus."

"Perfect. That's perfect."

Maybe I'll skip the session with Dr. Sherman. I never asked for it in the first place. I'm finished seizing the day.

"I'm going straight from here to class, so I won't be home until late, so please eat something. We've got those Trader Joe's dumplings in the freezer."

"Maybe."

"Did you finish writing that letter yet? Dr. Sherman's expecting you to have one."

It's official. The two of them definitely talked. "Yeah, no, I already finished it. I'm in the computer lab right now, printing it out."

"I hope it was a good day, sweetheart."

"Yeah. It was. Really great." Just two periods left.

"Great. That's great. I hope it's the beginning of a great year. I think we both could use one of those, huh?"

Yes is the answer, but I barely have time to think it, let alone say it.

"Shit, honey. I have to run. Bye. I love you."

Her voice disappears.

I'm left with a loneliness so overpowering it threatens to seep from my eyes. I have no one. Unfortunately, that's not fantasy. That's all-natural, 100 percent organic, unprocessed reality. There's Dr. Sherman, but he charges by the hour. There's my father, but if he really gave a shit he wouldn't have moved to the other side of the country. There's my mom, but not tonight, or last night, or the night before. Seriously, when it actually counts, who *is* there?

In front of me, on my computer screen, is just one name: Evan Hansen. Me. That's all I have.

I place my fingers on the keyboard. No more lies.

Dear Evan Hansen,

It turns out, this wasn't an amazing day after all. This isn't going to be an amazing week or an amazing year. Because why would it be?

Oh, I know, because there's Zoe. And all my hope is pinned on Zoe. Who I don't even know and who doesn't know me. But maybe if I did. Maybe if I could just talk to her, really talk to her, then maybe—maybe nothing would be different at all.

I wish that everything was different. I wish that I was a part of something. I wish that anything I said mattered, to anyone. I mean, let's face it: would anybody even notice if I disappeared tomorrow?

Sincerely, your best and most dearest friend, Me

I don't even bother reading it back. I hit print and pop up from my chair, feeling energized. Something happened just now when I was writing. What a concept, saying exactly what you feel without stopping to second-guess. I mean, *now* I'm second-guessing, but as I was writing it and as I was sending it to the printer, no hesitation, just one fluid motion.

Except, it's pretty clear that the letter should be torn up immediately and thrown in the garbage. I can't show it to Dr. Sherman. He keeps asking me to seek optimism, and this letter is nothing but hopelessness and despair. I know I'm *supposed* to share my feelings with Dr. Sherman, and make my mom happy, but they don't want my actual feelings. They just want me to be okay, or at least say that I am.

I turn around, eager to reach the printer, but instead, I almost run into Connor Murphy. I flinch, preparing for another shove, but he keeps his hands to himself.

"So," Connor says. "What happened?"

"Excuse me?"

He glances down. "Your arm."

I look down as if to check what he's referring to. *Oh, this?*

"Well," I say, "I was working as an apprentice park ranger this summer at Ellison Park, and one morning I was doing my rounds, and I saw this amazing forty-foot-tall oak tree, and I started climbing it, and I just—fell. But it's actually a funny story, because there was a good ten minutes after I fell when I was just lying there on the ground, waiting for someone to come get me. 'Any second now,' I kept thinking. 'Any second now.' But yeah, nobody came, so..."

Connor just stares at me. Then, realizing I'm finished, he begins to laugh. It's the reaction I pretended to want from my "funny" story, but now that it's happening, I have to admit it's not at all what I was going for. Maybe this is payback for me laughing at Connor before, but something about it doesn't sound like revenge.

"You fell out of a tree?" Connor says. "That is the saddest fucking thing I've ever heard."

I can't argue with him there.

Maybe it's the few light whiskers on his chin or the smell of smoke on his hoodie or the black nail polish or the fact that I heard he got expelled from his last school for drugs, but Connor seems like he's way older than me, like I'm a kid and he's a man. Which is sort of weird, because standing next to him I realize he's pretty scrawny, and if he weren't wearing those boots, I might even be taller than him.

"Take my advice," Connor says. "You should make up a better story."

"Yeah, probably," I admit.

Connor drops his gaze to the floor. So do I.

"Just say you were battling some racist dude." His voice is so quiet.

"What?"

"To kill a mockingbird," he says.

"To kill—oh, you mean the book?"

"Yeah," Connor says. "At the end, remember? Jem and Scout are running away from that redneck guy. He breaks Jem's arm. It's, like, a battle wound."

Most of us read *To Kill a Mockingbird* freshman year. I'm just surprised that Connor actually read it, and I'm also surprised that he wants to talk to me about it right now and so calmly.

After collecting his hair behind his ear, he spots something. "No one's signed your cast."

I take a hard look at my hard cast: still blank, still pathetic.

Connor shrugs. "I'll sign it."

"Oh." My gut says retreat. "You don't have to."

"Do you have a Sharpie?"

I want to say no, but my hand betrays me by reaching into my bag and presenting the Sharpie.

Connor bites off the cap and lifts up my arm. I look away, but I can still hear the squeak of the pen against my cast, individual sounds stretching out longer than you'd expect. Connor seems to be treating each letter like its own mini Picasso.

"Voilà," Connor says, evidently completing his masterpiece.

I look down. There, on the side of my cast that faces the world, stretching the entire length and reaching up to ridiculous heights, are six of the biggest capital letters I've ever seen:
CONNOR.

Connor nods, admiring his creation. I'm not about to burst his bubble. "Wow. Thank you. So much."

He spits the cap into his hand, slides it back onto the tip and hands over the marker. "Now we can both pretend we have friends."

I'm not exactly sure how to take this comment. How does

Connor know that I don't have friends? Is it because *he* has no friends and he recognizes me as one of his kind? Or is he just assuming it because no one else has signed my cast? Or, is it possible that he knows something about me? That would mean I made an impression on him. Sure, making an impression on Connor Murphy isn't ideal, and the impression I made on him isn't a flattering one, but still, it's an impression, and if a certain someone were actually trying to follow his therapist's advice and focus on the bright side, this development could be seen as something of a modest victory.

"Good point," I say.

"By the way," Connor says, reaching for a piece of paper tucked under his arm. "Is this yours? I found it on the printer. 'Dear Evan Hansen.' That's you, right?"

I'm screaming inside. "Oh, that? That's nothing. It's just this writing thing I do."

"You're a writer?"

"No, not really. It's not, like, for pleasure."

He reads more and his expression changes. " 'Because there's Zoe.' " He looks up. A cold stare. "Is this about my sister?"

His lips tighten and I see now that our momentary connection is broken. I step back. "Your sister? Who's your sister? No, it's not about her."

With one menacing stride, he swallows the space between us. "I'm not fucking dumb."

"I never said you were."

"But you thought it," Connor says.

"No."

"Don't fucking lie. I know what this is. You wrote this because you knew that I would find it."

"What?"

"You saw that I was the only other person in the computer lab, so you wrote this and you printed it out so I would find it." I look around the lab. "Why would I do that?"

"So I would read some creepy shit you wrote about my sister and freak out, right?"

"No. Wait. What?"

"And then you can tell everyone that I'm crazy, right?"

"No. I didn't—"

He shoves a stiff finger between my eyes. "Fuck you."

I'm expecting those two words to come with a red exclamation point, something painful, but they actually land weak. He turns around and heads for the exit. He doesn't think I'm worth the effort. I couldn't agree more. Anyway, I'm grateful. I'm not sure I could survive another fall today.

The air releases from my lungs, my body loosening. But the relief I feel lasts only a second. As I watch Connor Murphy stalk out, I call after him, but he's too fast. Clenched in his fist as he slips out the door is a totally different kind of red exclamation point: he still has my letter.

CHAPTER 4

My foot is a Weedwacker. I'm kicking at a patch of grass that's
overtaken a curb at my bus stop. Underclassmen watch with
worry and wonder. I know worry and wonder when I see it.
They might take me for a grass hater. Not in the slightest. It's
just that my medication isn't doing anything for me this morning. I can't calm down. I'm about to face the firing squad, and
there's nothing I can do about it.

I begged my mom to let me stay home from school, but convincing a nurse that you're sick demands powers of persuasion
I just don't possess. Truth is, I do feel sick. I checked the time
every hour last night. 1:11. 2:47. 3:26. When my alarm finally
sounded this morning, it felt like I'd just fallen asleep.

Dr. Sherman wasn't any help. I ended up going to the session yesterday, took the bus all the way out there after school.
I typed up a new letter that sounded upbeat and inoffensive,

and watched as Dr. Sherman read it on my laptop without comment.

I did attempt honesty. I spoke in a vague way about a certain issue that I'm struggling with. "Someone took something from me," I told Dr. Sherman, "something private, and I'm worried what might happen if I don't get it back."

"Let's play this out," Dr. Sherman said. "If this item isn't returned to you, what's the worst that could happen?"

True answer: Connor posts my letter online for the whole school to see, including Zoe, and now everyone knows that I write embarrassingly earnest letters to myself, which is just bizarre and disturbing, and all the days that were already an effort to get through become even more of a slog, and I feel even more alone and inconsequential than I already feel, which I didn't think was possible when I began my senior year yesterday.

The answer I gave Dr. Sherman: "I don't know."

So far, though, from what I can tell, the worst has not happened. Yet. There's no sign of my letter online. I searched my name and nothing new came up. No one's talking about it.

Jared Kleinman's last post: Just gave myself a dutch oven.

Alana Beck wrote: In Africa and Asia, children walk an average of 3.7 miles each day to collect water.

Rox liked a photo of a swimsuit model and started following the breakfast cereal Frosted Flakes.

Another food comes to mind: mashed potatoes. Last year, there was a fight during lunch between Rita Martinez and Becky Wilson. No one knows how it started, but everyone remembers what Rita said to Becky before she jumped on top of her: *I'm going to stick these mashed potatoes up your*...Rita garbled her last word, so it's unclear whether she was referring to Becky's front door or back, but it hardly mattered. A movement began. People started sending mashed potatoes to Becky's house. They'd mime explicit mashed potato acts at lunch. In our school, if you want someone to back off, you can just say "mashed potatoes." Or you can use the cloud emoji, which is the closest visual match. The letter that Connor stole from me is my mashed potatoes. It'll never die if it gets out. It will follow me wherever I go.

The bus turns the corner. I give my foot a break and start to wonder if my concept of *the worst that could happen* is naive and uninspiring. Maybe I'm not thinking like a true sociopath. What if Connor chose to go a more old-school route? For example, he could have printed up physical copies of my letter and stuffed them inside every student's locker. Or maybe he's at school right now, personally handing them out as my classmates enter the building. It makes perfect sense. He thinks my letter was setting him up to look crazy, and now, to get back at me, he will make it clear to everyone at school that the person who's *really* crazy here is the one writing weird letters to himself. *This* guy: Evan Hansen.

I step onto the bus, unsure if it's the engine that's rumbling or my insides. No fanfare as I slink down the aisle to my seat. The kid in the row across from me is horizontal, snoring. The bus lumbers forward. T minus ten minutes until my execution.

Or maybe sooner. Laughter draws my eyes away from my phone. Two rows ahead, a kid is cracking up. He leans across the aisle and presents his phone to his buddy. The buddy takes the phone. "No way," he says to his friend. Now they're both laughing.

This is it: *the worst that could happen.* Connor must have timed his attack for precisely this moment, when I was already on my way to school. He really is a maniacal genius. Any second now these kids will turn around and gawk at the saddest loser on the planet.

I close my eyes and prepare to open them to a new nightmare, but all I see when I finally look is the buddy handing the kid's phone back, and the bus returning to its former quiet.

Later, when I exit the bus, there are no photocopies with my name on them being distributed. No flyers flashing my face. Still, I can't catch my breath as I walk up the concrete path and through the metal doors of the school. What sort of dark surprise awaits me on the other side?

• • •

English: no tragedies. Calculus: no problems. Chemistry: no explosions.

I make it to lunch unscathed. You'd think I'd be relieved, but no, the anticipation is murdering me. I just want it to be over already.

The cafeteria is where my first altercation with Connor occurred. Finishing me off in this same place would provide our saga with a fitting symmetry. Besides, a true show-man would want to take advantage of this large and hungry audience.

Which begs the question: Why am I here? To which there is only one answer: I don't know. The choices always seem to be fight or flight, but I typically end up somewhere in between, doing exactly neither. I stay *and* I take the beating.

I creep along the back wall, partly searching for a safe table, but mostly scanning the room for Connor. No sign of him. I sit and eat. I try to. My teeth snap into a baby carrot and the sound echoes in my head like a gunshot. I swallow the one piece of carrot, and that's all I'm hungry for, because as I'm sitting here, something occurs to me. Something unsettling. Not only have I not seen Connor today, but I haven't seen Zoe, either.

Connor's absence, by itself, isn't unusual. But Zoe being out on the very same day? It's not like the Murphys would've scheduled a family vacation in the middle of the first week of school. Zoe doesn't even seem to get along with Connor, so she probably wouldn't skip with him. And besides, I can't remember the last time Zoe missed a day, and yes, this is something I pay attention to. Some people use energy drinks or coffee, but for me, a few glimpses of Zoe is the jolt I need to power through each day. I usually get my fix *at least* twice, once before homeroom (her locker is down the hall from mine) and then at lunch. I'd love to call her absence a coincidence. On a different day, maybe I could. But not after what happened yesterday. Connor and Zoe both being absent today of all days has to mean something, and not to be a total narcissist, but

I have this terrible feeling that that something leads straight back to me.

I hope I'm wrong. Maybe they're both in school and I just haven't spotted them yet. Or maybe they both have the flu and that's why they're out. A few tables away, Jared is half eating and half computer-staring. I tap him on the shoulder.

"What?" he says without looking up.

"Can I talk to you?"

"I'd rather you didn't."

Understood, but it's not like I have anyone else to turn to and this is serious. "Have you seen Connor Murphy today? Or Zoe Murphy?"

"Well, well, well. I saw you talking to Zoe yesterday. Finally making the move, eh?"

"No, it's not that."

"Do you need help locating the vagina?" Jared says. "I'm sure there's an app for that."

He laughs at his own joke. He still hasn't looked at me (or a vagina, I'm guessing). I scan the cafeteria for my dark nemesis or his much nicer sibling. It's hard to tell. They could be in here somewhere. I turn back to Jared. "I just want to know if you've seen her."

"No, I haven't," Jared says. "But I'll definitely tell her you're looking for her."

"No, please don't do that."

He finally looks up. "It's already done. Don't mention it."

As I'm leaving, he asks, "Or what?"

"Excuse me?"

He points to my cast. I purposely wore long sleeves today even though it's, like, ninety degrees out. Only the last two letters of Connor's name are visible, the O and R. Connor covered so much real estate with his signature I wasn't able to hide the whole thing.

"Death," I answer. "Life or death." I don't know why I say it, or what it means, but it feels true, and not just today, but always.

• • •

My cast is fully exposed in gym. Today is our physical fitness assessment. We take the test once at the beginning of every year and once at the end. Probably my two least favorite days of school.

Ms. Bortel has us in a row on the basketball baseline. Maggie Wendell, the captain of the girls' varsity soccer team, models each exercise as Ms. Bortel delivers instructions.

I look down at my arm. How am I supposed to do a pull-up? I mean, I can barely do a pull-up when I have two functioning limbs. Forget trying to do it with a cast covering half my hand. Actually, same goes for a push-up. I see my way out of this assessment. Finally this cast shows its silver lining.

When Ms. Bortel is finished with her speech, I walk up to her and display my cast. She seems repulsed by the sight of me, as if merely by standing next to my soft, broken body, her muscles might become infected. I have to admit, it's impressive, the work Ms. Bortel seems to put into her physique, especially for someone that age, probably older than my mom. Still,

I find it a little unfair that she's judging me without knowing exactly how I sustained my injury. What if I slipped off a roof while building a house for the homeless? Or what if I got injured while battling some racist dude?

Ms. Bortel asks, "Do you have a note for that?" For *that*.

"A note?" I say.

"A doctor's note."

"I think my mom emailed it to the office."

She mutters something that I can't make out. I do, however, hear her sigh as she sends me off to the bleachers. A few kids of a certain body type watch me with envy.

I manage to dodge one bullet, but the real shooter's still out there. Okay, I probably shouldn't joke about shooters, or even think it, but how can I not? We have lockdown drills to prepare just in case there really is an attacker in school. According to the statistics, it's usually not an outsider, but someone from the community. I sometimes imagine which one of us it would be coming through those doors. It's a simple process of elimination. In the past, when I've cycled through all the possibilities, my wheel of misfortune has, I must admit, on occasion, landed on Connor Murphy.

Honestly, I don't think Connor has it in him. He's not *actually* a violent guy. Sure, he shoved me yesterday at lunch, but that was because of a misunderstanding, just like this business with my letter. Then again, that's what people always think before something heinous happens. Then, after the fact, they say, *Oh, I always had a feeling.* Really, though, what do I know about what another person is capable of? I still don't have a clue what *I'm* capable of. I keep surprising even myself.

Connor and I were in the same class in first grade. I remember him crying a lot. I never knew why he was crying. I just know that I was never surprised when it happened. That's what Connor did: he cried. That was a long time ago, and Connor is way different now, but maybe I can find him and talk to him. He's unpredictable but not unreasonable. I think. If I explain what the letter really is, maybe he'd agree to keep it a secret.

I glance up at the clock behind the basket. The day's nearly over and the worst has yet to happen. Maybe for once I should really try to heed Dr. Sherman's advice and choose optimism. Connor could have tossed my letter in the trash right after he took it. Why do I think he cares about me at all? He's probably off getting high somewhere and has forgotten that I even exist.

All that sounds lovely. Except it still doesn't explain one thing: Where's Zoe?

It's obvious what (probably) happened: Connor showed her the letter and convinced her that I'm some creepy stalker, and the two of them spent the day downtown securing a restraining order against me. They think I'm a threat. Me! Hilarious.

If it wasn't that exactly, it was something equally disastrous. When the final bell rings, I skip the bus and walk home instead, trying to fend off all the terrible terrors in my head. I reach my house with no recollection of how I got there.

• • •

The next day is almost identical, but worse in a cumulative sense. Again, there's no sign of Connor Murphy. One moment I'm certain he's about to appear and humiliate me into oblivion, and the next I'm convinced I've blown this letter thing way out of proportion. In a single day filled with so many moments, the world ends and it carries on.

Now I'm home again and none of my usual methods of escape are doing the trick. I tend to watch a lot of movies. Ideally, documentaries about loners, outcasts, pioneers. Give me cult leaders, obscure historical figures, dead musicians. I want people with rare diseases and unusual talents. I want to see a misunderstood person who someone is finally taking the time to understand. One of my favorite documentaries is about this nanny named Vivian Maier, who happened to be one of the world's greatest photographers, except no one discovered her talent until after she died.

Tonight I tried watching a movie about Edward Snowden, the whistleblower who had to flee the United States and seek asylum in a foreign country. Seeing this guy have to live every day of his life in constant fear only amped up my nerves.

If I could just talk to someone. I've been stuck with my own thoughts for two straight days now. Dr. Sherman was no help, and even if my mom were home, I couldn't confide in her about this. I mentally flip through the (very short) list of people I could possibly turn to in my hour of need. There's really only one name that fits the bill.

Jared Kleinman may laugh at the Holocaust, but on the plus side, at least you never have to guess how he's feeling. I could use a dose of his unfiltered honesty. I message him and explain what happened with Connor.

A letter to yourself?
What the crap does that even mean?
It's like some kind of sex thing?

No, it's not a sex thing.
It was an assignment.

For what?

An extra credit thing.

Why are you talking to me about this?

I didn't know who else to talk to.
You're my only family friend.

Oh my god.

I don't know what to do.
He stole the letter from me,
and now he hasn't been at
school the last two days.

That does not bode well for you.

Neither has Zoe.

???

What is he going to do with the letter?

Who knows?
Connor is batshit out of his mind.
Do you remember second grade?
He threw a printer at Mrs. G because
he didn't get to be line leader that day.

I forgot about that.
I just don't want him showing
the letter to anyone.
Do you think he will?

He's going to ruin your life with it.
For sure. I mean, I would.

On second thought, maybe I prefer my honesty filtered.

I feel like Connor and I were actually having a civil conversation before he read my letter. It seemed like he might've even felt bad about pushing me earlier in the day. I mean, he didn't *have* to walk over and hand-deliver my letter to me. Or sign my cast. It was sort of classy.

An image appears on my screen, sent from Jared: a gorgeous, razor-thin girl leaning against a brick wall, windswept hair falling over one eye, provocative stare straight into the camera lens.

Who's that?

The Israeli chick I told you about.
The one I hooked up with.

The only time I've ever seen a girl hold out the end of her skirt like that is in a clothing ad. This photo has to be from a catalog or something.

She looks nice. Almost like a model.

Yeah, she's done a little modeling.
Definitely better than spending the summer hanging out with trees.
Who the hell becomes a park ranger anyway?

Apprentice park ranger.

Even worse.

The guidance counselor at school suggested it. Well, sort of. I met with her last year to go over my college plan, and she handed me a list of summer activities that would look good on my applications. Park ranger apprenticeship was really the only thing I thought I might be suited for.

When I told Dr. Sherman about my choice for a summer job, he didn't give me the reaction I'd been hoping for. He was concerned I was falling into old habits, retreating from the world instead of engaging with it. I admit, that was one of the things that first attracted me to being a park ranger, the idea of being alone with nature. It ended up being much more than that, but Dr. Sherman was right. Spending the summer away from my normal life made it way more stressful when it came time to go back. By mid-August I started to panic about the summer ending and the school year beginning.

Also, I realized that avoiding people didn't actually ease any of my anxieties. Out there in the woods, I still had to live with myself.

I shut my laptop and re-notice Connor's name on my cast. It's like he's taunting me from afar. I try to scratch the letters away with my nails. Obviously, it's no use.

I walk to my window. It's pitch-dark outside. For the most part, I've always preferred night to day. At night, it's okay to be hunkered down in your house. During the day, people expect you to be out and about. You can start to feel pretty guilty about wasting so much time indoors.

But right now, as I'm gazing out into the darkness, I don't feel any sense of comfort. I notice something out there: a shape. What is that?

What I originally assume is my neighbor's bush now resembles a figure. The figure just stands there, seeming to look right at me, through my window. I switch off my lamp to see more clearly, but when I turn back, heart racing, the figure, if that's what I really saw, isn't there anymore. Totally vanished from sight.

CHAPTER 5

The next morning, in AP English, as Mrs. Kiczek is rattling off the images, characters, and themes she wants us to look out for in "Bartleby, the Scrivener," an announcement comes over the loudspeaker. Everyone, all at once, turns and looks at me.

I'm already on edge, even more on edge than I usually am, because for the third day in a row, my letter is still not in my possession, nor has it been leaked, nor has the person who stole it shown his face, and neither has his sister. I would call this, what I'm in right now, full-on panic mode, but really I'm not sure I've ever felt this particular level of alarm. It's almost hallucinatory.

Even Mrs. Kiczek is looking at me. It takes more than a few seconds to realize why I'm suddenly the center of the class's attention: that was *my* name that was just called over the loudspeaker.

Me? Evan Hansen? I'm not the kind of person who gets called to the principal's office. Isn't that saved for, like, delinquents, class clowns, and fuckups? People whose actions affect others? I don't affect anyone. I'm nonexistent.

"Evan?" Mrs. Kiczek says, confirming that, yes, my ears are in working order. The principal wants to see me. Now.

My level of clumsiness is directly proportionate to the number of people watching. With roughly twenty-five sets of eyes now trained on me, I am squeaking my chair out, ramming it into the desk behind me, kicking the contents of my unzipped backpack onto the floor, and nearly tripping over someone's foot while making my way through the aisle.

My mind is a slide show of worst-case scenarios as I walk through the empty halls to the main office. The same *image*, *character*, and *theme* run through my mind: letter, Connor, shame. In three years, I've had only one interaction with the principal. When I was a sophomore, I placed third in some lame short-story contest and Mr. Howard presented me with an award at one of our general assemblies. My story was based on a childhood fishing trip I took with my dad and was basically a poor rip-off of Hemingway's "Big Two-Hearted River." I wouldn't be surprised if Mr. Howard had no recollection of that day, because, really, the contest was that forgettable and third place is essentially the same as losing. But why does Mr. Howard want to see me *today*?

Reaching the office, I try to wipe my palms on my shirt, but they won't get dry. I give my name to the secretary and she points at the open door behind her. I inch my way toward it like a cop nearing a dark corner. Except I'm not the cop in this scenario. Principal Howard is the cop, which makes me the criminal. Dr. Sherman says that I tend to catastrophize and that nothing is as bad as I imagine it will be, but this right here is proof positive that all my worrying over the past few days was warranted. All the parts of this equation—no Connor plus no Zoe plus my stupid letter plus my getting called to the principal's office—add up to an amount of humiliation and doom I can't even compute.

I poke my head into the room. I don't see Mr. Howard, but there's a man and woman sitting across from his desk. They look confused by my arrival. There's nothing important or official about the room, definitely not what I imagined for the headquarters of a principal. But that's Mr. Howard's face in all the pictures, so I must be in the right place.

The man is bent over in his chair, elbows on his knees, thick shoulders filling out every inch of his suit jacket. The woman is in a daze, her bloodshot eyes turned in my direction but not quite seeing me.

"Sorry," I say, because it feels like I'm interrupting something. "They said on the loudspeaker for me to come to the principal's office?"

"You're Evan," the man says. Not a question, but not *not* a question, so I nod in affirmation.

He sits up and finally takes a proper look at me. "Mr. Howard stepped out. We wanted to speak to you in private."

He gestures to a free chair. He wants me to sit down. I don't understand what's happening. Who are these people?

They look a little gloomy for college reps. Not that I have any clue what a college rep actually looks like. It's just, I heard Troy Montgomery, the star of our football team, had a few college reps come to our school to speak with him. He's an athlete, though, and apparently a very talented one, and I'm just a kid who placed third in a second-rate short-story contest once. So who are these people and what do they want with me?

I take a seat, even though the voice in my head is telling me to remain standing.

The man adjusts the end of his tie so it falls straight between his legs. "We're Connor's parents."

This is it: *the worst that could happen.* I waited and waited and it's finally here. But I still don't know what *it* is. Why do Connor Murphy's parents want to speak to me? And in *private?*

I can't believe these are the two people who made Connor Murphy. And Zoe Murphy, for that matter. It's hard to imagine that both Connor and Zoe came from the same source. Where does Zoe get that hint of red in her hair? And why is Connor so skinny when his father is built like a tank? When you look at my mother and father, I think it's pretty clear how that combination produced someone who looks like me.

Mr. Murphy places his hand over his wife's. "Go ahead, honey."

"I'm going as fast as I can," she hisses.

I thought it was uncomfortable, when I was younger, watching my own parents argue. Turns out, watching other people's parents do it is exponentially more awkward. I'm assuming I'm about to learn why both Connor and Zoe have been absent from school the last few days. And if they're interested in telling *me* of all people, then this can only relate to my letter. There's just no other link that connects all three of us.

But it's interesting, isn't it, how Mr. Murphy introduced himself and his wife as *Connor's* parents, as opposed to *Connor and Zoe's* parents. Of course this is about Connor. Of course. The question is: What did he do now?

After a long silence, Mrs. Murphy removes something from her purse and presses it into my palms. "This is from Connor. He wanted you to have this."

Before even looking, I know what it is. I feel it. My letter—it's back, finally, in my possession. But I can't exhale yet. Who knows what path it took to get here and whose eyes it fell under along the way. If Connor "wanted" me to have this, why didn't he give it to me himself? *Where is he?*

"We had never heard your name before," Mr. Murphy says. "Connor never mentioned you. But then we saw 'Dear Evan Hansen.'"

The thought of Mr. and Mrs. Murphy reading my letter is embarrassing, for sure, but it's not the same kind of embarrassing as having Connor read it. Or Zoe. That's what I'm really interested in knowing. Who else saw this letter? And how did it get inside Mrs. Murphy's purse?

"We didn't know that you two were friends," Mr. Murphy says.

I want to laugh. If these people knew the torture I've experienced over the last forty-eight-plus hours because of their son, they certainly wouldn't call us friends.

"We didn't think Connor had any friends," he says.

Now, that's a more accurate observation. From what I can tell, yes, Connor is a true loner. We do have that in common.

"But this note," Mr. Murphy says, "it seems to suggest pretty clearly that you and Connor were, or at least for Connor, he thought of you as..."

He pauses again. I thought I had trouble getting my words out, but Connor's parents are really having a difficult time getting to their point.

He gestures to the letter. "I mean, it's right there: 'Dear Evan Hansen.'"

I appreciate them returning my possession, but I'd rather not have to talk about what this letter actually says. It's humiliating enough just sitting here. Maybe it's humiliating for them, too. Maybe that's why they seem so agitated. Just like Zoe, they've probably had to apologize for Connor a thousand times and they're just plain tired of it.

At this point, I would very much like to take my letter and get out of here. Unfortunately, Mrs. Murphy has more to say.

"Go ahead, Evan. Read it."

I don't have to. I know every single word by heart. I've imagined what these exact words would look like running across the ticker display in front of our school. Or reproduced in the school paper. Or written in smoke across the blue sky. I've imagined every single possible way that Connor Murphy could use them against me.

I open my mouth for the first time since I entered the room. But I don't know what to say.

"It's okay. You can open it. It's addressed to *you*," Mr. Murphy says. "Connor wrote this to you."

I thought it was me who was confused. Turns out, they're way more lost than I am. "You think Connor..." Just when I thought this couldn't get any more uncomfortable, I now have to explain that I am my own pen pal. "No," I say. "You don't understand."

"Yes," Mrs. Murphy says. "These are the words he wanted to share with you."

"His last words," Mr. Murphy adds.

Again, the message doesn't arrive right away. I look to him. To her. What I understood to be humiliation on their faces a moment ago now, suddenly, resembles something very different.

"I'm sorry. What do you mean, *last* words?"

Mr. Murphy clears his throat. "Connor is gone."

I don't know what that means. Sent to boarding school? Ran away and joined a cult?

"He took his own life," Mr. Murphy says.

He clenches his jaw. She dabs her eye. Not humiliation. Devastation.

"He...what?" I say. "But I just saw him last night."

"What are you talking about?" Mrs. Murphy says with new energy in her voice.

"I'm not sure," I say. "I thought it was him. It was dark."

"It happened two nights ago," Mr. Murphy says, seeming to speak more to his wife than to me. "I know it's a lot to take in."

I couldn't sleep last night. I wondered if it had been Connor standing on my neighbor's lawn, looking into my window. But I guess it was just my imagination. My fear.

I need a minute. I need hours. This isn't real. This can't be real.

"The letter is all we found with him," Mr. Murphy says. "He had it folded up in his pocket."

I finally look at my letter.

"You can see," Mr. Murphy says. "He wanted to explain it. It's all there."

I read the words on the page. They're my words, the words I wrote, the words I've come to know by heart, but now they feel alien to me. It's like someone jumbled them up and tried to put them back in the same order, thinking no harm would be done, that it would be the same message, but it's not the same message. It's two messages, depending on how you read it, and Connor's parents are not reading it the way I intended. This letter, my letter—they think Connor wrote it. To me.

Mr. Murphy recites my words from memory. "'I wish that everything was different. I wish that I was a part of something.'"

"Let him read it by himself, Larry."

"'I wish that anything I said mattered—'"

"Larry, please."

"'—to anyone.'"

The room goes quiet.

I look around, for what, I'm not sure: help. There's no one. No sign of Mr. Howard.

I try to speak. I can't. That familiar rush—panic. It finds me every day, sometimes not so intense, but this right now is enough to overpower all my faculties.

"This letter. It isn't..."

"Isn't what?" Mr. Murphy says.

I catch my breath. "Isn't Connor."

Mrs. Murphy looks at me. "What does that mean?"

"Connor..."

"Yes?"

"Connor didn't..."

"Didn't what?"

"Write this."

"What does he mean, Larry?"

"He's obviously in shock."

"No, I just...he didn't." I'm trying to set them straight, but my thoughts keep coming out broken.

"It's right here," Mrs. Murphy says, pointing to the letter.

I hear a voice. It's been speaking this whole time but I'm only now paying attention. Coming from within, louder and louder. *Go*, it's saying. *Leave.*

"I'm sorry, but I should probably..."

Mrs. Murphy seizes me, gripping my hands, the letter held in our collective grasp. "If this isn't...if Connor didn't write this, then..."

"Cynthia. Please. Calm down."

I avert my eyes. "I should go."

"Did he say anything to you?" Mrs. Murphy pleads. "Did you *see* anything?"

"Cynthia, honey. This is not the time."

I loosen my grip and the letter is now in her hands alone. "This is all we have," she says. "This is the *only* thing we have left."

"I really should go."

Mr. Murphy turns to me. "Of course," he says. "We understand. We just wanted you to be among the first to know."

Mrs. Murphy hides her face. She's done her best to hold it together. So have I, but I can't help her, this woman; she's broken, completely, and I care, I really do, I understand, as much as I can, but I don't know how to be here with her, with them, with myself. I have to leave.

I start, but they catch me.

"Before you go." Mr. Murphy removes a business card from his inside breast pocket, flips it over, and begins writing on the back side with one of Mr. Howard's pens. He returns the pen and, with his eyes holding mine, hands me the card. I'm already reaching for it before I know what it is.

"The funeral is for immediate family only," Mr. Murphy says, "but here's the information for the wake tonight."

I don't know how to respond to this, nor do I have the time. Mrs. Murphy jumps up from her chair and grabs my outstretched arm.

"Larry. Look."

It happens so fast I can't stop it.

"Look at his cast."

He comes around to see what she sees. There, in permanent ink, is the name of their son.

Mrs. Murphy turns to her husband, an astonished smile forming. "It's true. It really is true. His 'best and most dearest friend.'"

• • •

From the principal's office straight to the bathroom. I lean over a toilet, but nothing comes out. My guts are swirling, round and round, like I just sat in the passenger seat of a car driven by a blind person, the wheel jerking left to right to left. I want to get past this dizzy feeling, force it out of me, but it won't come up.

I return to English class, but I never *really* return. I can't get back to where I was before I left. I can hear Mrs. Kiczek's voice, but not her words. The bell rings and I rise from my desk. I walk to my next class without my sneakers ever touching the floor.

My trance holds all the way to last period. Then, an announcement comes over the loudspeaker, repeating the news I learned hours ago but spent the entire day disbelieving. "It is with tremendous sorrow...one of our beloved students...services tonight from five to seven o'clock...any students who would like to talk to someone...Mrs. Alvarez will be available in the auditorium starting now."

The news begins to register in those around me. The shock in their faces breaks my daze. It's true. It's really true. Connor Murphy is dead.

I thought it was a dream. How could I know? It's not like some-one gives you a heads-up: *Hey, just so you know, you're dead.*

The day started like any other. The whole happy family seated at the kitchen table. Eating breakfast. I wasn't really eating. Neither was Larry: too busy with his phone. Neither was Cyn-thia: too busy serving the rest of us. (My parents love it when I call them by their first names.) Zoe was the only one actually consuming food.

I didn't want to go to school. My mother wouldn't hear it. Said it was the first day and I had no choice. School would do me good, she said. She watched me sleep all summer. She was des-perate to get me out of the house.

But really, what was the point of going to school? They never knew what to do with me. If you don't fit into one of their boxes, you get tossed aside. I could learn way more at home. Reading my own books and watching *Vice*. At least when I was at Hanover I could mention Nietzsche without a teacher star-ing back with a blank look.

(Unfortunately, the whole private school experiment was a bust. Apparently, Adderall to get through finals—or the day—is perfectly OK. But a little weed in your locker is unforgivable. Hypocrites. Maybe now they'll see how ass-backward they are. Hey, geniuses, no one dies from marijuana. Pills, though? Yup, you guessed it.)

Then Cynthia tried to get Larry involved. That's always good for a laugh. *You're going to school, Connor,* was all he could muster. This really set off my mother, that my father couldn't be bothered. They went at it for a while, talking like I wasn't there. Welcome to the Murphy household. If your name is Zoe, strap in for the ride of your life. If you happen to be Connor, well, you're going to want to stay good and numb.

I ended up going to school. Some fights aren't worth the effort. I got a lift from Zoe. Yet another perk of being me. Your little sister drives you around. All because the Subaru that Larry Luxury handed you like an olive branch is in a recycling heap somewhere.

(There was no deer in the road that night. I can come clean about that now. I crashed into that tree because I felt like it. My messiest decisions were always like that. Made in a split second. Nine times out of ten I'd walk away only wounded. Then, on the tenth time . . .)

Turns out I was right to want to skip school. I got singled out in homeroom (even though I wasn't the only one on my phone). Got messed with in the cafeteria. Messed with again in the computer lab. I'm just trying to mind my own fucking business. Not even allowed to do that.

And that was only day one. What about the rest of the year? One hundred seventy-something days left. How am I supposed to get through?

I couldn't.

I skipped my last two classes. Walked right out of the building. I couldn't shake the feeling—free-falling. Like there's nothing to hold on to. I reached out to the only person I thought might help. And then, when that didn't work...

I woke up in the hospital. My family was there. All of them, looking at the floor, their phones, the insides of their eyelids— anywhere but at one another or me. I knew what was coming. I'm a fuckup—I know. Spare me. I got out of bed before anyone could say a word. Just left the room. No one bothered to come after me.

At the front desk, there were two nurses. One said, *Room 124. So sad. He's the same age as Evan.*

I know, the other nurse said, sighing.

The first nurse made a call, left a message: *Hey, honey, just checking in. I wanted to hear how the rest of your day went. Did you get any good signatures on your cast? You'll probably be sleeping when I get home, but I'll see you in the morning. I love you so much. I just want you to know that.*

She put down her phone. Hands on her forehead. Soothing her temples. I couldn't believe it. Who this woman was.

I think I know your son, I said. *I signed his cast today.*

She didn't answer, just walked away. Another fan of mine. I figured Evan had told her what happened between us. Probably made it seem like he was innocent. Just standing there like a saint and here comes big, bad Connor Murphy. But he's the one who messed with me.

(I didn't really mean to push him. Another one of those split-second decisions. Honestly, they're more like knee-jerk reactions. Or something deeper. Part of my nature. That's just what I do. I ruin things. Always. Whether I want to or not. The thing I'm ruining can be the best thing in my life. And I'll know it, too. And I'll still be powerless to stop it. Or too scared.)

I turned back down the hall, vowing to be more patient with my waiting family. I reached my room. Room 124. I looked in. That's when I saw him. The kid in the bed. It was me.

I bent over him—the other me. Skin gray. Mouth sagged open.

I got what I wanted, I guess.

I'm free now. No one in my way. No one waiting around a corner, setting a trap. No one checking for redness in my eyes. Asking where I've been all night. Making promises.

I've been hanging here at the hospital. Everyone is beaten up and broken, just like me. Even the staff. They just hide it better than the patients do.

Especially that one nurse. Evan's mom. She's kind of a disaster, always rushing around the halls. But she seems decent. Today, on her break, she barely touched her sandwich. She was looking up college stuff for Evan. I can't picture Cynthia doing that. Even though I was her life's work.

My mother preferred to delegate. She treated me like one of her home renovation projects. Hire help. Call in the specialists. The best in the business. Let's get this kid fixed up. Do whatever you've got to do. Take him overnight, or for weeks at a time. Pump him full of meds. Solo sessions. Group sessions. We've got money, as much as it takes. Spare no expense. Just solve this problem of ours. And hurry. My husband's growing impatient. Losing faith. Asking, why throw good money after bad? It hasn't worked so far, after all these years. Maybe it's best to abandon the project. Stop the work. At least for the time being. Let's wait this thing out. See what happens.

And here we are.

CHAPTER 6

Once I'm home, I message Jared and tell him in a hurricane of words what happened with my letter, how it was finally returned to me (temporarily) by Connor's parents, who were under the impression that it was a letter written *by* Connor *to* me, and how they now think that Connor and I were best friends, and how that ridiculous belief was then corroborated when they caught a last-minute glimpse of my cast. After I see all this typed out on my screen, Jared's response seems like the only appropriate one:

Holy. Shit.

I know.

Holy. Fucking. Shit.

I know.

I tried to tell them the truth.

I did.

I tried.

Holy. Motherfucking. Shit.

I can't believe this happened.

I mean, about Connor.

He's really gone.

I spoke to him just a few days ago. Now I'll never speak to him again. Or walk past him. Or hear a rumor about him defacing school property. Never. I've known this kid since we were in grade school. He disappeared for chunks at a time, and we weren't friends or anything, but he was still part of our whole group, our class, our year.

No one I know has ever died before. All my grandparents are still alive. I've never even lost a pet. I guess the closest thing I can relate to is when a famous person dies. You feel like you've spent so much time with this person, watching their movies, listening to their music, and then they die and you feel this swift loss of air and this powerful, full-body sadness, but then, pretty soon after, within minutes even, the feeling passes and you go on with your life. But it's been hours now since I spoke with Connor's parents and I still can't calm the waves in my stomach.

Of course, Connor's death is just the half of it. The other

half is what's really making me uneasy. This whole misunderstanding about us being friends. I have to fix it.

Are you going to the wake?

No. Why would I?

I don't know. Isn't it the right thing to do?
I feel like maybe I have to go.

You realize you weren't actually
friends with him, right?

I know that.
But you should have seen their faces. His mom . . .
And his dad gave me this look as I was leaving.
I think they expect me to be there.
What am I supposed to do?

You stay home.
That's what you do.

But what if I run into them one day
and they ask me why I never
came to Connor's wake?

How often do you run into the Murphys?

What are you supposed to wear to a wake?

How the fuck should I know?
My people don't do it that way.
We hang at someone's house
and load up on pastrami and bagels.

It starts in two hours.
Can you meet me there?

I wait for Jared's response, but it never comes.

Who am I kidding? I'm not going to Connor's wake. I'll stay home. It's fine. It's a wake for their son; they won't even notice I'm missing. Besides, it's not my responsibility to be there. Like Jared said, we weren't actually friends.

I kick off my sneakers and open my laptop. The goal is to get my mind off Connor, but that's impossible. Everyone at school is talking about him.

Rox: Rest in peace bro!

Kristen Caballero: So sad right now 💔

Kayla Mitchell: Never thought CM would go out like that.

Alana Beck: Still can't believe the terrible news about Connor Murphy. He looks so happy in this photo. It really shows his spirit. This is how we should remember him. Share this post if you agree.

Everyone seems to be circulating the same photo of Connor. It must be from a couple years ago, because Connor's hair is short and it makes his ears more pronounced. He's wearing a button-down shirt in light blue, a color I'm not used to seeing on him, and even weirder, he's got a big smile on his face. His arm is wrapped around someone, another guy, it looks like, but the other guy has been cropped out of the photo and all you can see is his shoulder. The whole thing is just odd because when I close my eyes and picture Connor, the image I see is pretty much the total opposite of this photo.

Why would he do this? I mean, I understand how low a person can get. I also know that when you're not in the best headspace, the trivial can turn into the insurmountable and all of a sudden you're heading down a dark path and you can't find your way back. But what if *I'm* the thing that happened to Connor? What if he did it because of me and my letter? That pointless letter. I should have never written it in the first place. I finally expressed the truth, and look what happened: it got turned into a lie.

I look down at my cast. If I could rip it off my arm, I would. I don't care if I'm not fully healed yet. I want it off. I want *him* off.

As I'm staring at Connor's sloppy signature, I'm reminded of what's in my pocket. I pull out the business card that Connor's father gave me and flip it over to reveal his handwritten message:

McDOUGAL FUNERAL HOME
BOWERS + FRANKLIN
5–7 PM

Not only handwritten, but hand-delivered, too. That look in his eyes when he gave it to me was so primal. Deeper than words. It was as if he was reminding me that attending Connor's wake was my duty as a man.

I look again at the address. The funeral home is within walking distance from my house.

How could I *not* show up? His parents are expecting me. I don't want to let them down. Or Connor. I owe it to him, don't I? I didn't know him well, but I still feel some kind of connection with him, after all this, and it's the right thing to do, to pay your respects when someone passes. I'd want others to do the same for me. Actually, now that I think of it, I wonder who would even come to my funeral. My mom, obviously. My grandparents, yes. But who else? Would my dad fly in or would he just send flowers?

I stand up from my bed and swing open my closet door. Buried somewhere in here is a pair of black dress shoes. I can't remember the last time I wore them. Who knows if they still fit.

I'll just go for a few minutes, make an appearance. I can clear up this misunderstanding quickly and leave. It's really nothing. And it's the right thing to do. And maybe it's the only thing that will finally exorcise these demon butterflies from my stomach.

• • •

According to the map on my phone, I've arrived. It's a non-descript one-story building set back from the road, a parking lot in the rear. I must have passed this place a thousand times on my way to and from school and never once thought about its purpose. Now I'm pretty sure I will never *not* think about it.

On my way up the path, I roll down my sleeves and cover as much of my forearms as possible. After much debate about what to wear, I settled on khakis, my nicest dress shirt, and the black shoes from my closet, which I had to wipe clean with a kitchen sponge (sorry, Mom).

Before I even get close to the building, the front door opens and a suited man steps aside, waiting for my arrival. I had planned on stalling a bit more, lingering until I could follow someone (anyone) inside, but it's too late now. I've been spotted. I pick up my pace. The suited man bows his head as I pass and closes the door behind me.

Inside the well-lit hallway, I'm met with light chatter and a trail of perfume. On a side table is a family photo. In it, Connor is just a boy, pale and slight, maybe ten years old. Zoe stands obediently by her brother's side, hiding behind his shoulder. I miss seeing her face. Maybe it's an inappropriate thought for this moment, but it's true. I wonder how she's been taking this. I hope she's okay.

Next to the photo is a guest book that's been signed by a dozen people. I don't recognize any of the names. I look back to the suited man, who's busy window watching. I write my name in the book. In case the Murphys don't spot me in the crowd, at least there will be proof that I attended.

When I reach the end of the hall, my legs shaking, I realize instantly that there is no chance of my presence going undetected. I had thought, as I was nearing this back room, how remarkable it was that my classmates, even at such a somber event, were able to keep their voices so low. Now I know why. They aren't talking, because they aren't here. None of them.

Leave. Immediately. Of course that's what I should do. It's obvious. But there's no time. My sudden appearance in the doorway is observed by all. Mrs. Murphy, midconversation, makes eye contact with me. There's no way out now.

I order my leg to step forward, and then my other leg after that, and pretty soon I'm walking from one end of the room to the other like a regular, functioning person. On my way to find a seat, I spot a familiar face that interrupts all the momentum I've built.

"Mrs. G? What are *you*—" I stop myself. I didn't mean to say any of that out loud. It came out in a spill of surprise, and now I have to clean up my spill. "It's good to see you. I mean, you know, it's good that you, that...you're here." I don't know what I'm saying.

She seems unfazed, lost in her own thoughts. For a second, I wonder if that ponderous look on her face is her trying to identify me as one of her former students. But when she finally speaks, it has nothing to do with me or the clumsy words I've just mumbled.

With a stoic smile, she says only, "Connor was a special boy."

I nod in agreement and hurry away, finding a seat in the last row of chairs. I stare at the back of Mrs. G's head, the veins in her neck, her short gray hair. She's the last person I would have expected to be here. I never had her for a teacher, and was glad for it, because she was super intimidating and had a reputation for being strict. If she saw you in the hall, even if you were barely moving, she'd tell you to slow down. It's no surprise that she and Connor were a combustible combo. And yet, even after he threw a printer at her, she's here.

Which is saying something, because there can't be more than twenty people total in attendance. Nearly everyone is an adult. All the men are wearing suits. I'm the only idiot who looks like a waiter. I check around for a hint of red hair. Zoe isn't here, and I can't fathom why that would be.

Most of the attendees are gathered around Connor's parents at the front of the flower-filled room. Behind them is the casket. I wasn't expecting to see it. I assumed caskets were reserved for funerals. Thankfully, it's closed. Still, it's hard to ignore its presence. His presence.

Where is everybody? Connor Murphy wasn't popular or well liked, but I assumed *some* people would be here. We all knew the kid, grew up with him, passed him in the halls. Doesn't that count for something? Where are Rox and Kristen Caballero and Alana Beck? They'll post something about Connor online but couldn't be bothered to pay their respects in person?

I should have listened to Jared and stayed home. I'll slip out the back door when no one's looking. Pretend like I'm going to the bathroom and just keep going. I give my legs a mental heads-up, needing them to buy in to my plan.

But I don't get a chance to refine my exit strategy. Mrs. Murphy's hand goes up and starts swiping at the air. I turn around. There's no one behind me. Her eyes enlarge to better signal her intentions. Yes, it's me she wants. I wish she'd come over to me, instead of making me go to her—and all those people.

Slowly, carefully, strenuously, I stand and will myself to the aisle, past Mrs. G, and up to the front of the room. I practice the script I came up with on the walk over: *I wrote the letter. We weren't friends, but I liked him a lot. I'm sorry for your loss.*

I'm missing a few lines. Some key explanatory words. My brain is overheating. My socks feel soaked.

Mrs. Murphy clears a path, beckons me into her huddle.

Mr. Murphy reaches out his hand. "It's good to see you, Evan. Thanks for coming." His grip is scary strong. I apologize for my sweatiness, but he doesn't seem to hear me.

Mrs. Murphy wraps me in her arms, squeezes me harder than my own mother would. Her jagged necklace impales my chest.

I'm sorry for your loss.

"Oh, you're shaking, you poor thing."

I wrote the letter, not Connor.

She eases up and holds me in such a way that I have no choice but to look her in the eyes. She forces a smile, then turns me around by the shoulders so that I'm facing the others. "This is Evan, everyone."

"Hi, Evan."

"Evan was Connor's closest friend," Mrs. Murphy says.

We weren't friends, but I liked him a lot.

"We're so sorry for your loss."

They say this to *me*. I'm the one they feel sorry for.

Mrs. Murphy guides me away from the others and plants me directly in front of Connor's casket. I turn away and face the room.

"I'm so happy you're here," Mrs. Murphy says, and yet absolutely nothing about her or this place feels happy.

I wrote the letter for my therapist. Connor took it from me.

The words are right there, but they won't come out.

"Larry and I were talking," she says, stopping to take a long and deep breath, her hand almost helping her chest draw in the oxygen. "We would love to have you over to the house for dinner. We have so many questions about..." She pauses again, ingesting more air. Clearly, I'm not the only one having trouble speaking right now. "About everything. About you and Connor. Your friendship. If you could find a free night to spend with us, we would be so grateful. *So* grateful. Just to sit down with you would mean so much."

"I..."

"Think about it. No rush."

She exhales and hugs me again before returning to the group. Escape is now possible. I turn for the door, and in my haste, I nearly run into someone: Zoe.

I regain my balance as she works through her confusion. "What are you doing here?" she asks.

Such an astute question. If only I had a good answer.

She's been crying. I can tell by her puffy pink eyes.

"I'm sorry," I say. "About your brother."

Arms crossed, crossed so tightly, giving herself a hug. She nods, just once, and walks away.

I take one more look—at him, or the box he's in—before letting myself out.

Mrs. Gorblinski. She actually gave a shit. Other people assumed she was a nemesis. Because of the story, I guess. The legend. That's what happens with legends. The facts get pushed aside and replaced with something more dramatic.

I'm guilty of it, too. I've heard the story so many times, even told it myself. I began to believe the simple version: *Connor Murphy threw a printer at Mrs. G.* Well, yeah, but...

It was a long time ago. Second grade. I only remember bits and pieces. We all had jobs. On the wall was a chart: lunch helper, schedule announcer, board eraser, nurse buddy, recycler. The most prized job of all, really the only one that mattered, was line leader. *Everyone* wanted to be line leader. For me it was the idea of being in charge. Controlling things. (We weren't curing cancer or anything, but trust me—this was all very serious at the time.)

Each day, Mrs. G moved our names one spot. I waited my turn, watching my name advance. Finally, I was one spot away. The next day, I came to class, dressed up probably—that's how excited I was. But something was wrong. I wasn't line leader. I had a different job. It was supposed to be my day.

The class was lining up behind someone else. I called out to Mrs. G.

Connor, it's not the time for questions.

She was a real no-nonsense type, everything by the book. There was a right way to do things. An order. And that order was now out of whack. There had been an oversight. Mrs. G would fix this right away. She'd appreciate what was at stake.

I told her, *I got skipped.*

Get in line, Connor.

But it's my turn to be—

You heard me.

No. It's not fair.

I stepped in front of the line. One of the kids pushed me. I tried to explain. I felt myself getting hotter. The room closing in. Tears forming.

Connor, please find your place in line.

But...

Connor, I won't tell you again.

But it's my turn to be line leader!

I reached out for the first thing I could find. Felt the printer with both hands and swept it off the desk. It slid across the floor, stopping at Mrs. G's feet. The tray broke off, flew to the other side of the room.

The room went silent. All eyes on me.

Ms. Emerson escorted the class out. Mrs. G stayed with me, tried to calm me down. I couldn't even look at her. And that's it. As far as everybody knows, that's where our story ends. I freaked out and threw a printer at Mrs. G.

But it wasn't the end.

The next day, the printer was back in place. Back on the desk, minus the tray. And on the job chart: I was line leader.

And Mrs. G had moved my seat closer to her desk. She gave me a little pad. If I had a problem or question, I could tear a blank page from the pad, crumple it into a ball and place it in the glass jar on her desk. She wouldn't stop teaching the class on my behalf. *I won't tolerate any more disruptions,* she said. But she promised that if I placed a ball in the jar, she'd see it. And when the time was right, she would get to me. But I had to be patient. If I was, she would listen. She would hear me. I would be heard.

Everyone in school knew about the printer. It became this thing that followed me around. The logline to my movie, telling people what to expect of me. Telling me what to expect of myself. I was the villain. That was my role. And Mrs. G was the victim. And for years, that's been our story. But it demands a correction. She made a mistake. And so did I.

CHAPTER 7

On my way home from Connor's wake, I text Jared, typing faster than I can walk.

Why did I go?

I told you not to.

I was just trying to do the right thing.

Who told you to do that?

They invited me over for dinner.
They want to know more
about Connor and me.
About our "friendship."

This is getting good.
When are you going?

I don't think I can do it.

Take pictures.
I'd love to know what that house looks like.

I stop at a busy intersection, cars whizzing by. It's after seven now. My oxford shirt feels like it's strangling me. All I want to do is climb into bed and hide under the covers. Lately, every time I leave the house, I only end up making more trouble for myself.

The signal changes and I resume walking (and typing).

So you think I should go to dinner?

Now you have to.
What are you going to tell them?

The truth.
I need to tell them the truth
once and for all.

The truth. Really?

Yes?

You think you're going to go
to the Murphys' house and
explain to them that the only thing
left they have of their son is some weird
sex letter that you wrote to yourself?
You do realize you could go to jail for this
if you get caught, right?

                                        But I didn't do anything.

Yeah, I hate to tell you this, Evan,
but you may have already perjured yourself.

                            Isn't that only when you're under oath?
                                        Like, in a courtroom?

Well, weren't you under oath?
In a way?

                                        Um, no, actually.

Look, do yourself a favor and listen to me this time.
Do you want to have another meltdown
like last year in English when
you were supposed to give that speech
about Daisy Buchanan,

but instead you just stood there
staring at your note cards
and saying, "um, um, um," over and over again
like you were having a brain aneurysm?

What do you expect me to do?
Just keep lying?

I didn't say lie.
All you have to do is just nod and confirm.
Whatever they say about Connor, you just nod.
Don't contradict and don't make shit up.
It's foolproof.
Literally, nothing I tell my parents is true
and they have no idea.

I absorb Jared's instructions. I'm trying to accept what he says I have to do while also thinking of ways to not have to do it. At the moment, the only house I want to be in is my own.

It's nearly dark by the time I get there. The driveway is empty and the lights are off. I ignore the envelopes and flyers spilling from the mailbox. None of it is for me.

The front door whines as I push it open. I'm inside now, finally, but I'm missing that sense of relief I was hoping to find.

There's a note on my door: *Sit tight. Take hold. Thunder Road!* When it's not a horoscope, my mom is often quoting a Bruce Springsteen lyric. It's like she has no idea how to talk to me.

I crumple the note and stare at my wrongly dressed reflection in the mirror. Even if I had known that a suit was the thing to wear, I don't own one. The last time I wore a suit was at my dad's wedding and that was a rental. My mom and I flew out to Colorado. She didn't want to go to the wedding, but I did. I don't know if she went just for me or if she also wanted to prove to my dad that she had moved on. She certainly didn't prove it to me. When we got back to the hotel after the reception, she took the heel of her shoe and started hammering it into our picture-frame wedding favor until the carpet was covered with tiny pieces of glass. At the time I thought she just hated picture frames. I was only ten.

Right now it's almost six o'clock in Colorado. My dad has probably just arrived home from his accounting job. He hangs his coat up on the rack. Theresa already has dinner on the table, lasagna or a juicy prime rib. Everyone sits, and Theresa's older daughter, Haley, leads the family in a prayer, even though my dad was at one time an atheist. Haley's little sister, Dixie, sits there all cute with her milk mustache. Dad gives his second wife a wink and his second kids a hearty smile, and as they dig into the home-cooked meal Theresa slaved over all afternoon, each member of the family takes a turn talking about his or her day.

Hey, Dad, I say to the empty hallway as I head to my room, *want to hear about my day?*

Interrupting this quality chat with Dad is the familiar whine of the front door. It sends a horror-film shiver down my spine. By the time I hear my mom's voice, I'm already kicking off my dress shoes and stuffing them into my closet. One of the buttons on my shirt refuses to open before finally doing me a solid and coming undone. I slide under my covers, still in my khakis, just as my mom appears in my doorway.

"Hi, honey."

"You're home early," I say.

"Not really. It's eight o'clock."

"Oh, wow, I didn't notice. I was so busy."

"Oh yeah? Doing what?"

I'm not exactly sure what I'm trying to hide. I haven't had time to figure that out. It just seems like the most prudent thing to do is to say as little as possible.

"Just thinking," I answer.

Her expression changes. "About what happened?" She enters my room and perches awkwardly on the edge of my bed.

"What do you mean?" I glance over at my crumpled shirt on the floor. It's only a matter of time before she starts poking around my room and inquires why I unearthed that never-worn piece from my closet.

"I got an email from your school," she says. "About the boy who killed himself? Connor Murphy?"

There's something about hearing my mother say it out loud. "Right, yeah."

"Did you know him?"

"No," I say quickly, clearly, definitively. If only I could have shown such decisiveness with Connor's parents.

"Well, if you ever want to talk about anything, I'm here.

And if I'm not *here* here, I'm a phone call away. Or text. Email. Whatever."

I was just thinking about how far away Colorado seemed, and here's my mom, living with me in the same house, and I honestly can't say she feels any closer.

She bows her head and starts fiddling with the drawstring of her pants. I can see the deep brown roots at the top of her head. They seem to be spreading and negating her most recent trip to the hairdresser. I'm not sure when she last visited the salon, but she's constantly saying how her next appointment is long overdue.

"Your cast," she says.

I try to shove it under my blanket, but I'm too slow. She grabs my arm. This damn cast should be on my foot—it's become my Achilles' heel.

"It says, 'Connor.'" She sharpens her eyes. "You said you didn't know him."

"Yeah, I don't. I didn't. This is a different Connor." As someone who's always been bad at lying, I can honestly say it never gets easier. "He's new this year, so yeah, I let him sign my cast. Putting myself out there, y'know?"

She breathes out and places a palm over her heart. "For a second there, I was worried."

I still am.

"Hey, you know what?" she says. "Why don't we go to Bell House tomorrow?"

Breakfast at Bell House used to be our Saturday morning ritual, but with my mom's busy schedule, we haven't been back in a while. When we do make plans, something usually comes up. As much as I love the pancakes at Bell House, I feel like the smart thing to do right now is stay home and recharge. "I think I have a lot of homework," I say.

"Come on," she says. "You've been back at school for a week already and I've barely seen you."

One suicide and all of a sudden my mom is paying attention. Seriously, though, considering what she sees at work— stabbings, burns, overdoses, gunshot wounds, induced comas, not to mention untold numbers of soiled bedpans—I'd assumed she was numb to tragedies by now. But this one obviously hits close to home. Even closer than she knows.

I guess having a little company on a wide-open Saturday wouldn't be the worst thing. I do love those pancakes. "Okay. Yeah. That would be good."

"It's a date, then," she says, tapping a spirited drum fill on my leg. "I can't wait."

I think I'll save my enthusiasm for when we're in the car and I actually believe we're going.

She stands up and grabs my Ativan off the nightstand. "You okay on refills?"

She says this so often now it's almost become a stand-in for *goodbye*.

"Yup," I say, which is my standard reply. Although the way today went, I might need a refill sooner than usual.

"Good. Well, don't stay up too late. "

"I won't," I say, eager to end this conversation.

She pauses in my doorway. "I love you."

I look at her. "You too."

An unsteady smile and she finally shuts the door. I jump out of bed and put my dress shirt back on its hanger and into my closet. While I'm up, I pause, overcome with a feeling. I step to the window, raise the blinds, and look out. The street appears empty. The neighborhood is completely still. There's no one out there. Of course not.

•••

The Bell House hostess tells us to sit wherever we'd like. My mom looks to me to pick a table, but "wherever we'd like" is way too open-ended for a mind like mine and I become paralyzed. So, with a barely perceptible shake of her head, my mom leads the way.

Breakfast is not the main meal on my mind this morning. From the moment I woke up, I've been obsessing about this dinner with the Murphys. Jared says I have no choice but to go, and I really wish I could think of a reason for why he's wrong about that.

"You're so far away," my mom says when we're seated. "I feel like I want to come sit on your side."

"Don't," I beg. I already feel like we're on a date, with my mom wearing tight jeans and a low-cut shirt instead of her standard (and appealingly baggy) scrubs. If she sits next to me in this small booth, I may have to begin emancipation procedures.

I can't recall the last time my mom went on an actual date with a man. There was a leather-jacket guy named Andreas many moons ago, but I'm not sure what happened to him. I like to think he died while attempting a motorcycle stunt.

The server comes and I give her my order without even opening the menu: pancakes, hash browns, OJ. (I'm my most efficient when I don't have to think and I'm barely aware of what's happening.) My mom gets an omelet.

Once our menus are cleared, my mom reaches into her purse and pulls out a folder. "Hey. Remember that short-story contest you won a few years ago?"

"I didn't actually win. I came in third place." Why is she bringing this up now? Has she officially run out of things to talk about with me?

"Third place in the whole country."

"Actually, just the state and only in my age bracket."

"Well, it was very impressive." She places the folder on the table and flings it open. "I found these online: college scholarship essay contests. Have you heard of these? NPR did a whole thing about it the other morning. There are a million different ones you can do. I spent my whole lunch break looking these up." She hands me a piece of paper and starts reading from the others. "The John F. Kennedy Profile in Courage Essay Contest—ten thousand dollars, college of your choice. Henry David Thoreau Scholarship—five thousand dollars." She hands me the entire stack. "With the way you write, you could really clean up here."

Now I know why she defied expectations and followed through with our breakfast plans. It wasn't simply to spend time with me, but also to give me another assignment.

"Wow," is the only response I can manage.

She grabs the folder and places it back in her purse. I think I've hurt her feelings. That tends to happen.

"I just thought it was a neat idea," she says. "You've always been a wonderful writer. And we're going to need all the help we can get for college. Unless your stepmother has a trust fund for you I don't know about, with all those fabulous tips she made cocktail waitressing."

She will never get over the fact that Theresa went from being a cocktail waitress to a woman whose only job now is to be a mother. And she did it by stealing my mom's husband. Sometimes I feel like my mom works so hard just so she can hold up an invisible cross-country middle finger to her younger replacement.

I get the resentment, especially with how much she has to work and for so little. She's like an indentured servant, always rushing off to the hospital whenever she's called, never able to say no. If she did, they'd find someone else. And it's not like she has anything to fall back on. The degree she's been working toward at night seems a long way from bearing any fruit.

A heap of pancakes appears before me. It's the add-ons that make Bell House's pancakes memorable. The house syrup, the strawberry butter, the powdered sugar. The pancakes themselves are pretty standard.

"College is going to be so great for you, honey. How many times in life do you get to just start all over again?"

That does sound tempting, actually. Can I start over today?

"The only people who like high school are cheerleaders and football players, and those people all end up miserable anyway."

"Weren't you a cheerleader?" I point out.

"For like a week. That doesn't count."

Over the years, my mom's stint as a cheerleader has gotten shorter and shorter. She used to claim she cheered a whole season, and now she cheered only a week. All I know is she was around long enough to be photographed with the rest of the team. I guess I could ask my dad for the truth—my parents dated back in high school—but when he and I finally get a chance to talk, the last person either of us wants to talk about is my mother.

She takes my hands before I can dig into my food. "What I'm trying to say is that you've got so many wonderful things ahead of you. Just remember that. It's a long way to the top, but the journey is totally worth it."

I nod and reclaim my hands for eating. My mom, however, is frozen, staring through her food. It lasts longer than I'm comfortable with.

"Mom."

She snaps awake, surprised. "Sorry." She unfolds a paper napkin and lays it on her lap. "I was just thinking."

"About?"

"About that boy who..."

The pancakes in my mouth suddenly lose their appeal. I keep wondering how he did it. Razor blade? Pills? Noose? Carbon monoxide? The casket was closed at the wake, so maybe he used a gun? I know he didn't jump off a bridge, considering the pristine condition of my letter. I can't find any details about his death. People online keep saying it was probably an overdose, which would be fitting. And peaceful. But maybe not. I wonder if at any point he regretted it. If there was a moment between deciding and dying when he changed his mind.

She lifts her fork. "Those poor parents. I just can't imagine."

I can. I witnessed it. The sadness in them, in his parents, was beyond what I've ever known or imagined, something total and unending. His mom was just destroyed, flattened. And right now, the two of them are probably sitting there, alone and confused, asking themselves the same sorts of questions I'm asking. The really messed-up part is that some of these questions will never have answers. Knowing that must be the worst.

But then there's my letter. Giving them the wrong answers, but still answers. Still something.

"If I ever lost you," my mom says, taking her first bite. "I just don't know what I'd do." She smiles helplessly.

For my mom, it's only a hypothetical. But for Connor's?

One dinner. Two hours, max. Jared's message repeats in my mind—just nod and confirm.

CHAPTER 8

The bus ride to the Murphys' house takes forty minutes. In a car, it would take half that, but I don't drive.

At first, I couldn't wait to get my license. I longed for the ability to just get up and go whenever I wanted. But any romantic vision I had of the road was quickly spoiled. In driver's ed, they show you nightmarish videos of car crashes and alarming statistics about mortality rates, and then they hand you a learner's permit and throw you behind the wheel. Sure, you've got an "expert" coaching you from the passenger seat, but you're the one in charge, struggling to remember all the rules you learned, and then just as you're getting the hang of it, you realize that even if you drive flawlessly, you have to trust that everyone else on the road will do the same.

But they don't. It's chaos out there. No one seems to use a blinker or come to a complete stop or yield to pedestrians.

The light is still turning green and the person in the car behind you blares their horn. Then there are animals running into the road, cops waiting around bends, and drivers staring at their phones. It's a miracle that anyone gets where they're going without harming themselves or others, because so many of the worst things that could happen—paralysis, disfigurement, brain damage, accidental manslaughter, drowning, decapitation, pulverization, incineration, bleeding out while waiting for help—can happen in a car.

On the day of my driver's test, I locked myself in the bathroom. Through the door, I heard my mom talking not so quietly on the phone: "What kind of kid isn't excited to get their license?" At one point she tried to hand me the phone. "Your father wants to speak to you." I hated her for calling him.

When I finally opened the door, my mom was in tears. "We can't keep doing this," she said. "You don't have to feel this way. Don't you want to feel better?" I must have said yes, because a week later I had my first appointment with Dr. Sherman. A few months after that, with the help of my pal Lexapro, I was able to get my license. I never actually use it, though. Lucky for me, we can't afford a second car.

The Murphys live in the newer part of town, where the houses are bigger and the lawns are wider and the driveways are longer. As the bus passes the front entrance of Ellison Park, I see the well-lit WELCOME sign that I spent so much of my summer refurbishing. I always knew Zoe lived over here by the park, but I wasn't sure exactly where. I must have passed by her street every day on my way to work and never knew it.

It's a short walk from the bus stop, but still, by the time I arrive, my armpits are drenched and the paper wrapped around my flower bouquet has become a soppy mush in my hands. On the porch, I tear the paper off the flowers, roll it into a ball, and shove it into the pocket of my pants.

The Murphy house sits peacefully between two majestic beech trees at the end of a wide cul-de-sac. The front door is painted a storybook red. It's time to ring the bell, but for some reason I can't lift my arm. These flowers should be for Zoe, as a gesture of, well, my affection or whatever, but instead I'm giving them to her mother because she lost her son. The only reason I'm here is because Connor isn't. How am I supposed to feel about that?

I'm so busy not ringing the doorbell that I barely notice the front door swing open to reveal Connor's mom, a confused smile on her face.

"What are you doing out there?" she says.

"Good night. I mean, good evening, Mrs. Murphy."

"Come on in. And please call me Cynthia."

I present the flowers.

"Oh. That is very sweet, Evan. Thank you."

She pulls me in for a hug, holding on a little too long. I worry that she can feel my heart slamming out of my chest. And then, over her shoulder, I see Zoe coming down the stairs. Unlike her mother, she does not look happy to see me. Her eyes seem to know who I am, a big non-truth teller, and also a fool to have ever agreed to come here tonight.

• • •

In the center of the table is a bowl of apples. They're so shiny and perfect I assume they're fake. But now, after staring at them for the past ten minutes, I'm convinced they're edible.

So is the food on my plate, but I'm finding it hard to breathe, let alone swallow. I've been trying to trap single pieces of rice between the tines of my fork, just a little game to pass the time.

"It's hot in here," Mrs. Murphy says, fanning herself. "Is anyone else feeling hot?"

I'm melting, but I keep my mouth shut.

"It's muggy for September," Mr. Murphy says. "I can lower the AC, if you want."

"No, it's fine." She dabs her head with her napkin.

Zoe hasn't spoken since I got here. Last week we finally talked after so many years (twice!), and now it's looking like the first two times may also be the last. I thought she'd be back at school today, it being Monday, but she was absent again. I wonder if she's ever coming back.

Mr. Murphy lifts a platter. "Would anyone else like more chicken?"

"I think you're the only one with an appetite, Larry," Mrs. Murphy says.

He hesitates for a moment, then forks a piece of chicken onto his plate. "Well, I'm not going to let it go to waste. It was very considerate of the Harrises to bring it over."

I cut off a bite of chicken, but I don't actually bring it up to my mouth.

"Did Connor tell you about the Harrises?" Mrs. Murphy asks me.

Part of my apprentice training at the park was learning the ranger code of ethics. There's a part in the handbook about being *honest in thought and deed*. Unfortunately, the park ranger handbook makes no mention of how to survive the jungle of high school, or how to not make a bad situation worse. For help with that, I've looked instead to Jared for advice. As terrible as that decision might prove to be, if I had just listened to him in the first place, I never would've gone to Connor's wake and I never would've been invited to tonight's dinner.

In response to her question, I simply nod and take a sip of water. I'm going with Jared on this—it's not the same as lying. I'm not actually speaking words.

"They're very old friends of ours," she says.

I can tell she's waiting for me to say something. I'm not supposed to—that's the plan—but now that I'm actually face-to-face with this woman and her needy eyes, making it through the whole night without words seems unrealistic, not to mention rude.

"Mmm," I say, which isn't technically a word. Even if it is, it's barely a word, and besides, it could be referring to the food that I'm pretending to eat.

"Our families used to ski together," Mrs. Murphy says. "We had some really nice times out there on the slopes."

I nod and nod and nod, and then, before I can stop myself, I open my mouth. "Connor loved skiing."

"Connor hated skiing," Zoe says.

I can feel Zoe's eyes on me, but I don't dare look over. Why did I think I could handle this? If I sense even a hint of pressure, I immediately buckle. Pressure is my kryptonite. Connor hates skiing like I hate pressure.

"Right, he *hated* it. That's what I meant. It was, yeah, just pure hate whenever skiing was the topic. He *loved* talking about how much he hated skiing."

"So you guys hung out a lot? You and Connor?" Mrs. Murphy asks.

It's a mistake to tear my eyes away from the bowl of apples, but I do it anyway. Mrs. Murphy's face is begging for even the tiniest bit of information. Something. Anything.

What I come up with, finally, is, "Pretty much," and I'm actually proud of this answer, because it's not *yes* and also because *a lot* means something different to different people. Do I speak to my father *a lot*? Compared with how often soldiers in Afghanistan talk to their dads, yeah, probably, I think that's fair to say.

But Zoe wants clarification. "Where?"

"You mean, where did we hang out?"

"Yes, where?"

Jared never specified what to do about questions that required more than a simple yes or no. It turns out this is not true/false. This is an essay exam.

"Well," I say, forcing a quick cough, "we'd do most of our hanging out at my house. I mean, sometimes we'd go to his house—I mean, here—if nobody else was here." She's about to call me a liar and a phony—I know it. I'll be thrown out of this house, and then I won't just be invisible, I'll be a pariah, too. I'll be homeschooled and my only connection to the outside world will be social media and email. Oh! "Email," I say. "We would email a lot, mostly. Sometimes he didn't want to hang out in person. Which I understood. We had that in common, I guess."

"We looked through his emails," Zoe says. "There aren't any from you."

Maybe I'm just excited that she's talking to me again. Maybe that's why, against my better judgment, I keep stringing more and more words together. "Well, yeah, I mean, that's because he had a different account. A secret account. I should have said that before. That was probably very confusing. Sorry."

"Why was it secret?" Zoe asks.

"Why was it secret?" I repeat. Now seems like a good time to start eating. I shovel some rice into my mouth and gesture to the others that I'll be ready to answer Zoe's perfectly reasonable question after I've swallowed all my food, just because it's poor etiquette to talk with food in your mouth, as everyone knows, obviously. I swallow and wash it all down with some water.

"It was secret because it was just . . . he thought it would be more private that way."

Mrs. Murphy shakes her head. "I told you, Larry. He knew you read his emails."

"And I don't regret it," Mr. Murphy says, reaching for his wine. "Somebody had to be the bad guy."

They stare at each other, continuing their conversation with silent, powerful words. I look away, allowing them privacy.

"It's just weird," Zoe says. "The only time I ever saw you and my brother together was when he shoved you at school last week."

Shit. She remembers. Of course she remembers.

Mrs. Murphy leans over. "Connor shoved you?"

"I wouldn't say it like that, Mrs. Murphy. In that way. I tripped, is what really happened."

"Please, Evan, call me Cynthia."

"Oh, right, I'm sorry." Relief at the change of subject. "Cynthia." I smile at her.

"I was there," Zoe says. "I saw the whole thing. He pushed you. Hard."

A drop of sweat falls from my armpit all the way down my torso to the waistband of my jeans. No mere subject change will get me out of this.

"Oh, I remember now," I say. "About what happened. That was a misunderstanding. Because, the thing was, he didn't want us to talk at school, and that's exactly what I did. I tried to talk to him at school. It wasn't really a big deal, seriously. It was my fault."

"Why didn't he want you to talk to him at school?" Zoe says.

It never ends. The more I answer, the more they ask. I have to stop this. But how?

"He didn't really want anyone to know we were friends," I tell them. "He was embarrassed, I guess."

"Why would he be embarrassed?" Mrs. Murphy—I mean, *Cynthia*—says.

I wipe my forehead with my napkin, not sophisticated but so necessary. "I guess because he thought I was sort of..."

"A nerd?" Zoe says.

"Zoe!" Her father shoots her a look, but Zoe ignores him, not about to let up on me. "Isn't that what you meant?" she says.

"Loser, I was going to say, actually. But *nerd* works, too."

Cynthia places her hand on my arm. "That wasn't very nice."

"Well," Zoe says, "Connor wasn't very nice, so that makes sense."

Cynthia sighs. "Connor was...a complicated person."

"No, Connor was a bad person. There's a difference."

"Zoe, please," Mr. Murphy says.

"Dad, don't pretend like you don't agree with me."

"It's too hot in here," Cynthia says, which is exactly what I was thinking.

"I'll lower the AC," Mr. Murphy repeats, but he doesn't leave the table.

I can now appreciate at least one plus side of having divorced parents and never actually sitting down to eat dinner with my mom at home—not having to endure this.

Cynthia wipes her brow. "You refuse to remember any of the good things. Both of you. You refuse to see anything positive."

"Because there were no good things," Zoe says. "What were the good things?"

"I don't want to have this conversation in front of our guest," Cynthia says.

I drink more water and I keep pretending to drink long after my glass is empty.

"What were the good things, Mom?"

"There were good things," Cynthia insists.

"Okay, then say what they were. Tell me."

"There were good things."

"Yes, you keep saying that. What *were* they?"

Cynthia doesn't answer. Mr. Murphy looks down at his plate.

The question hangs in the room, a thick, hot smog that no one can get out from under. I watch them all, struggling to breathe, struggling to be. Struggling.

"I remember a lot of good things about Connor."

All eyes turn. That was me who just spoke. I said that. Why did I just say that? How did those words come out of my mouth?

"Like what?" Zoe wants to know.

"Never mind," I say. "I shouldn't have... I'm sorry."

"Again you're sorry," Zoe says, dismissing my entire existence.

"Go ahead, Evan. You were saying something," Cynthia says.

"It doesn't matter. Really."

"We want to hear what you have to say. Please, Evan."

I don't know how to do it, how to let this woman down after all she's been through. Her heart is in my hands. That's what it feels like. Even her husband is standing by, all alert, his fork down, just waiting. I glance at the last person at the table: Zoe. Her expression is softer now, as if her curiosity has briefly overpowered her doubt. They need something, this family. They need me to say *something* that will make them feel better.

"Well," I begin, "Connor and I had a really great time together, this one day, recently. That's something good that I remember about Connor. That's what I keep thinking about. That day. That one day."

I already know that what I just said won't be enough. They'll want more. I keep painting myself into a corner. They want specifics, details. They *need* them. I'm scrambling for the next tidbit, the whole time staring at that bowl in the middle of the table.

"Apples," I say, before thinking it through. "We went to the apples...place." I look up. "Anyway, I knew it was stupid. I don't know why I even brought it up." I need to leave. Right now. I squeeze my fists in my lap, my nails digging into my palms. How can I get away from here without being rude?

"He took you to the orchard?" Cynthia says.

I scan her expression. It looks like I've touched on something. There's a new brightness in everyone's eyes. Their faces encourage me. I can't leave now. "Yes, he did."

"When?" Cynthia asks.

"Once. It was just that once."

"I thought that place closed," Mr. Murphy says. "Years ago."

"Exactly, which is why we were so bummed when we got there, because it was totally closed down, and Connor said the apples there were the best."

Cynthia is smiling, but also tearing up. "We used to go to the orchard all the time. We'd do picnics out there. Remember that, Zoe?"

"Yeah," Zoe says, her expression somewhere between wistful surprise and forced indifference.

Cynthia looks to her husband across the table. "You and Connor had that little toy plane you would fly. Until you flew it into the creek."

Mr. Murphy almost smiles. "That was an emergency landing."

"Oh, Evan, I can't believe Connor took you there," Cynthia says. "I bet that was fun. I bet you two had some real fun."

"We did. The whole day was just...amazing. That was back in the spring, I think."

"Larry, what was the name of that ice cream place out there we loved?" Cynthia asks.

"À La Mode," he answers.

"That was it," she says with genuine appreciation. "À La Mode."

"That's where we went, actually," I say, my enthusiasm getting the better of me. "We got ice cream at that À La Mode place."

"They had that homemade hot fudge," Mr. Murphy recalls.

"We would sit in the meadow with all the sycamores," Cynthia says, smiling at Zoe. "And you and your brother would look for four-leaf clovers."

"I'd completely forgotten about that place," Mr. Murphy says.

"Well, I guess Connor didn't," Cynthia says. "Isn't that right, Evan?"

I look at her and then Mr. Murphy and then Zoe, and I release all the air from my chest, and I tell them exactly what they are aching to hear: "That's right."

The air releases from their chests, too. It feels that way. There's relief, real relief, small but tangible, in the room. What I'm doing, what I'm saying, is working, it's helping, and that's all I want, to help.

"We would do that sort of thing all the time, actually," I say, not knowing how to stop myself now. "Just go somewhere and talk." Like buddies. Like friends. "We'd talk about movies and people at school. We'd talk about girls. You know...just normal stuff. Connor was easy to talk to."

I see how much my words mean to them. It feels good to make them feel good. It's the right thing for me to be doing, to be making their hurt go away, even for a moment.

"That one day," I say, "at the orchard, I remember, we found this field, and collapsed on the grass, and we looked up at the sky, and we just...talked."

About our lives. Where we were. Where we were going. What would happen after school. We didn't know exactly. We just knew we'd figure it out. We'd have each other's backs. Whatever it was...

"...anything seemed possible."

I pause, thinking I've lost them, that I've lost myself, but it's too late now. My mouth forges on without my mind, the words arriving as if they've been waiting a lifetime to be spoken.

"And the sun that day, I can picture it, it was so bright. And we were lying there, looking up at the sky. It looked endless, like it went on forever."

And the tree.

"We saw this tree. This incredibly tall oak tree. Bigger than all the others. We got up and we ran over to it and we started climbing it. We didn't even think."

The Murphys climb with me, hanging on my every word.

"We kept climbing. Higher and higher." Climbing and climbing, almost at the top, but then... "The branch gave way."

I fell.

"I'm on the ground. My arm is numb. I'm waiting."

Any second now. *Any second now.*

"And I look, and I see..."

I see...

"...Connor. He's come to get me."

I stop talking, finally. They're all looking at me, as if waiting for me to say more. But I can hardly comprehend what I've already spoken. It's like I'm waking from a dream. I was sitting here, describing that day, that nightmare day, except it wasn't that day, not exactly. This time Connor was there. I mean, he wasn't really there, but in my mind, it was like he was, and all of a sudden that same day wasn't such a nightmare. It was something else.

In my periphery, I see Cynthia reaching over and then I feel her arms wrapping around me.

"Thank you, Evan," she says. "Thank you."

It's the best feeling. And the worst.

● ● ●

Zoe follows me out of the house. "I'll take you home," she says.

I never thought there'd be an instance where I would deny Zoe Murphy, but all I want right now is to be alone. "You don't have to."

"I need to go for a drive. Hop in."

She loops around the horseshoe driveway and zips out into the street. I thought I'd finally be able to breathe out for the first time in hours, but no. I'm now sitting shotgun in Zoe Murphy's blue Volvo.

I have literally dreamed about this moment, having a chance to be alone with her like this, just a few inches away. But right now I'm in no condition to be *on*. Someone, please, turn me off.

The silence is begging me to kill it. "This is a nice car. What is it, German?"

"It's a piece of crap," Zoe says. "There's always something wrong with it."

The engine growls as Zoe picks up speed. She doesn't say another word to me the whole ride home, even when I'm telling her which streets to take to my house. The quiet ride gives me the opportunity to review the night and arrive at the assessment that it was a complete and unequivocal failure. At one point, when the speedometer is up past sixty, I imagine unbuckling my belt, pulling the door handle, and tumbling out onto the busy road. What a tragedy.

Once we're parked outside my unlit house, Zoe finally turns and acknowledges me. "You probably think I'm just a junior and I'm clueless, but I know what's really going on."

A frightening sharpness to her expression. "I don't know what you mean."

"You and Connor weren't sending secret emails because you were friends."

I should have done it, jumped out of the car when I had the chance. "What?"

"I've been racking my brain all night trying to figure out why you two would possibly be talking to each other," Zoe says. "Let me guess. Was it about drugs?"

"*Drugs?*"

"That's what he was mad about the other day at lunch, isn't it? When he pushed you? Be honest with me, please. I just want to know the truth."

"No. Are you crazy? Me? I would never. That's not something I'm involved in. I swear." Finally, a truthful truth.

"Oh yeah? You swear?"

Zoe's mother keeps showering me with hugs, but Zoe only douses me with suspicion. "I swear."

She studies me for a moment, and then turns away, making it clear I'm dismissed.

I try to open the door, but it's locked. She hits a button, but at the same time I'm pulling the handle. I release the handle so she can now unlock the door without my stupid hand getting in the way. When I finally hear that heavenly click, I throw open my door and inhale a whole chestful of fresh air. I shut the door gently behind me and watch her accelerate into the night. How wrong I've been about everything from the very start. *The worst that could happen.* It's still happening.

CHAPTER 9

I'm not sure why I keep reporting back to Jared after every new disaster. I never feel better after our chats. Jared has a way of highlighting my errors so they seem even worse than I first realized.

But I'm so lost right now, sitting alone on the couch in my dark living room. Jared is the only person in the entire world who has even the slightest appreciation for where I am. I'm floating through space and he's the voice in my earpiece from central command. I might not agree with his tactics, but without him, there's a good chance I may never get back home.

I bring Jared up to speed with what happened at the Murphys. As usual, I somehow fail to anticipate where he'll focus his critique.

His parents think you were lovers.

You realize that, right?

What? Why would they think that?

Umm. You were best friends,
but he wouldn't let you talk to him at school?
And when you did, he kicked your ass?
That's like the exact formula for
secret gay high school lovers.

Oh my god.

I told you what to do.
What did I say?
Nod and confirm. That's all.

I tried. You don't understand.
It's different when they're looking you in the eye.
I got nervous. I just started talking,
and once I started

You couldn't stop.

They didn't want me to stop!

It's true. I don't think I realized it until just now, but it's
like they were helping me along, filling in the gaps when I
didn't know where the story should go next. I'm not blaming

them. Obviously. I know this is all on me, but I also know, from the looks on their faces, that they wanted me to keep going. They *needed* me to.

The thing is, I tried to tell them the truth. I mean, I *did* tell them the truth. I told Connor's parents that he wasn't the one who wrote the letter. I told them, point blank, but they wouldn't listen.

So what else did you completely fuck up?

Well, I'm pretty sure Zoe hates me.
She thinks Connor and I
were doing drugs together.

You're the best.
I really mean that.
What else?

Nothing.

Nothing?

I mean, I told them we wrote emails.

Emails.

Yeah. I told them that Connor and I emailed.
And that he had a secret email account.

Oh, right, one of those "secret"
email accounts. Sure. For sending pictures
of your penises to each other.

It's all just a big joke to him. I really don't know why I keep
turning to Jared for advice.

No, I just said he had this secret account
and we would send emails to each other.

I mean, honestly?
Could you be any worse at this?

Is that so bad?

They're going to want to see your emails.

Oh no.

Oh yes.

Oh shit.

Of course they're going to want to see our emails. What's
wrong with me? Seriously. Why do I keep fooling myself into
thinking that the worst that could happen has already happened? Things *always* get worse. It's guaranteed. That's how

life works. You're born and you keep getting older and grayer and sicker, and no matter what efforts you make to reverse the process, you die, every single time. To repeat: worse, worse, worse, and then death. I have a long way to go before the worst. This is only the beginning.

I'm so screwed.
What the hell am I going to do?

I can do emails.

What do you mean?

I can make the emails.

You can? How?

It's easy. You make up an account
and backdate the emails. There's a reason
I was the only CIT with key card access
to the computer cluster this summer:
I have skills, son.

I'd be giving them what they want—what they *need*. I'd be helping them.

It's tempting. It really is. But it's also…sick? I can't keep doing this, deceiving these poor people. I'm not cut out for it.

At one point tonight it felt like I was sweating from my eyes—that's how anxious I was. Had I perspired another drop, I might have mummified. I can't go on like this. I'm all drained out.

I turn my phone over so it's facedown. The light from the screen waves over my cast. The memory of the story I conjured up for the Murphys hits me anew. They were talking about the orchard, and I guess the way they were talking about it made me think of Ellison Park. And I can no longer think of Ellison Park without thinking of the tree and my fall. Connor wasn't there that day, of course. But I guess...he could've been.

I leave the dark living room and head upstairs. Once in bed, I put on my headphones and stream a playlist called "Jazz for Newbies." I can't say I totally get jazz, but I've been trying. I wait for the music to take me somewhere, but it never does. I'm too invested in what I'm listening to for my mind to escape. Frankly, only one of the instruments even interests me. I keep waiting to hear what the guitar is going to do.

My mom appears at my doorway, forcing my head up off the pillow. I remove my headphones to hear her.

"Did you eat already?" she asks.

"Um. Yeah." I already know what she'll ask next, so I quickly cycle through potential answers: made a sandwich, warmed up frozen pizza, grabbed Chinese.

But instead, she says, "Darn," and it almost sounds like maybe she was hoping I *hadn't* eaten yet.

"That was fun the other day, right?" she says. "Going out for breakfast?"

So much has happened since our breakfast it already feels like ages ago. "Yeah. Definitely. It was."

"I was thinking, how about I bag one of my shifts this week? When's the last time we did a taco night?"

I can't remember, but I'm pretty sure those tortillas in the freezer have officially turned by now. "Oh. You don't have to."

"No, I want to. Maybe we could even start brainstorming those essay questions together."

The essays. Of course. Her face waits expectantly. "Sure," I say. "That would be great."

"Oh. That's exciting," she says, looking victorious. "I'm excited now. Something to look forward to."

"Yeah."

• • •

The next day, I see Zoe walking through the cafeteria, joining friends at a table. If I weren't already seated, I would've had to sit down. It's that much of a shock to my system. I haven't seen her in school since the first day.

So much has happened in a week. I've interacted with Zoe more than ever—at the wake, at her house, in her car—but all those moments were under the worst of circumstances. This, seeing her right now, seated at a table in the school cafeteria, feels right and normal. This is how I'm used to seeing her. This makes sense.

Zoe must have felt my stare from across the room, because now she's staring back at me. She's staring so intensely that it's almost as if she's daring me to turn away. I can't. I don't want to. I don't know what I'm supposed to be doing. I smile, hoping she'll do the same. She does not. It's like she couldn't do it even if she tried.

She lifts her tray and leaves her friends at the table. Her food goes into the trash, and without even a peek in my direction, she walks out of the cafeteria.

I'm much better at interpreting books and stories than I am at understanding the decisions made by living, breathing people. But in this case, I can easily apply Mrs. Kiczek's strategies for critical analysis to the real-life behavior I just witnessed. The action of our beautiful and righteous heroine Zoe Murphy throwing her food in the garbage is really a metaphor for how she feels about our narrator. In Zoe Murphy's eyes, Evan Hansen is trash.

There I go again, overestimating my importance. How quickly I forget *meh*-self. Why should I assume this has anything to do with me? Her brother is *dead*. Maybe she just doesn't have an appetite. I can relate to that. It's just that it's hard to see her look so troubled, especially after the way she began to lighten up at dinner. Her mood shifted when we were talking about Connor. When I was telling her and her parents things they didn't already know. Filling in missing pieces. It's like I was able to make them forget the weight of their misery. I brought them some relief.

I look across the cafeteria to where Jared's sitting. Leaving my stomach with only my morning medication to feed on, I pack up my lunch and head over to his table.

"How do the emails work?" I ask.

"Well, *email* is short for 'electronic mail,'" Jared says. "Ray Tomlinson is credited as inventing the technology in 1971, but we all know it was really the brainchild of Shiva Ayyadurai."

"This is serious." I keep my voice as low as possible.

Jared leans back conspiratorially. "It's going to cost you."

"How much?"

"Two grand," Jared says.

"Two thousand dollars? Are you insane?"

"Five hundred."

"I can give you twenty."

"Fine. But you're a dick," Jared says. "Meet me at four after school. I'll text you the location."

CHAPTER 10

Jared's SUV swerves into the lot of Workout Heaven and slams into a parking spot. He walks past me and through the revolving door of the gym.

I follow him inside. "Why are we here?"

Jared flashes a membership card to the muscled bro at the front desk and identifies me as his guest. After filling out some paperwork, I follow Jared through a loud and cavernous room.

Everything about Workout Heaven makes me anxious. The bright fluorescent lights. The intense volume. The amount of exposed skin. I still don't know what we're doing at a place like this.

"Do you work out here?" I ask.

"No, but my parents think I do," Jared says. "Trust me, this is a great spot to do homework. Have you ever watched a woman run on a treadmill?"

"That is not—I don't feel—"

"Look, for this kind of job, I can't be on my home network. Think of it as an extra precaution. Being on open Wi-Fi will make it harder for anyone to trace this back to us."

He really makes what we're doing sound extra unseemly. "I don't know about this. What if someone from school sees us?"

"I would never let that happen. I have a reputation. Besides, no one from our school comes here. Look around. It's all moms and shit."

I scan the gym. As loud as it is, it's actually pretty empty. I guess it's just the booming music and high ceilings. "Still, maybe we shouldn't be doing this. There's got to be another way. If the Murphys ask me about the emails, I just won't respond. It's not like they're going to hunt me down, right?"

"If you back out now, you still owe me the twenty dollars," Jared says, sitting down on a back bench.

I picture Zoe's face, the look she had at lunch. Her parents probably have that same look right now, heavy and defeated.

"Let's just try one email and see what happens," I say.

Jared opens a blank file on his laptop and begins typing.

Yo Evan,

Sorry it's been a minute. I been all crazy and shit. You feel me?

"Why are you making him talk like that?"

"Like what?" Jared says.

"You know, like that. Just make him talk normally."
Jared erases everything and starts again.

> **Dearest Mr. Hansen,**
>
> **I am terribly sorry, alas, that I have failed
> to maintain contact. Life has been most
> challenging of late.**

"Okay, now he sounds like a prince or something. Just have him speak like you and I do. And it has to match my letter exactly. Make it say 'Dear Evan Hansen.'"
"Why would you guys refer to each other by your full names?"
"I don't know. It just has to be that way, okay?"
"Suit yourself."

> **Dear Evan Hansen,**
>
> **Sorry I've been out of touch. Things have been
> crazy.**

"That's perfect," I say.

> **I want you to know that you've been on my
> mind this whole time. I rub my nipples every
> night as I picture your sweet, sweet face.**

"Why would you write that?" I ask.
"I'm just trying to tell the truth."

"You know, if you're not going to take this seriously, then forget it. These emails have to prove that we were actually friends. They have to be completely realistic."

"There is nothing unrealistic about the love that one man feels for another."

"Just write down exactly what I say. 'Life without you has been hard.'"

Jared laughs under his breath. "'Hard'?"

"Fine, change it to 'rough.'"

"Kinky."

"Here, let me type."

> **Life without you has been difficult. I really miss talking to you about life and other stuff.**

"Very specific," Jared says.

"Shut up."

> **I like my parents.**

"Who says that?" Jared asks.

> **I love my parents, but I hate how much we fight. I should really stop smoking drugs.**

"'Smoking drugs'?" Jared shakes his head at me in disappointment.

"Just fix it."

"This isn't realistic at all."

"How do you know? You barely knew Connor."

He gives me another look.

"The objective here is to show that I was a good friend. That I was really trying to help him."

"Oh my god." He grabs the laptop back.

> **I should really take your advice and stop smoking crack.**

"Crack?" I say. "That's a little extreme, no? Do people in our school actually smoke crack?"

> **I should really take your advice and stop smoking pot. Maybe then everything might be okay. And I'll try to be nicer. Wish me luck.**

"That's not bad, actually," I say. "Now sign it at the bottom 'Sincerely, Me.'"

"Not even gonna ask," Jared says. "Are we done yet?"

"I can't just show them one email. We need a reply from me back to Connor."

There's a loud clang as a tattooed man lets his heavy weights crash to the floor. Even with the thick padding, the impact reverberates under our feet. The man, now pacing around, resembles a rabid MMA fighter primed for battle. This guy could yank someone's head clean off their neck if he felt like it.

I can relate. Not the roid-rage aggression part, or the strength to carry out manual decapitation, but the sensation of being a match strike away from full explosion. I'm actually jealous of this man that he's found an outlet for all his energy. I don't exercise or play sports or participate in any physically demanding hobbies. I did a ton of walking over the summer, but that's about it. I think Dr. Sherman was hoping that writing letters would offer me that same sort of deep release. It hasn't worked out that way.

"Okay," I say. "You ready?"

Jared is gazing across the room. "Look at the bumper on that one."

I resist the temptation to look. "All right. Write down what I say. 'Dear Connor Murphy, I just got back from the gym.'"

"The gym?" Jared says. "Seriously?"

"'I just got back from a hike.'"

"That's more believable," Jared says.

"'I took pictures of the most amazing trees.'"

"No," Jared says.

"But that really happened."

"Sometimes you truly break my heart."

Dear Connor Murphy,

I'm really proud of you for pushing through this tough time. It really seems like you're starting to turn things around. You know I'm here for you whenever you need me.

Sincerely,
Me

"I have to say, the friendship you guys had is just precious," Jared says.

"Yeah, it does seem nice, doesn't it?"

I can see from Jared's smirk that he wasn't serious. I just meant that a friendship like this would probably be nice. Having someone to talk to about things, someone who would listen.

P.S. Your sister's hot.

"What the hell?"

"My bad," Jared says, erasing that last line.

"Okay, let's do another one."

We get into a groove. *Dear Evan Hansen, I'm so lucky to call you a friend. Dear Connor Murphy, I'm always on your side, brother. Dear Evan Hansen, I owe you big time. Dear Connor Murphy, don't even mention it. Dear Evan Hansen, you know I've got your back.*

All told, we churn out a dozen emails, six from Connor and six from me. I feel as exhilarated and out of breath as the bald guy hyperventilating over by the water fountain. We slap on a fake email address for Connor and then Jared uses his technical wizardry to time-stamp the emails to land within the spring.

"I need to print these out," I say.

Jared shuts his laptop. "There's an office supply store in this strip mall."

"Perfect," I say, standing up. "After that, there's one more favor I need."

"Sorry, your twenty dollars is all used up."

"Are you sure? I thought you said you wanted to see where the Murphys live."

Later that evening, Jared eases up to the end of the Murphy driveway. I lower my window and place the emails into their brick mailbox. Driving away, Jared presents his fist and waits for me to bump it. He wants to celebrate what we just pulled off, but I leave him hanging. As I watch the Murphys' house diminish in my side mirror, I'm in no mood for celebration.

"Pull over," I say.

"Why?"

"Seriously, pull over. I think I'm going to puke."

My family is gathered in the living room, looking all Norman Rockwell. (I wasn't planning on coming home. I left this house for a reason, didn't I? Turns out, I just couldn't stay away.)

Larry is nursing a scotch. Cynthia and Zoe are reading through the same stack of papers.

I never realized Connor was so interested in trees, Cynthia says.

Speak of the devil. I can't say I'm surprised about being the topic of conversation. They loved talking behind my back when I was alive, too.

I'm pretty sure they're talking about weed, Zoe says.

Where? I don't see that, Cynthia says.

When they say trees?

Oh, Cynthia says. *Oh.*

I lean over my mother's shoulder, see my name on the paper. I also see the name Evan Hansen.

You have to read these, Larry.

Larry nods, sips his Laphroaig. (A scotch habit doesn't count, you see. It's part of the job. Hell, the old man's firm gifts him a new bottle every Christmas. I sampled my father's collection. Not my thing. Alcohol was always my least favorite buzz.)

He seems, just, I don't know, different, Cynthia says.

They're reading emails. From me to Evan. From Evan back to me. What is this? "I loved that documentary you told me about. It was delightful." Who talks like that? "I'm excited to go on long walks with you this summer." It's like a whole creepy story. "I've given serious thought to what you said. Family is definitely most important."

I've been good and gone too many nights to count. I've been up late and baked, and I'd scribble out wacky shit. But never have I come up with anything this bonkers.

"Dear Evan Hansen, you're the man."

Amazing.

"Life is looking up. Way up."

I take it back. This shit is brilliant.

"I'm ready to make a change. All thanks to you."

Why is Evan doing this? First he plants a letter for me to find. Now he's got my family involved, feeding them lies? Guess what, Mom. The reason I seem "different" is because this isn't fucking *me*.

My mother takes off her reading glasses, the ones she never wanted to be photographed wearing. *I never knew how much our trips to the apple orchard meant to him.*

The apple orchard. Haven't thought about that place in years. Thinking about it now, I have to say, nothing terrible comes to mind. No blowup fights or traumatic episodes. That's usually what happens when I dig too deep into memories. The worst stuff pops up first. But those orchard trips were pretty uneventful. In a good way. We acted like a normal family. My mother would pack lunches. Zoe and I would roll down that bumpy hill. My father put work aside. Paid attention. Why couldn't that happen more often? Why couldn't we carry that feeling home with us?

He says here that when it closed, he felt like his childhood ended. It makes sense when you think about it. That's around the time his behavior really started changing.

Um, no. If it's answers you want, Mom, you're digging in the wrong place. That's one thing about my mother. You see, my father is convinced there's only one right answer to every question. But my mother will keep searching forever. She'll try anything and everything. Sounds noble—and maybe it is—but even that approach can start to feel like torture. Especially when you're the lab rat.

I can't do this, Zoe says. She drops the papers and rises from the couch. Thankfully, someone in my family seems to have a functioning bullshit detector.

But she can't escape. Larry hits her with one of his stock questions: *How's school?*

Amazing, Zoe says. *All of a sudden, everyone wants to be my friend. I'm the dead kid's sister.*

The dead kid. Me.

I'm sure Mr. Contrell is happy to have you back at practice, my mother says.

You guys really don't have to do this, Zoe says.

Do what?

Just because Connor isn't here, trying to punch through my door, screaming at the top of his lungs that he's going to kill me for no reason, that doesn't mean that all of a sudden we're the fucking Brady Bunch.

Not the most comfortable thing to hear your little sister say. But actually, I think there's a compliment in there somewhere. Some vindication, at least. Because I've often said: maybe it's not me contaminating the family pond, but the other way around.

She storms off. Not much of a storm, in truth. If it were me, I probably would've smashed something. (Then, afterward, I'd feel bad about it. But not bad enough to apologize. Or not do it again.)

She'll be all right, my mother says. *We are all grieving in our own way.*

Larry knocks back his scotch.

My mother returns to the emails. *I feel like I'm seeing a new side of him. He seems so much lighter here. I can't remember the last time I heard him laugh.*

I laugh plenty. I mean, I *laughed* plenty. I laughed at how absurdly fucked everything is. I laughed because there's not much else you can do. You can laugh or you can cry. I'd do plenty of both. But see, any time my mother got a glimpse of the raw me, she couldn't take it. There'd be so much fear in her eyes. There was love, too—I saw it. But the fear...that's what stuck with me. You catch that look, and it's not like you're itching to open yourself up. No, you shut down pretty quick.

I'm going to bed, my father announces.

Come sit with me.

I'm exhausted.

You know, Larry, at some point, you're going to have to start—

Not tonight. Please.

I suppose this is what I get for building my walls so high. My family never actually knew about my life. Occasionally I'd reference *a friend* (going out with *a friend*; got it from *a friend*). But I don't think they believed me. Especially when I never forked over a name.

(Even now, I don't like saying his name. I wonder: Has he even noticed I'm gone?)

I wander upstairs to Zoe's room. I find her strumming her unplugged electric guitar. What she said about me is only partly true. I screamed at her a few times. Banged on her door.

I never threatened to kill her, though. Does she really believe that? Of course I'd never actually hurt her. It's like that quote: "full of sound and fury, signifying nothing." That was me. (That was also Shakespeare. Just because I didn't hand in my essay on *Macbeth* doesn't mean I didn't pay attention. Maybe I paid too much attention.)

She's on the carpet now, her back against the bed. Her strumming stops. She props her pick in her mouth and scribbles in a notebook.

I can't remember the last time I was in her bedroom. We were next-door neighbors who just stopped saying hello. I thought she was the clean one, but this is chaos in here. Clothes scattered. Blurry still-life photos from an instant camera. A pile of loose guitar strings. Old toast on a plate, next to a dirty knife.

(Lady Macbeth is another famous suicide. There's a line of hers I underlined. Something about how you get no lasting satisfaction from causing destruction. In the end, the only real solution is to destroy yourself.)

A new sound. Zoe is talking. Not talking, actually. Softly singing:

> *I could curl up and hide in my room*
> *Here in my bed still sobbing tomorrow*

She mutes the chord. More scribbling in her notebook. She sings a cappella:

> *I could give in to all the gloom*
> *But tell me, tell me what for?*

She hums while she writes. It's a developing melody. She retrieves her pick. Nestles the guitar to her chest like that raggedy bear she used to tote around.

Early on, we got along fine. Backseat passengers on the same ride. We'd share beds on vacations. (Before Larry had his name on the letterhead, we'd all pile into one hotel room.) We'd feed the cats under our deck. (This was back at our old house. Cynthia didn't want us letting them inside. *Diseases*, she said.) We'd trade Halloween candy. (Zoe liked chocolate. I was all about the sours.) She'd want to do everything I was doing. Play with my cars and X-Men. Pretend she was a soldier in my army.

At some point, though, she stopped fighting for me. Where's the loyalty? The other day at lunch, when Evan and I had that argument, she went to see if *he* was OK. What about me? Who was checking up on *me*?

> *Why should I have a heavy heart?*
> *Why should I start to break in pieces?*
> *Why should I go and fall apart for you?*

I never knew she was singing in here. Now that I'm hearing her, there's no way to unhear. She enunciates each syllable, commanding my attention. A private moment unknowingly shared. There's so much hurt in her voice. Even more of it in her words.

> *Why should I play the grieving girl and lie?*
> *Saying that I miss you and that my*
> *World has gone dark without your light*
> *I will sing no requiem tonight*

I wouldn't call it a lullaby.

CHAPTER 11

Mr. Lansky collects our papers and promises that the results of the quiz we just took won't count toward our final grade. It's a relief, considering I could barely concentrate. Mr. Lansky wants to see what each of us already knows and doesn't know about the different states of matter. I'm more focused on what I know and don't know about my own life.

What I know: Jared and I delivered a packet of emails to the Murphys on Tuesday. It's now Thursday.

What I don't know: Whether the Murphys received the emails. Whether they read them. What they thought of what they read. Whether the emails helped them or not. What they want from me now.

I can't even remember what Jared and I wrote. The words arrived in a mad, inspired rush. I handed over my only physical copy to the Murphys. I was going to ask Jared to send me the files, assuming he didn't already get rid of them, but I decided I don't want to see them. I'm trying to forget that they exist. That we did what we did.

The bell rings and it's off to lunch. I lag behind my classmates. What's the hurry? Before all this, I was alone, but I still had a few squeezes left in my tube of hope. Connor Murphy wasn't a part of my daily life. He, like me, existed in the background. Our paths didn't cross, and if they did, neither of us noticed. I was able to sit in the back of the cafeteria, sneaking glances at Zoe and imagining the possibility, however farfetched, that one day we might be together. Now I don't even lift my head at lunch. I'm too scared to catch another one of her icy stares from across the room.

I enter through the open double doors into an onslaught of aromas and sounds. I'm the last one to arrive, it seems, which is fine, because I don't need much time to eat, if I eat at all. My usual table has plenty of open seats. I take one. As I'm sitting down, someone says, "Hey, Evan."

The kid seated across from me looks familiar, but I don't know his name.

"Sam," he says. "We have English together."

"Oh. Right. Hey."

Sam resumes eating. I stare into his thick forest of hair. Where did he come from? Has he always been here? I've basically gone all of high school as a nonentity. Being acknowledged all of a sudden fills me with a strange and unsettling sensation.

Since my eyes are already raised, I keep them up for just a

moment longer and take stock of my surroundings. As I feared, I'm getting stared at. But this time not from Zoe. The stares are coming from all over the cafeteria and not all at once. They're not quite stares, actually, more like brief glances. A head turn here. A peek over there.

I lower my head and start unpacking my sandwich. At this point, just the sight of my SunButter standard fills me with dread. When I was working at Ellison Park over the summer, my boss, Ranger Gus, and I would grab lunch at one of the nearby food trucks. My favorite was the Korean tacos. I'm practically salivating right now thinking about those tacos. That, right there, was living. It actually makes me excited for dinner. Tonight is taco night with Mom.

I take a chomp out of the flavored Styrofoam in my hands. The bench shakes as someone takes a seat next to me.

"Oh my god, how *are* you?" Alana Beck says. "How is everything?"

My reaction time in social situations is always slow, but with Alana it's even more delayed. Her brightness is like the sun reflected off snow.

I'm not sure why she's so interested in how I'm doing, but it's nice that she's asking. "I'm okay, I guess."

She cringes, as if in pain. "You are amazing."

"Me?"

"Jared has been telling everyone about you and Connor, how close you guys were, how you were, like, best friends."

Now I'm the one cringing in pain. Can an ulcer form instantaneously?

"Everyone is talking about how brave you've been this week," Alana says, her hands clasped, a nun consoling a bed-ridden patient.

"They are?" My voice cracks and I almost crack with it.

I scan the room. Is that why everyone keeps looking at me? Sam delivers a miraculously timed nod.

"I mean, anybody else in your position would be falling apart," Alana says. "Dana P. was crying so hard at lunch yesterday she pulled a muscle in her face. She had to go to the hospital."

"Isn't Dana P. new this year? She didn't even know Connor."

"That's why she was crying. Because now she'll never get the chance. Connor is really bringing the school together. It's pretty incredible. People I've never talked to before, they want to talk to me now, because they know how much Connor meant to me. It's very inspiring. I actually started a blog about him, a sort of memorial page."

I open my mouth to speak but can't. My heart rate has tripled. A long drink of water barely helps. "I didn't realize you were friends with Connor."

"Not friends, really. More like acquaintances. But *close* acquaintances."

My heart rate drops to merely double speed.

"He probably never mentioned me or anything," she adds.

I can't tell if she's asking a question or making a statement. Either way, my lips are sealed.

"Truthfully?" she says. "I think part of me always knew you two were friends. You did a really good job of hiding it, but I totally knew." She leans in. "Tell me something."

"Tell you what?"

"The photo everyone keeps posting of Connor? The one where the other guy is cropped out? The other guy is you, isn't it?"

She studies me. I'm too frightened to even breathe.

She smiles. "I knew it."

Sam smiles, too.

I didn't say anything. I didn't do anything. Not a nod, wink, or twitch.

"Hang in there, Evan," she says before departing.

I want to be somewhere else, anywhere else. I gather my lunch and head for the doors.

Jared appears in my path, his arms spread open, welcoming me. I go in for a hug.

"What are you doing?" he says, throwing me off him.

"Sorry. I thought..."

"I'm trying to show you something, asshole." He points to his chest. Over his heart is a button with Connor Murphy's smiling face on it. It's that same photo of Connor. Jared reaches into a canvas bag slung over his shoulder and removes an identical button, which he pins onto my shirt. "I'm selling them for five bucks each, but you can have yours for four."

"You're making money off this? Off Connor's..." I can't bring myself to say it.

"I'm not the only one," Jared says. "Haven't you seen the wristbands with Connor's initials on them that Sabrina Patel started selling during free period? Or the T-shirts Matt Holtzer's mom made?"

"No, I haven't. I can't believe people are doing that."

"It's simple supply and demand, my friend. Right now we're at the peak." He pats his bulky canvas bag. "I have to move these buttons before the bottom drops out of the Connor Murphy memorabilia market."

He walks away. I call after him. "I'm not wearing this thing." I can't get the button off fast enough. I toss it at him. As I do, I see, over his shoulder, the glare of Zoe Murphy. She just watched me tear Connor's button off my shirt and launch it across the room with contempt.

Jared saunters off and Zoe takes his place, standing right in front of me. "What's wrong?" she says. "You don't feel like wearing my brother's face on your chest?"

What if I took one of the buttons and stabbed the needle point in my eye? Would that be justice?

Zoe scans the room. "He would have hated this." And then, returning to me, "Don't you think?"

It sounds sincere, like she's seeking my insight. Then again, it could be a test.

"Probably," I say.

There's so much weight in her eyes. I can't decipher what any of it means or what particular shape it takes, but the overall heft of it, the total sum, it's colossal and I'm staring straight at it.

She's about to step away, but her retreat is interrupted. I look down to see what she sees. It's my cast, what's written on it. When I go to check her face, it's too late. She's already halfway across the room, swallowed by the masses.

• • •

It's an eerie feeling, being back in the computer lab. It was only last week when Connor Murphy stole my letter. I wasn't even aware he'd been in the room at the time. I look, now, over my shoulder, checking who's here. A few kids. I don't see Connor. Obviously, I don't see Connor. He's not alive. You can't see people who aren't alive.

Maybe he could be alive right now if I hadn't printed that stupid letter. As soon as I hit return on my keyboard, it's like I started a tragic chain reaction. If the Wi-Fi connection failed and the command never reached the printer, Connor could be alive. If my mother didn't schedule that appointment with Dr. Sherman for that specific day, Connor could be alive. Also, if I never broke my arm, there would be no cast for Connor to sign and maybe I could have debunked this myth before it hardened like plaster.

Considering how far I fell from that tree, I could have broken a whole lot more. I was lucky. That's what everyone told me. I didn't feel very lucky, lying there in the most excruciating physical pain of my life. But I guess I was. I could have wrecked my back. Cracked open my head. Even worse.

Ranger Gus drove me to the hospital. He kept asking what I was doing up there in that tree. I didn't know how to tell him that I suddenly felt like climbing a tree when I was supposed to be working. I made up a story on the spot, what I hoped might sound better, something about finding a loose dog on my sweep. How it ran away before I could grab it and how I chased after it. I thought I could get a better view of everything if I was higher up.

"You call me on the walkie," Ranger Gus said. "How many times have I told you that? Anything out of the ordinary, you call me on the walkie." He was angry.

There were several instances over the summer where Ranger Gus's sudden shift in tone caught me off guard and I had to remind myself that as much as he felt like my friend, he was actually my boss. One of those instances was when I tried calling him Gus, without the *Ranger* part, and he immediately corrected me.

"The rules are in place to keep you safe," Ranger Gus said from the driver's seat of one of the park's pickups. "To keep everyone safe, including the park. It seems to me you just tossed all that out the window."

He was right. Truthfully, I didn't care one bit about safety in that moment. That's not where my head was.

"Look, I know you're in pain," Ranger Gus said. "But if you don't learn from this, then all that pain is for nothing."

I didn't mind Ranger Gus coming down hard on me. I was sort of grateful for it, actually.

"Did you call your folks?" he asked.

Ranger Gus's reaction was better than what I got from my dad. When I talked to him the next day, my dad started telling me about how his older stepdaughter, Haley, broke her wrist last year. He described how quickly it healed and how Haley was back to playing sports in no time. If he was trying to make me feel better, it didn't work. I would have preferred any other response than the one he gave me. He could have ridiculed me for being clumsy, or sympathized with a simple *That sucks*, or he could have shared a story about a bone break that *he* had when he was little. I definitely didn't want to hear about Haley right then and there.

"I left my mom a message," I told Ranger Gus. "I think she's in class." Coincidentally, she wasn't at the hospital that day when we arrived. I remember feeling relieved when I realized that.

I haven't spoken to Ranger Gus since my apprenticeship ended. I was with him five days a week for two months, and now we have nothing to do with each other. I don't know. It just seems sort of messed up. One minute we're a team or whatever, and now he's probably busy teaching a new recruit.

I awaken my computer's screen. I could send Ranger Gus an email and ask how he's doing. But considering how rarely he's online, he probably wouldn't see my email for weeks. I tried to get him to create a social media profile for himself and the park, but it did not go over well. Ranger Gus is one of those off-the-grid types who thinks technology is ruining society. Besides, if I emailed him to ask about his life, I'd also have to fill him in on mine.

• • •

That evening, I'm busy trying to bang out some homework before dinner when I notice a new email in my inbox. The subject reads: *Thank you.* I open it and realize that it's a message from Cynthia Murphy. The sight of her name nearly strikes me blind. Why did I include my real address in those emails I gave her? I should have made up my own fake account, too.

I begin to read:

Dear Evan,

We received the package you left. We can't thank you enough for trusting us with these private exchanges. They certainly provide us a view of Connor to which we were never privy, one that we can hardly reconcile with the boy we knew.

You mentioned there were more emails. We'd be grateful for whatever you choose to show us and at whatever pace you decide. Reading over these emails is almost like seeing Connor live on, and part of me wants to stretch out the experience forever.

I do have one favor to ask. I'm wondering if you have any additional emails pertaining to Connor's unfortunate struggle with substance abuse. In particular, did he ever mention by name any of the people who supplied him with drugs? Would you go back and check? Of course, my husband thinks I'm wasting my time, but I would just sleep more soundly at night knowing you looked over everything and could confirm that there was nothing there.

Finally, when will we see you again? Are you free tomorrow night? We'd love to have you over for dinner again.

With the deepest love,
Cynthia

The emails didn't satisfy her. She wants more. This will never end.

Names? Why is she asking me for names? So she can give them to the police? It's definitely not so she can send out gift baskets. No, she wants justice. That's my interpretation of this reading, and when it comes to English skills, I feel, for once, confident. Here's what else I feel confident about: Cynthia Murphy going to the police is officially *the worst thing that could happen.*

On my nightstand, next to the waiting pile of college essay scholarships, are two bottles. One is full of water, the other Ativan. I swallow one of the latter and down some of the former. I close my eyes, willing the chemicals to course through me. My shoulders slacken and my breath slows as I wait for myself to reset.

Okay. This has to stop. I have to *make* this stop. I'll just tell Cynthia that there are no names. It's the truth. (I've started keeping track of truths like they're bread crumbs that might lead me out of this.) But what if it's still not good enough for her? What if she won't take no for an answer? This is a grieving mother we're talking about. This woman lost her son. This isn't a game for her. It isn't for me, either.

That's it. I can't go on like this. It's time to come out with the truth. The *whole* truth. It's what I tried to do from the start, but I didn't speak loudly or clearly enough. I'll fix it. I'll go back to their house and I'll look them in the eyes and I'll just do it: I'll confess.

"You okay there?"

It's my mom in my doorway. I swear she possesses some kind of superpower for suddenly and inconveniently appearing outside my bedroom.

"Yeah. I'm okay. Of course." That Ativan can't kick in fast enough.

"You had a very focused look on your face." She squints, doing her best impersonation of me. "Let me guess." She comes closer. "Is it math? That was always my worst subject."

I shut my laptop before she can reach it. She stops in her tracks and we share a look.

"I was just...emailing Jared," I say, hands shaking. "He had a question about something."

I avoid her eyes and notice that she's wearing her scrubs.

"It seems like you and Jared are spending more time together." She seems relieved. "I've always said he's a great friend for you."

"Yeah, really great." Her purse hangs over her shoulder and she's holding her car keys.

"I'm proud of you. Putting yourself out there."

"Right," I say dispassionately.

"Well, I'm leaving, but I left money on the table." She turns to go. "Order anything you want, okay?"

A sick, swelling feeling mixes in with what was already there. I wish I didn't even care. "I thought we were doing tacos tonight. Looking at the essay questions."

Her eyes widen. "That's tonight. Oh my god. Oh, honey. I completely forgot. Shit." She bangs her keys against her head.

"That's okay," I say, because, well, what else can I even say?

She sits down on my bed and looks at the pile on my nightstand. "You know what? You should go ahead and take a look at the questions without me. And then, if you have any ideas, you can email me, and I can write back with any ideas that I have. That's better anyway, isn't it? That way you can really take your time?"

I nod, ready to be done with this whole conversation. "Yeah. For sure."

"We can do tacos another night, Evan. We could do tomorrow night. How about tomorrow night?"

"I can't tomorrow. I have...I'm busy."

My mom doesn't hear me. She's looking at the time on her phone. "Shit. I'm late."

I get out of bed. "You should go." Those bedpans aren't going to clean themselves.

"No, let's figure this out."

"It's fine."

"Evan..."

I head for the door. "I'll make dinner for myself," I say, leaving her alone and late in my bedroom.

CHAPTER 12

This is the double bed that Connor Murphy slept in. The wooden floor his boots scuffed up. The white walls he did his best to smother. Standing out amid movie and band posters, homemade works of art, and a joke award ribbon that says I PUT ON PANTS TODAY is a close-up photo of a hand with its middle finger extended. The middle finger is painted black with tiny white lettering on it. Only when you press your face up close to the photo can you read what the white letters say: BOO!

I'm scared, all right. But I was already scared before I entered Connor's bedroom. Cynthia told me to come up here while she finishes preparing dinner. Apparently, in my panicked state, I arrived an hour earlier than I was supposed to. I offered to stay downstairs with her and help set the table, since she seemed to be doing it all by herself, but she insisted that I go and spend some "alone time with Connor."

It's almost eighty degrees outside, but inside the Murphy home, I'm shivering. That woman downstairs is about to have her heart broken for the second time and I'm the one who's going to rebreak it. She told me again how much the messages between Connor and me meant to her, how they're helping to keep Connor alive. I can see a new lightness in her tonight, and yet here I am, about to rip Connor away from her all over again and reveal myself to be a terrible, terrible person. I hate to do this to her, but what choice do I have? It's even worse to keep feeding her lies about me and her son.

As torturous as it feels to be here in Connor's private space, it's probably the closest I've ever been to the truth of who he was. Besides the obvious differences between his bedroom and mine—my bed is half the size, my floors are carpeted, and my walls are painted light green—there are some striking similarities. Nowhere in this room is a single hint of anything sports related. I've always felt out of step with kids my age for having zero interest in playing or watching sports.

Also, like me, Connor has shelves crammed with books. I see *The Hitchhiker's Guide to the Galaxy, The Catcher in the Rye, The Great Gatsby,* and *The Mysteries of Pittsburgh.* Some of the stuff I've never heard of, some I have. I see a school copy of *Macbeth* from our junior year. He's got at least half a dozen Kurt Vonnegut novels. A few have Dewey decimal numbers on the spines. It seems like a contradiction: Connor Murphy in a library.

One of the titles I own: *Into the Wild* by Jon Krakauer. I saw the movie first and then went back to read the book. It's about a guy in his early twenties who tries to live on his own in Alaska. When it came to nature, the guy knew his stuff. He would have made a superb park ranger. Unfortunately, he ended up committing a critical mistake and perished out there in the wild.

It's a weird feeling, knowing that Connor and I both read the same book. It's possible I had more in common with him than I have with most kids at school. If the two of us had sat at the same lunch table, we could have talked about other books we've both read, like *Slaughterhouse-Five*. Who knows, maybe we could have actually been friends. So it goes.

One of Connor's hardcover books has no jacket or title. I remove it from the shelf. It's a journal full of sketches. They're bizarre and unnerving, but also intricate and skilled. This one features a man in galoshes holding an umbrella. Rats and spiders are falling from the sky. The ground and trees are also covered in rats and spiders. A caption at the bottom reads: *Crittercism*. It's kind of funny.

"Why are you in my brother's room?"

I practically throw Connor's sketchbook back onto the shelf before facing Zoe. "I showed up too early and your mom told me to come up here."

"Don't your parents get upset that you're here all the time?" she asks.

I'm not here all the time. I've only come twice. But I'm not about to contradict Zoe Murphy in her own home (or anywhere, for that matter).

"It's just me and my mom," I say, "and she works most nights. Or else she's in class."

She leans against the doorframe. "Class for what?"

"Legal stuff."

"Oh yeah? My dad's a lawyer."

"Oh," I say, scratching my ear. I don't even have an itch, but I suddenly have a very strong urge to scratch.

"Where's your dad?" Zoe asks.

Now I'm clearing my throat. Clearing my throat and scratching. Not weird at all. "He lives in Colorado. He left when I was seven. So. He doesn't really mind if I'm here, either."

Her eyebrows jump. "Colorado's not close."

"No, it isn't. Eighteen hundred miles away, actually. Or something like that. I haven't calculated it or anything." (Of course I have.)

She steps into the room, and I step back, accidentally kicking a metal garbage can. It might as well be a cymbal, that's how loud it seems to reverberate around us.

We stand there awkwardly at opposite sides of Connor's room. The only places to sit are the bed and the desk chair. I make no move toward either.

"Anyway, your parents seem really great."

"Right," Zoe says, amused. "They can't stand each other. They fight all the time." She comes even closer and takes a seat on Connor's bed. Her rust-colored corduroys hike up just enough to reveal her naked ankles.

I try to retreat even more, but there's a wall behind me and I almost end up knocking something off it. "Well, everyone's parents fight, right? That's normal."

"My dad's in total denial. He didn't even cry at the funeral."

I have no idea how to respond to this. But that is definitely *not* something you reveal to someone you hate. Even if she doesn't hate me now, she will definitely hate me later. "Your mom said we're having gluten-free lasagna for dinner," I say. "That sounds really..."

"Inedible?"

I try not to laugh. "Not at all. You're lucky your mom cooks. My mom and I just order pizza most nights."

"You're lucky you're *allowed* to eat pizza," Zoe says.

"You're not allowed to eat pizza?"

She rolls her eyes. "We can now, I guess. My mom was Buddhist last year, so we weren't supposed to eat animal products."

"She was Buddhist last year but not this year?"

"That's sort of what she does. She gets really into different things. For a while it was Pilates, then it was *The Secret*, then Buddhism. Now it's free-range, *Omnivore's Dilemma* or whatever. It's hard to keep track."

Besides my mother's fascination with astrology and arena rock, she doesn't really have any interests or hobbies. I tried to get her to come on a few hikes with me, but she said she doesn't like bugs.

Zoe scratches her freckled shoulder and then leans back with both hands propped behind her. She smiles at me, and my body reads it as an invitation. I look down and try to recall what we were just talking about. "I think it's cool that your mom is interested in different kinds of stuff."

She seems confused that I'm confused. "She's not. That's just what happens when you're rich and you don't have a job. You get crazy."

"My mom always says, it's better to be rich than poor."

"Well, your mom's probably never been rich, then."

"And you've probably never been poor."

Did I just say that? I feel my face begin to radiate red heat.

"I'm so sorry," I say. "I didn't mean to—that was completely rude."

She laughs. "I didn't realize you were capable of saying something that wasn't nice."

"I'm not. I never say things that aren't nice. I don't even *think* things that aren't nice. I'm just, I'm really sorry."

"I was impressed. You're ruining it."

Oh shit. "I'm sorry." Shit.

"You really don't have to keep saying that."

I want to. So badly.

She sits up on the bed and grabs a solved Rubik's Cube off Connor's nightstand. "You want to say it again, don't you?"

"Very much so, yes."

She smiles at me, a real and full smile, the kind Zoe seems reluctant to hand out freely to anyone, and I feel myself bask in it. Like: I made that happen.

She spins one panel of the cube and then, thinking better

of it, spins it right back into place, as if not wanting to spoil its perfection. She slides it back where she found it on the nightstand.

"I should probably apologize about my mom emailing you. I told her not to." Zoe looks up. "I don't imagine you found what she wanted."

I shake my head.

"I didn't think so. My mom's clueless when it comes to that stuff. She never knew when my brother was high. He'd be talking so slow and she'd be like, 'He's just tired.'" She pauses and stares at the Rubik's Cube. "Why did he say that?"

It's almost a whisper. She's lost me.

"In his note," she says. "'Because there's Zoe. And all my hope is pinned on Zoe. Who I don't even know and who doesn't know me.' Why would he write that? What does that even mean?"

"Oh. Um." The letter. She has the letter memorized.

She stares at me, waiting for a response. When I don't provide one, her head drops and her legs angle away. I recognize that feeling, when your body tries to fold in on itself in the hopes that it can go unseen.

I can't stand to see her like this. So in need.

"Maybe," I say. "I mean, I'm not one hundred percent sure about this, but thinking about it now, Connor always felt like, you know, if you guys were just closer—"

"We weren't close," Zoe says. "At all."

"No, I know. But he used to say that he wished you were. He wanted you to be."

Her chin comes up. Just like that, she seems resuscitated. "So you and Connor, you guys would talk about me?"

"Oh, yeah, definitely, sometimes. I mean, if he brought it up. I never brought it up. Obviously. Why would I have brought it up? But yeah, he totally thought you were awesome."

She smells something foul. "He thought I was *awesome? My brother?*"

"Yeah. Of course. I mean, maybe he didn't use that exact word, but—"

"How?"

"How did he think you were awesome?"

"Yeah," she says, pulling up her knees and sitting cross-legged on the bed. I gulp, hopefully not audibly.

"Well, okay, let me try to remember. Oh. Okay." How Zoe is awesome happens to be a subject I know a lot about. "So, whenever you have a solo in jazz band, you close your eyes— you probably don't even know you're doing this—but you get this half smile, like you just heard the funniest thing in the world, but it's a secret and you can't tell anybody. But the way you smile, it's sort of like you're letting us in on the secret, too."

"Do I do that?"

"Totally. At least that's what Connor told me."

"I never knew he was even awake at any of my concerts. My parents always made him go."

I laugh, like, *Of course he was awake! That is so funny and ridiculous, what you just said!*

She looks down and scratches the stitching in Connor's quilt. I did it again. I took it too far. I shouldn't be doing this, digging myself in deeper when the whole reason I came here was to finally break free. Just tell her. Do it. Now.

"You know the first time he ever said anything nice about me was in his note," Zoe says. "A note he wrote to you. He couldn't even say it to me."

"Oh. Well. He wanted to. He just...he couldn't."

She takes it in for a long moment. Shyly, she asks, "Did he say anything else about me?"

How do I answer this question?

Before I can formulate a response, she jumps back in. "Never mind. I don't even care."

"No. It's not that. It's just, he said so many things about you."

She peeks up. Her eyes move through me. *What am I doing?*

"I know he thought you looked really pretty—I mean, sorry, what I meant to say is that he thought it was pretty *cool* when you dyed your hair blue."

"Really?" She stares into space, seeming to travel back in time to sophomore year when her hair had lines of blue in it. "That's weird, because he used to make fun of me all the time."

"Well, he liked to tease you. You know that."

"Yeah," she says, nodding to herself.

"He noticed all kinds of things about you. He'd watch you all the time. Just keeping track of you, I guess."

Again, I have her full attention.

"He noticed how you scribble on the cuffs of your jeans when you get bored."

A sheepish smile. I finally cross the divide between us and sit down on the bed, facing her.

"And how you chew on the caps of your pens. And how your forehead crinkles when you're mad."

"I didn't think he paid any attention to me."

"Oh, he did. He couldn't *not* pay attention to you."

She seems troubled. "I just wish I knew."

I take a hefty breath. "I know. It's just, he didn't know how to say all this to you. He didn't know how to tell you that... he was your biggest fan. No one was a bigger fan than him. He knew how great you are."

Her eyes. Looking into mine.

"You are so great, Zoe."

Freckled nose.

"I can't even tell you."

Shimmery hair.

"I mean it."

Lips like pink pillows. Smiling at me.

"You're everything."

I feel them. Even softer than I imagined.

Her hand on my chest, pushing me back.

"What are you doing?" Zoe says.

"I don't... I didn't... I'm so..."

I can't speak words. *What the hell am I doing?*

She jumps up, forehead crinkled, staring, processing.

"I'm sorry. I didn't mean—"

"Dinner's ready," Cynthia yells from downstairs.

I see Zoe's anger, confusion, hurt, all these emotions arriving at once, because of me.

"Tell them to eat without me."

She's out the door before I can stop her. Before I can clean up this brand-new mess I've made.

• • •

You *what*?

Is it that bad?

You tried to kiss Zoe Murphy.
On her brother's bed.
After he died.

It looks really bad when you type it out like that.

Grapefruits.
Your balls are the size of grapefruits.
How do you walk around
with those things in your pants?

I didn't mean to do it.
It just happened.

I just got caught up in the moment. It felt like she, like we, like *something* was happening. When I leaned in, it was as if my body was working without my mind, like we were being drawn together.

I don't know how long I sat on Connor's bed before Cynthia

appeared at the door, announcing for the second time that dinner was ready. It could have been two seconds or twenty minutes. I thought about jumping out the window. Just one story down. I could have made it. I've survived falls from greater heights. I could have disappeared into the night and never looked back.

Somehow I willed myself off that bed and down those stairs and sat at that table. When Zoe didn't show up, I suggested to her parents that she probably wasn't feeling well.

As expected, over a home-cooked meal the likes of which I've never seen in my house, Cynthia asked if I happened to find anything in the emails. Larry seemed annoyed that she was even bringing it up. As they bickered, I reminded myself that this was my chance to come clean. At least I wouldn't have to do it in front of Zoe, which was a small but not insignificant relief. I desperately wanted to. My stomach was a hot puddle of nerves, had been for a week straight. I couldn't take it anymore. But to get rid of it once and for all, I had to do the brave thing. That's where my plan failed. I couldn't do it. I'm not brave. I'm extremely not brave.

Being not brave is just about as easy as breathing. Here's how I did it. First I shook my head. Then I said, "I didn't find anything." That was it. The moment passed. Connor's parents were content to move on to another topic and so was I. I can't remember what the new topic was. It hardly mattered. Eventually, we returned to the topic of Connor. They asked me questions. I told them what I thought they wanted to hear. What I thought would make them happy.

I wish someone could do the same for me.

CHAPTER 13

On the bus to school, I write a new letter for Dr. Sherman:

> **Dear Evan Hansen,**
>
> **Today is going to be a good day, and here's why. Because it isn't supposed to rain like yesterday and that's good because I didn't have to pack my umbrella and my backpack feels a little lighter.**
>
> **Sincerely,**
> **Me**

It's short and underwhelming, but factual. If Dr. Sherman asks me about it at our session today, at least I'll be able to stand behind it as the honest truth.

I'm done being ambitious. Jared was wrong—my balls aren't grapefruits. If ball size equates to confidence, then I've got the smallest ones you can have and still qualify as a man. My balls are poppy seeds.

It's been four days since I tried to kiss Zoe Murphy. I mean, I *did* kiss her. It was just really brief and she didn't reciprocate, but it did, in fact, happen. I wish it hadn't, but it did.

It was only my third kiss ever, and my first two barely counted as kisses. Pretty depressing when you consider I'm old enough to drive a car and donate blood and get my own passport. My first kiss was with Robin, who lived in the one-story home across the street. It happened in her pool. It was a lightning-speed peck, more funny than anything, just because we both wanted to find out what it felt like. And my second kiss was from Amy Brodsky when I was ten. She just leaned over at recess one day and I instantly fell in love with her, until I saw her do the exact same thing to two other boys over the course of the next week.

I haven't been the same since kissing Zoe. I can't eat or sleep or think. I try to read, but the lines in books start to vibrate and turn blurry. I put on movies, but I can't pay attention to what's happening on-screen. When my mom gets home from work at night, I pretend I'm already asleep, but really I'm just lying there in the dark. I can't even stand being on the computer. I'm too worried I'll find a new email from the Murphys, asking me to come over for another dinner or send them more emails or both. They haven't contacted me since I saw them the other night. Maybe they finally have what they need. Maybe they're done with me.

That's what I wanted, right? I've been telling myself that. Then why am I sitting here now, feeling something that seems awfully similar to disappointment? The plan, if there ever was a plan, was to offer the Murphys solace in whatever way I could and then for me to go back to living my normal life. But now, after everything, that just doesn't feel right.

The bus bumps along. I picture, for a moment, the driver steering us off a cliff. Unfortunately, there are no cliffs in town. Maybe she could drive us off Xavier Bridge instead. Or take us under an overpass that's too low. Trouble over.

The small comfort I get from this brief death fantasy is outsized by my guilt. I shouldn't be daring mortality. Connor Murphy is actually dead, and I'm sitting here pretending like I want to be. I don't want to be dead. I'm finally sure of that. I just wish that life, for once, for a day or even a few hours, would go smoothly. I can never just sit back and sail. People like Rox can put their feet up and let the water carry them along. Not me. I'm constantly on the verge of sinking.

The bus jerks to a stop and we all file out. Thankfully, I haven't seen Zoe at school. I've tried to avoid her, and I think she's done the same with me. Still, I keep fearing I'll turn the corner and she'll be there. You want to know what's really fun? When your nerves are so fried that the sweat from your hand drips down your pen and onto your paper, making the surface so moist that the next time you try to write a word, you accidentally shred the paper with the tip of your pen. It's the best.

I'm too wrapped up in my own thoughts to notice the

commotion up ahead. Students step aside to make way for the freight train that is Ms. Bortel. She's coming at a clip, a cardboard box in her chiseled arms. Chasing behind is Principal Howard. "You're making this worse, Bonnie. That's school property."

"This is *my* stuff."

"Bonnie, please."

Ms. Bortel turns to face Principal Howard. "John, get ready, because I'm suing your ass."

Our collective jaws drop as Ms. Bortel strides into the parking lot and into her black sports car.

Principal Howard, donning a professional smile, encourages us to keep moving. But we can't unsee what we just saw. What *did* we just see?

• • •

Already, yesterday, I noticed there weren't as many people staring at me during lunch compared with when the news first broke about Connor and me. Now it's down to a few passing glances. Those few glances may not even be aimed my way. It's hard to tell.

As I'm inspecting the room, as surreptitiously as I can, I spot Sam. My fellow lonely loner. Except he's seated at a table across the cafeteria. The last few days he sat at my table. We even chatted a little bit. Meaning, we said "Hey" to each other a few times. I figured we were the same kind of person. We both pack lunches from home. We both prefer to keep to ourselves. We both have nowhere better to sit in the cafeteria.

Turns out I was wrong about that last one. Apparently even Sam has options.

I return to my sandwich. Again, that disappointed feeling. This is the existence I'm used to, being overlooked. I didn't want people staring at me while I eat my lunch. I should feel relieved right now, shouldn't I? I guess, as uncomfortable as I felt being watched, it was also kind of nice, for a change, to actually be seen.

I wonder how Connor Murphy got through lunch each day. Where did he sit? With whom? What did he eat? I never paid attention. Just like no one's paying attention to me.

I take out my phone, just to have something to do. I scroll past everything. Most of the news is about a celebrity sex scandal or an upcoming election. There's a big movie coming out this weekend that I'm interested in, but it's the third installment in a trilogy and I still haven't seen the first two.

I'm surrounded by voices, hundreds of them, and these voices combine to form a wall. I can't break through the wall. This, what I hold in my hand, is the only way inside, the only way I can learn what's going on in my own world.

According to my phone, the major news at school, unsurprisingly, centers on one single name. It's just not the name I've grown accustomed to seeing.

●　●　●

I shut my locker and Alana Beck is waiting there. My rib cage does its best to hold back my skittish heart. "Jesus. You scared me," I say.

"I need to show you something."

Every time Alana opens her mouth I feel like I'm being scolded. She dresses like she's the dean of a small liberal arts college, and she probably could be. Not only does she relish following the rules, but she's also the only one who even knows what they are.

Her backpack sucker punches me as she does an about-face. I follow her down the hall. We stop in front of a trash can and Alana points inside. Resting on top of a pile of debris is one of the Connor Murphy pins that Jared was selling.

"It's the third one I've found," Alana says. "The first one was on the ground in the parking lot. Someone apparently ran it over with their car. And there was another one in the toilet in the girls' bathroom."

That can't be good for the plumbing.

"Why are you showing me this?" I say.

"I was already noticing that people were mentioning Connor less, and now this. People don't care anymore. All anyone wants to talk about is Ms. Bortel. Some people are saying she slept with a student, but I also heard she might have had an affair with Principal Howard."

"No way."

She shakes her head at the shame of it. "People have totally forgotten about Connor Murphy. You can't let this happen, Evan. You were Connor's best friend."

It doesn't sound so crazy to hear Alana say that. I mean, it's not true, I know, but also, when you think about it, it might be *kind* of true. There's a good possibility that I was the last person Connor spoke to the day he died. We had an authentic exchange. For guys like Connor and me, that type of interaction is rare, and it definitely forged a bond between us. I'm probably the only one who had any clue how he was truly feeling that day. Who else, besides me (and maybe Alana), even thought about him for a second in the last week? No one. Seriously, as absurd as it sounds, is there anyone in this entire school who was closer to Connor than I was?

"Maybe you can ask Zoe to do something," Alana says.

Okay, obviously I wasn't counting Zoe.

"Zoe is the perfect person to help get people interested again," Alana says. "She was literally his sister."

"I'm sorry. I can't—I just don't think that's the best way for us to get people to remember him."

Alana gives me a look that reduces me to half my size. "Well, I guarantee that if you don't do something, no one will remember Connor. Is that what you want?"

She hurries off without waiting for a response. I look down at Connor's face in the trash. I don't want it to be this way, either, but what am I supposed to do?

• • •

I bite my nails as Dr. Sherman reads over my letter. The few strands of hair on top of his head resemble cracks in a wall. One of the reasons my mom chose Dr. Sherman, other than the fact that he was covered by our health insurance, was because he's young. He looks old to me, but my mom says he's "only" thirty.

Dr. Sherman hands back my laptop. I snap it shut and wait for him to say something. Typically, that can take a while. Dr. Sherman prefers that I do the talking. I do not share his preference. Sometimes I feel like we're playing a game of chicken, each waiting for the other to utter the first word. In normal social situations, I can't stand silence, but here I get a slight thrill from seeing how long I can stretch it out. I think my ideal session would include only "hello" and "goodbye." I'm not trying to waste Dr. Sherman's time. It's nothing against him. I just have this feeling sometimes that even the best therapist in the world couldn't fix me.

A few minutes later, Dr. Sherman gives in. "How's your day been so far?"

Let's see. Not amazing? Not good? Not *not* terrible? In some ways it was exactly like so many other days of my life and in other ways, vastly different. So much has happened and so fast. I just wish I could slow everything down somehow. Because it's unfair, how the world keeps on going no matter what happens, and people like Connor just get left behind. Literally one day he's pinned over someone's heart and the next he's tossed in the garbage. How can that be?

I think myself into such a twister that it's no wonder some of my thoughts start flying right out of my mouth. "It's just not right."

I look up, shocked by my own voice. I feel this sudden sense of relief, having said only that much.

I want to release more. I can't share all of it, but there's plenty I *can* say. I give in to the temptation. I tell Dr. Sherman about Connor Murphy, how he died and how everyone was talking about him for a while, how they seemed to care one minute, and now they don't care anymore because they're on to something new.

"And this bothers you?" Dr. Sherman asks.

"Well, yeah," I say. "It does. I don't think it's right to just brush someone aside like that. One minute they care about him and the next they don't. It's like he's just being... forgotten."

Dr. Sherman shifts in his chair. I notice he does this when he feels we've finally hit on something that deserves more exploration. I glance up at the clock to see if our time is up yet.

"I was reminded, Evan, when you were speaking just now, about what happened with your father."

Now I'm the one shifting in my chair.

"When you first found out that his wife was pregnant, that your father was going to have another son, it seemed to trouble you a great deal. You seemed to think it reflected on your father's feelings toward *you*."

Dr. Sherman consults his notes.

"That was about a month ago when we discussed that," he says. "You haven't mentioned it since. So, I'm just wondering, how have you been coping with that?"

• • •

I'm in bed watching a movie I've already seen. The bottom of my computer warms my thighs, definitely giving me cancer. My eyes are trained on the screen, but I'm barely watching. I'm too busy ruminating on what Dr. Sherman brought up at our session. It's something I try not to think about or talk about, which is exactly the type of thing that Dr. Sherman loves to harp on.

Fine, Theresa's pregnant. My dad is going to have a new son. What's the point of even bringing it up? What does Dr. Sherman want me to say about it? He won't be born for many more months, and when he gets here, he'll be in Colorado. He won't know me and I won't know him. When I was young, I begged my parents for a sibling. I'd dream about having a brother or sister. But now? No thanks.

The mattress sags beneath me. My mom is suddenly by my side, propping a pillow behind her back. I didn't hear her come home. She focuses on the computer screen as if it's broadcasting the secret of life.

She was not happy when she found out about the baby. She tried to pretend like she didn't care, but then I heard her on the phone with a friend saying, *I could have a baby right now if I wanted to. Right now!* And later, *Isn't he a little old to be having a new baby?*

"What are you watching?" she asks now.

It's the documentary about Vivian Maier, the nanny who no one realized was also a brilliant photographer until after she died.

"And who's the kid talking?" she asks.

"That's the guy who discovered all her photos after she died. He's the one who made the film about her. He paid for it with Kickstarter."

"This guy's impressive."

"Not *he*. She. Vivian Maier is a woman."

"I know that. Jeez. Give me some credit. I'm talking about the guy who put the whole thing together."

Oh. Right. The filmmaker. His name is John Maloof and the movie is also about him. I guess my mom's right. He *is* impressive. Without him, no one would know about Vivian Maier.

I take a closer look at the guy on-screen. He's not a star or anything. Far from it. He's dorky, actually, with glasses and bad skin. He looks really young, too. He just cared enough to do something. He made it his mission to make sure that the world appreciated Vivian Maier. Vivian Maier was a nobody. But John changed that. He wouldn't let her be ignored or forgotten. He *made* people pay attention. He saved her.

I lift my arm out from under the blanket and read once again the name written on my cast.

CHAPTER 14

My mom enters the kitchen and freezes in her clogs. "You're up early," she says.

I press one more key on my laptop and slam it shut. The printer croaks awake in the living room. I stand up from the table. "I had to finish something."

My mom inserts a pod into the coffee maker. "It wouldn't happen to be one of those scholarship essays, would it?"

"Um. Not yet. But I've been, like, brainstorming a ton of ideas and stuff." I totally forgot about the essays.

"That sounds so exciting," she says, sliding our only clean mug under the spout. "And you're sure you don't want to plan another night to do them together? I told you, this time I'll just tell my boss I don't even exist. I am nonexistent on that day. Except to you. I promise."

She's already apologized fifty times about blowing taco

night, and I appreciate the effort, but right now those essays are the last thing on my mind. "Maybe. I'll definitely let you know."

"Wait. Where are you going?"

I can't delay. I need to retrieve the papers coming out of the printer. The last time I printed out something private it fell into the wrong hands.

"Is everything okay?" she asks.

I turn around in the doorway. "Yeah, it's just this thing for school."

"No, I mean in general. Your session with Dr. Sherman went well? And before you answer, I want you to know that I was going to ask you about it last night, but I didn't because I know you need time to process. How's *that* for Mother of the Year material?" She laughs awkwardly.

"You're a shoo-in," I say, scratching loose paint off the wall. "Actually, I think I might have had a little breakthrough with Dr. Sherman."

You would think I just handed her a winning lottery ticket. She shoots up two thumbs and dances her fists in the air. "That's what I'm talking about."

Another happy customer.

● ● ●

I catch Alana as she's heading into homeroom. On the way to school, I folded each piece of printed paper twice to form three equal sections. They're supposed to resemble pamphlets. Alana takes one of my pamphlets and reads the front panel.

"'The Connor Project'?" Alana says.

"It's the first thing that came to me," I say. "It doesn't have to—"

"I love it. What is it?"

"Well, it would be a student group dedicated to keeping Connor's memory alive and showing that he... mattered. That everyone matters."

Alana is silent. I repeat to myself what I just said aloud. It sounds preposterous now that I'm hearing it back. There are at least a dozen more of these prototype pamphlets in my bag. I wonder if the school has a paper shredder I can borrow. "It's just a rough idea. It doesn't have to be that, obviously."

"I'm so honored," Alana says. "I would *love* to be vice president of the Connor Project."

"Vice president?"

"You're right. We should be co-presidents."

I guess that means she's into my idea. "So you think we should actually do this?"

"Are you kidding, Evan? We *have* to. Like you said, not just for Connor. For everyone." She holds up my pamphlet next to her face. "Excuse my language, but screw Ms. Bortel."

No plan I've made for the future has ever actually panned out. I'm not sure what I'm supposed to do next. "I was thinking we'll probably need a good website. I know someone who could help with that. But it might cost us."

• • •

"Tech Consigliere," Jared says when Alana and I approach him during lunch.

"What's that?" Alana asks.

"It's a *Godfather* thing, right?" I say.

"Precisely," Jared says. "I will forego my normal fee in exchange for being referred to as Tech Consigliere of the Connor Project."

"Fine, whatever," I say. "You can list it that way on the website."

"No, you need to call me that in normal conversation, too."

"Jared, come on."

"How about we give you the additional role of treasurer?" Alana offers. "It'll look great on your college applications."

Jared studies Alana's face. Alana holds his stare.

"That would please my parents," Jared says.

"I'm sure it would," Alana says.

"Fine. Can I eat my lunch now?"

"Wait," Alana says. "Shouldn't we get the Murphys' blessing before we move forward?"

I thought about that, too. "I just figured it might be a little early for that, since we're only in the setup phase."

"There's really no point in putting a lot of work into this until we know we have the Murphys on board," Alana argues. "We should pitch it to them immediately. Like, tonight."

"You mean, all of us, together?" I ask.

Jared nods. "Yeah. Let's go to their house."

"I guess we could," I say, overwhelmed but excited.

"A team outing." Alana goes to squeeze my arm, I think, but then seeing the cast thinks better of it. "I love it. Great for morale."

"I'll drive," Jared says. "Just text me a pickup time."

"One more thing," Alana says before Jared can leave. "How about we organize a school-wide assembly to kick this thing off?"

I knew Alana would be the right partner, that she'd be able to take the ball and really run with it. "Yeah. That sounds... great."

"Perfect. I'll speak to Principal Howard about it. See you guys tonight." She walks away and so does Jared.

Last night it was just a vague, unsure concept in my mind. Now it's this real thing that feels like it might actually happen. It's sort of thrilling to watch it come alive so fast, and yet I'm suddenly looking around for a place to sit. My legs have gone numb.

• • •

Despite my insistence that he park on the street, Jared dumps his SUV smack in the middle of the Murphys' C-shaped driveway. On our way to the front door, Alana flips open a folder and shows off two thick rubber-banded bundles of multicolored pamphlets. My Connor Project heading has been restyled, the small and modest font I used replaced with something thick and bold.

"I had a window in my after-school schedule," Alana says when she catches me looking at the pamphlets.

"Shouldn't we wait to hear what they say first?" I say.

"We have to go in there like the position is already ours."

"But this isn't, like, an interview."

Alana pulls at the cuffs of her shirt so they reach down to her wrists. "Life is an interview, Evan."

Where do you learn something like that? Alana's parents must be supersuccessful people. I bet one is a judge and the other is a surgeon. From the moment she was born she's been training to kick life's ass.

"Is the maid going to answer the door or what?" Jared says, sounding the doorbell.

"They don't have a maid," I say.

"Look at the size of this pillar. I bet you the Murphys are swingers."

"What? No. They're just normal."

Jared pretends to laugh. I notice he's wearing one of the Connor buttons he's been selling at school. Before I can tell him to take it off, the front door opens.

It's Connor's mom. "Evan, what a surprise."

"Hi, Mrs.—Cynthia. I have something really exciting I want to share with you," I say.

"Oh," she says, smiling at Alana and Jared. She spots the image pinned to Jared's shirt. I can't read her expression before she invites us inside.

She plants us around the dinner table with miniature bottles of water and excuses herself. Alana hides the folder with all the new pamphlets on her lap under the table. Meanwhile, Jared is threatening to steal a splash of something fun from the cabinet in the corner. He also assures us that the slot in the living room ceiling houses a retractable screen for a movie projector. I wait in my seat, wiping my wet hands on my jeans. I'm nervous, but also full of anticipation.

Cynthia returns to the kitchen with Larry. I wasn't sure Larry would even be home from work yet, but the way he's dressed, in a polo shirt and cap, who knows, he might have skipped work and played golf instead.

Zoe arrives just behind her father and takes a seat at the table directly next to me. She doesn't greet me with words, just a look, and as usual I'm unable to decipher what her look means.

Once everyone is settled, I take a drink of water and begin the presentation that we only vaguely sketched out on the way over. "I've been thinking a lot lately. I keep asking myself, what if there was a way to make sure that Connor was never forgotten? That he was *always* remembered? And that the memory of him could help people?"

I study our audience. I have their undivided attention.

"Connor is gone," I say delicately. "But his legacy isn't. It doesn't have to be."

I remember to breathe. There are so many things to cover.

"Okay," I say. "Imagine, first, a beautiful and informative website designed by Jared here, our tech consigliere."

Jared nods. "Yup. I can have that up pretty quickly."

"This website would have links to educational materials and meaningful calls to action," Alana says, barely able to contain herself.

"Right. Yes. And that's just the beginning." I start running through the list that we brainstormed. "There would be steady outreach through social media...community events..."

Alana takes over. "Partnerships with strategic sponsors... a massive fundraising drive...suicide prevention resources... mental health education."

"This way we can try to help people just like Connor," I say.

"Exactly," Alana says. "And it's all part of this new initiative we've come here to present to you. We're calling it—"

"The Connor Project," I say.

While I do value Alana's enthusiasm, this whole thing *was* my idea. Also, I didn't mean to say it so loudly.

"The Connor Project," Cynthia says, turning to her husband.

"Yes," I say. I glance at Alana, signaling that it's time.

She opens her folder and hands everyone a pamphlet. I'm surprised, when I get mine, how substantial the paper feels.

"We want to kick off the Connor Project in the right fashion," Alana says. "I already spoke to Principal Howard about doing a memorial assembly this Friday. Students, teachers, whoever wants to, they can get up and they can talk."

"About how all this has been affecting them," I say.

"Right. How they're feeling."

"About Connor."

"Yes. What he meant to them."

"What he meant to *all* of us."

It seems a good place to stop, and somehow we all sense it. I turn to Alana and Jared, feeling a sense of pride and accomplishment. The room is eerily still and mute until the ice maker produces a loud *clink*. It takes a few sips of water and more inspection of the pamphlets before Connor's parents are ready to speak.

"I didn't realize Connor meant this much to people," Larry says.

"Oh my god," Alana says. "He was one of my closest acquaintances. He was my lab partner in chemistry, and we presented together on *Huck Finn* in English. He was so funny. Instead of calling it *Huck Finn*, he switched out the *Huck*, you know, and he called it..." She catches herself. "Nobody else in our class thought of that."

Zoe hasn't looked up from her pamphlet since she got it. If she's not on board with our plan, I'm not sure I can be, either. "I was thinking," I say, "for the assembly, maybe the jazz band could do something."

Zoe glances up. "Oh. Yeah. Maybe. I can ask Mr. Contrell."

Jared slaps me on the back. "Great idea, Evan."

"Thank you, Jared," I say through clenched teeth.

"Honey?" Larry says, touching Cynthia's shoulder. "What do you think?"

Usually Cynthia is the one who does most of the talking for the Murphys, but she's been awfully quiet. She's looking straight at me, but not at my eyes. It's like she can't see past the space between us.

And then, she emerges from her waking sleep. "Oh, Evan. This is just...this is wonderful. Thank you." She grabs my hand from across the table and squeezes it. It feels so nice that I almost forget to be embarrassed.

•••

Once again I'm in Connor's bedroom, only this time with his mother. Alana and Jared already left. We were all getting ready to leave together when Cynthia pulled me aside and asked if I could stay a little longer. I don't mind taking the bus home.

Now she's looking in Connor's closet. Through the walls, I hear a voice singing over guitar. After a few stops and starts, I realize it's not a recording.

Cynthia turns around. She's holding a tie. After studying the tie a moment, she extends it to me. "For the assembly."

"Oh."

"When Connor started seventh grade, all my girlfriends said, 'Here comes bar mitzvah season. He's going to have a different party every Saturday.' I took him to get a suit, some shirts…a tie." She pauses. "He didn't get invited to a single one."

We both look down at the tie in her hands. Connor's tie. His only tie. He never wore it. Never had a reason to.

"I thought you could wear this for your speech," she says.

The taste of panic on my tongue. "My what?"

"Well, Alana said that anyone who wanted to would have a chance to say something at the assembly. I think we all assumed that you would be the first to sign up."

"I don't…"

Panic has a salty taste. It's like I'm standing in a small glass tank and the tank is filling up with water. I'm guessing the water is coming from the sea, because of the saltiness. The seawater rushes into my tank. It's already at my mouth, and in a moment it will cover my face and I'll drown. There's no way out of the tank. All I can do is wait as the water surrounds me. I stretch my neck up for that last bit of air. I'm gasping. And then, when I can barely catch my breath, it stops. The water recedes, always. I never end up drowning, but it doesn't matter. The feeling of almost drowning is even worse than actually drowning. Actually drowning is peace. Almost drowning is pure pain.

"The thing is just, I don't really do very well with, um, with public speaking. I'm not very good at it. You wouldn't want me to. Trust me."

"Of course I would want you to," Cynthia says. "I'm sure the whole school wants to hear from you. I know Larry and I do, and Zoe..."

She puts the tie in my hands.

"Think about it."

She leaves me alone in Connor's room. I stand there, paralyzed, waiting for all the water to drain away.

I stare down at Connor's tie. Thick and rough. Navy with light blue diagonal stripes running down it. Like rolling waves through a dark, violent ocean. The water came for Connor, too. He must have fought for air until he just didn't feel like fighting anymore. If I can understand anything, I can certainly understand that.

187

A sound in the doorway. Zoe stands there with her arms crossed.

"Sorry," I tell her. "I'm leaving. Your mom and I were just talking."

She steps into the room and makes a slow circle around me before finally resting on the bed. The last time we were alone like this in Connor's room I apparently lost my mind. I'll keep better track of it this time.

Zoe didn't say much after our presentation. When it was over, she just disappeared upstairs. I wait for her to speak, and when she doesn't, I proceed with extreme care. "Was that you playing guitar just now?"

She nods.

"I didn't know you sing," I say.

"I don't. I mean, I'm not very good. It's sort of a new thing. Actually, this past Sunday I played my first open mic night at Capitol Café. Just a few songs."

"Wow. No way. Like, covers or...?"

"My own stuff," she says, looking a little hesitant but fighting through it. "It's weird. It's like I've had these songs waiting inside me. And now they're finally ready to come out."

I understand. I'm jealous, actually. I wish I had some way of releasing all the stuff that's been churning inside *me*.

I sit down on the bed, as far away from her as I can possibly be without falling off. "That's awesome."

She turns to me. "You shouldn't have kissed me the other night. That was annoying."

Damn. I sat myself right into that one. "I know. I'm sorry."

"But," she says, "I shouldn't have freaked out. I overreacted."

"No, you underreacted. I don't even know why I did it."

She stares down at the floor, her shoes scrunched up, as if they're trying to push right through the wood. "I think grief can make you do weird things. Things you wouldn't do normally."

I give her the only answer I can. "I think that's probably true."

She stands up and paces around. I follow her movements until she stops and faces me head-on. "Why did he push you that day?"

"What? Oh. I mean. I think..." The seawater returns. I was just starting to dry off. "Didn't I tell you before?"

She shakes her head. "I don't believe you."

My heart cracks. I look away, studying Connor's wall as if it were a cheat sheet, but what I see only confuses me more. I close my eyes and search inward instead. "I sometimes...I get scared talking to people, I guess, sort of." The truth of it calms me down. I slowly open my eyes. "Connor was always trying to get me to be more outgoing. And he'd get annoyed sometimes. If he thought I wasn't trying hard enough. That sort of thing."

She takes it in. "Well, my mom is in love with you. This whole Connor Project thing, too, she's obsessed."

I feel my heart gluing back together again. "She's really awesome."

Zoe glances at the open door, seeing something I can't see. "She likes you being here. You make her feel like Connor is still here, I think, in a way. Like you bring him with you somehow.

But not like how she remembers him. Different. Better than she remembers him."

"That's what happens when people leave, I think. When they're gone, you don't have to be reminded of all the bad things. They can just stay the way you want them forever. Perfect."

I'm not sure if that made any sense. I watch Zoe, waiting for some kind of reaction. She stands there for a moment, saying nothing. Finally she nods, turns, and goes.

A flyer stapled to a telephone pole: CONNOR PROJECT KICKOFF CEREMONY.

And so, here I am. How could I miss it? An event in my honor. Students. Teachers. Local paper. Even the folks are in attendance.

There are speeches. A slide presentation. A performance by Zoe and the jazz kids. This is really something. I mean it—I'm almost flattered. And yet, call it habit, but I can't shake the feeling that they're only fucking with me.

How can I not? They stand here, talking about how much I meant to them. How much they relate. How they *feel* the things I felt. The isolation, unworthiness, loneliness. But how the hell do they know how I felt? I had to die for them to notice I was ever alive.

I'm ready to leave. But a new speaker is being called to the stage. He's being referred to as "Connor's best friend."

I tremble. Could it really be him? Maybe my absence finally registered. I move closer, searching. But as soon as the speaker hits the stage, I see it's not a match. Just from the walk, stiff and unsure—nothing like him. (Stupid to even dream it.)

Instead, it's my other bestie: Evan Hansen. What's the deal with this kid? And why the fuck is he... wearing my tie?

I'm positive it's mine. I picked it out myself, years ago. My mother took me shopping for a suit. She said it would be good to have one for a special occasion. Always the dreamer, my mother. Rather than burst her bubble, I went along with it. I let her believe my special occasion was coming.

Curiosity draws me closer to the stage. It's a totally different show up here. A little too intimate. I can see the beads of sweat on his forehead. Hands fumbling on his stack of index cards. He won't even look at the crowd. Been a minute and he hasn't even said hello.

Finally, he moves his lips. Voice so frail, even with the microphone. You have to lean in to hear him. And I'm only a few feet away. It's hard to imagine anything more fragile. Honestly, it wouldn't shock me if he burst into flames under that light.

With shaking uncertainty, he reads through two index cards:

Good morning, students and faculty. I would just like to say a few words to you today about... my best friend... Connor Murphy.

I'd like to tell you about the day that we went to the old Autumn Smile Apple Orchard. Connor and I, we stood under an oak tree, and Connor said he wondered what the world would look like from all the way up there. So we decided to find out. We started climbing slowly, one branch at a time. When I finally looked back, we were already thirty feet off the ground. Connor just looked at me and smiled, that way he always did. And then... well, then I...

He wipes his hand on his shirt.

I fell.

He keeps wiping.

I lay there on the ground and then...

He turns to the next card.

Good morning, students and faculty, I would...

The entire stack drops to the floor. Cards everywhere. I turn to gauge the crowd. My fellow spectators have lost their patience. Scattered whispers build to a steady rumble. Phones alight, the drama onstage filmed, immortalized. Poor guy, aware but oblivious, down on his knees, collecting his words. I can see the tears forming. I know that look. When your insides are about to pour right out of you and it's too late to stop it. You're naked, everyone watching. They see you there, defenseless, and they pounce. No mercy.

CHAPTER 15

A silence over everything. Not sure when it arrived, if it's been here the whole time. I squint past the lights to see if I'm suddenly alone. But no. They're all still here. Hundreds of them. Staring. Waiting. For me to do something. To say something. To stop drowning.

I'm on the ground, knees vibrating against the stage. I can't stop shaking. My cards scattered, out of sequence. Everything, out of sequence. I fight back the tears.

Bringing my gaze in, I notice, running down my chest: the tie.

I slide my fingers over it. Feel its weight. Soak up its power.

I have to finish this.

Legs wobbling, my whole body a convulsing mess, I rise to

stand. It takes every ounce of power and adrenaline to make it to my feet. To lift.

The cards remain on the stage. I don't need them. I've told the story so many times I could recite it in my sleep. I just have to open my mouth and *speak*.

Slowly, I raise my chin and lean into the microphone.

"I fell," I say, my voice carrying off into the distance.

I push out the words one by one.

"I lay there...on the ground...."

I shut my eyes. *Any second now.*

"But see, the thing is, when I looked up...Connor was there."

He always is. Somehow. Day after day, he comes, the thought of him. Visions in the night. His name on my arm. No matter what I do, where I go, a constant reminder. Of what? Of who I am. Of who I could be. Who I *should* be.

I open my eyes. "That's the gift that he gave me...to show me that I wasn't alone. To show me that I matter."

I do. Don't I? And not just me.

"That everybody does. That's the gift that he gave all of us. I just wish..."

It's the worst part. How unfair it is.

"I wish we could have given that to him."

It grips me. Sinks in. A slow sobering.

Then, terror returns. Realizations. Where I am. What I'm doing. What I'm saying. What *am* I saying?

I listen for the echo of my voice in the auditorium, trying

to make out my own words, trying to catch up with myself. But my voice is long gone. There's only silence.

Did I speak at all just now? Or did I only imagine it?

I look up, blinded by the lights. What have I done?

Leave. Now.

Panic-stricken, I turn, and I go, and I don't look back.

He steps away from the mic and hurries off the stage.

A pause, everywhere: What *was* that?

Again, my default reaction: this has to be a joke. I'm being messed with. But my gut says otherwise. I mean, the story he told wasn't real. It never happened. But the spirit of what he was saying, *how* he was saying it—in some weird way, it felt true. Like he actually meant it.

There hasn't been much encouragement these last few years. Even when I'd get the occasional compliment (*Connor, you're so artistic; funny; passionate*), I never believed it. Against all the negative feedback, a few nice words didn't register. Also, it depended on who was giving the compliments. They meant less from my mother (who overdid it), more from my father (who underdid it), and the most from . . .

That's the fucked-up part about this speech. It would've really meant something coming from a true friend. He should have been the one standing up there, saying those words. Because for him, I actually did show up. For him, I risked it all.

Around me, there's a growing sound.

(And as usual, I only ended up hurting myself.)

First sparse.

(What difference did any of it make?)

Then steady.

(Did I even matter at all?)

Hitting me. Slowly. What I'm hearing. Like an answer.

Applause.

CHAPTER 16

Even with my pillow covering my face and pressed against my ears, I can still hear my phone vibrating against my nightstand. It's the third time it's done this dance this morning. I would have buried it in my sock drawer before bed if I thought anyone might try to get in touch with me today. But no one ever tries to get in touch with me. And anyway, if there was ever a morning where I didn't want the world to find me, this is the one.

I suppose the universe has shown me some small mercy by making yesterday's assembly fall on a Friday, which means I don't have to show my face at school today. Disturbing images from the event flash in my memory. My index cards flying everywhere. Dropping down to my knees. The deafening silence. But one thing that I can't recall is what I actually said up there.

I didn't even wait to see how the assembly ended. The thought of having to face people, especially the Murphys, sent me fleeing. In a blind panic, I walked right out of school and skipped my last few classes. I couldn't bear the idea of riding the bus home, being trapped with my classmates as they offered reviews of the travesty they had just witnessed onstage. *I know it wasn't supposed to be a comedy, but I thought parts of it were hilarious. The name* Evan Hansen *shall hereby be used as a verb meaning "to crash, to burn, to meet with disaster."* No thank you.

I walked home and when I got here, I crawled right under the covers. I left my sneakers next to the bed, laces loosened, just in case I had to take off running in the middle of the night. For weeks now, I've been waiting for the worst to come, thinking it would be something unexpected and beyond my control, and in the end I basically chased it. I walked right onstage wearing Connor's tie directly into the worst thing that could happen.

My phone is still vibrating. I remove the pillow from my face. It's Alana calling. If I weren't so busy hating myself, I'd be hating her instead. It was her idea to have that assembly. She should have never encouraged me in the first place when I told her about the Connor Project. She should have been straight with me. *Sorry, Evan, but you should drop this immediately. It's way beyond your skills as a human being.*

"Where have you been?" Alana says when I finally pick up. "You haven't responded to any of my emails or texts."

I give no response.

"Hello?" Alana says.

I drop an Ativan into my mouth and flush it down with two-day-old water. "I'm here."

My speech lasted twelve hours. That's how long it felt, standing on that stage, under those blazing lights. I couldn't make out their faces, but I knew they were out there. I've never almost-drowned for such an extended period of time. I'm exhausted. I might never get out of bed again.

"Have you seen it?" Alana says.

Here we go. Why did I pick up the phone? "Seen what?"

"What's happening with your speech."

Now it's too late. Now I need to know. "What's happening with my speech?"

"Someone put a video of it online," she says.

"My speech?" I'm awake now. Every cell in my body is wide awake. It's officially over for me.

"Evan, it's totally insane. People started sharing it and now it's everywhere. Connor is everywhere."

"What do you mean, *everywhere*?"

"This morning, the Connor Project page had fifty-six people following it."

That's not bad, actually. Last I checked we were in the teens. "How many does it—"

"Now it has over four thousand."

"Did you say four..."

"Thousand," Alana says.

That's more people than we have in our entire school.

I sit up and open my laptop. Alana is still talking, but I'm barely listening. I refresh my browser. She's not lying. Actually, we're almost at six thousand now. What is going on?

I see a message from Jared waiting for me.

Dude. Your speech is everywhere.

"I'll call you back," I tell Alana.

My inbox is brimming with new emails. I find the first one that Alana sent and click the link to the video. I stop the video before it plays. I don't need to see my speech.

Under the video, though, is a long string of comments and I can't stop myself from looking. A few of the posts are from names I recognize, but most are from strangers. Some of the comments have links to other pages. I click on those links and I wander over to other websites and to new conversations among more people who I definitely don't know. I'm bouncing through space, from star to star, drawing lines that form a picture. I'm starting to see the picture as a whole, but I don't understand what the picture means, or how it came to be. It's not what I expected.

Oh my god, everybody needs to see this

I can't stop watching this video

Seventeen years old

Take five minutes, this will make your day

Share it with the people you love

RePost

The world needs to hear this

A beautiful tribute

Favorite

I know someone who really needed to hear this today

Thank you, Evan Hansen, for doing what you're doing

Yes, yes, yes

I never met you, Connor. But coming on here,
reading everyone's posts

It's so easy to feel alone, but Evan is
exactly right, we're not alone

None of us

We're not alone

None of us is alone

Like

Forward

Share

Especially now, with everything you hear in the news

Why can't there be more of this kind of thing?

Share

Sending prayers from Michigan

Richmond

Vermont

Tampa

Sacramento

Kansas City

Forward

Thank you Evan Hansen

Love

The best

I'm so in

Why do I have tears in my eyes?

I feel like I've been found

Thank you, Evan

Watch until the end

Thank you, Evan Hansen

This video is everything right now

Thank you, Evan

All the feels

This is about community

The meaning of friendship

Thank you, Evan Hansen, for giving us
a space to remember Connor. To be
together. To find each other. To be found.

Thank you

Thanks to Evan

Thank you Evan Hansen

It's true. My speech is everywhere. And not just that. People like it. They really like it.

A ringing startles me. It's the front door. The doorbell.

My mother will get it. I return to my inbox. It's full of emails from actual people, not companies. Here's one from my English teacher. And somehow Sam from lunch got my email.

The doorbell rings again. I crawl out of bed. I hear the shower running and my mom saying, "Evan, I think someone's at the door." I look out her bedroom window and see a car in the driveway. A blue Volvo.

A quick glance in the mirror. My hair is unacceptable, but I have no means to correct it. The one time when I could use a little moisture on my hands, they are completely dry. Conveniently, though, I'm already fully dressed.

Why is Zoe here? She can't be here right now. My mom has no idea what's been going on with her and the Murphys. I didn't intend to keep it all a secret. It just happened that way.

I'm already running down the stairs and opening the front door before I realize I should have at least taken a second to gargle some mouthwash.

The sun roars behind her.

"Hi," I say.

"Hey," she says.

She looks as exhausted as I feel. Somehow it looks good on her.

"I would invite you in, but my mom is really sick and I'm taking care of her. I'm sorry. Why are you here?"

She lowers her eyes.

"That sounded rude," I say. "I didn't mean it that way."

Great, I did it again. She won't even look at me. I Evan Hansened it.

She wipes her eye.

"Wait. Are you crying?"

Zoe nods.

"Why? Why are you crying?"

She shakes her head. Because she can't speak. Or because she doesn't know why she's crying. Or because it doesn't even matter.

"Everything you said in your speech. Everything you've done for all of us, everyone. My family. Me."

"No, I..." What am I trying to say? I don't even know. My brain has shut down. Do I want to apologize? Do I want to tell her the truth? Do I want the ground to swallow me?

She looks up. She takes a step. And then, my lips and her lips, again. Only this time it's not my doing.

She pulls back and exhales.

"Thank you, Evan Hansen," she says.

She turns and walks away, leaving me alone on the doorstep, exploding.

PART TWO

CHAPTER 17

"Hey, everybody, it's me, Alana, co-president, associate treasurer, media consultant, chief technology officer, and assistant creative director slash public policy director for creative public policy initiatives for the Connor Project."

"Hi, I'm Evan. I'm co-president of the Connor Project."

I see my face on one side of the screen and Alana's on the other. I'm assuming it's the same visual Alana is seeing on her screen at home, and the same one our audience is seeing, too, but this being our first-ever live-streamed update, I'm not positive.

"I wish I could see all of your amazing faces out there," Alana says.

"I hope you're having an amazing day," I add.

It's crazy to think how many people are waiting right now to hear what we have to say. Our viewer count is currently in the high hundreds and climbing. Wildly successful in my book, but Alana assures me that it's not really about the people watching live; it's about the traction we get after the fact. Once we log off this morning, the video will be watchable on our website and spread-ready through all social channels. Thanks to Jared, we'll even have usable data about who's engaging with our video.

"I know a lot of you have seen the inspirational videos on our website," Alana says.

"Thank you for checking out the awesome videos we put up last week with Mr. and Mrs. Murphy and Connor's sister, Zoe—"

"And Connor's best friend, my co-president, Evan Hansen."

I smile. (Awkwardly, I assume.)

There was no way I was going to allow anyone to be in the room with me when I did my video. I shot it myself and ended up doing seventeen takes before I had something I was willing to share. Alana wanted each of us to talk about the one big thing we learned from Connor. For Cynthia, it was patience. For Larry, empathy. My answer was hope. It was the only thing I could think of that was, and still is, totally and completely true.

Zoe might have been more nervous doing her video than I was doing mine. She said she knew what she wanted to say, but every time I started to record her, she'd clam up and go silent. Eventually, she talked about the importance of being independent and self-sufficient. I wonder if that was the answer she originally intended to give or if she changed her mind at the last second. I never asked. It didn't seem like she wanted me to.

"As you know, Connor's favorite place in the entire world was the incredible Autumn Smile Apple Orchard," I say.

"Tragically," Alana says, "the orchard closed seven years ago. This is what the property looks like now."

Onto the screen pops a photo of an empty overgrown field with tree stumps. A FOR SALE sign hangs on a rotting fence.

I've never actually laid eyes on the orchard. I know where it is, but I've never been there, not with Connor (obviously), or anyone. I never imagined it being so dilapidated and depressing. In my mind it's green and alive, rows of trees dotted with red apples.

The photo vanishes and our faces reappear. I perk up my sagging smile and make a contribution. "Connor loved trees."

"Connor was *obsessed* with trees," Alana says. "He and Evan used to spend hours together sitting at the orchard, looking at the trees, being with the trees, sharing fun facts they knew about the trees."

"That's true. For example, did you know that if you hang a birdhouse on a branch, it won't move up as the tree grows?"

"I did not know that," Alana says. "That is so interesting."

According to the script Alana sent me, it is now time for me to tee up our big announcement. It's been a learning process these last few weeks figuring out what exactly the Connor Project is and what it should be doing. At the outset we had only a few pamphlets, parental approval, and a kickoff assembly, which went way better than any of us expected. We weren't prepared for the reaction to my speech, either in a practical sense (our website crashed twice; Jared seemed stumped) or emotionally.

Jared and I were blown away to a degree that no one else could fully appreciate, and it caused us to stop and acknowledge what, until then, had gone unspoken. We both agreed: no one could ever know the truth. This thing we had started was actually helping people. The truth now would only cause harm.

A whole week went by after my speech before we realized that we weren't capitalizing on all the attention. New followers were still jumping on board, but some of our original followers had already lost interest and left. People kept arriving at our online door inspired by this newfound belief that they were not alone, that they didn't have to live with that burden anymore, that they could lessen it by sharing it with so many others who felt the exact same way. And we'd invite them into this new home of ours, except we soon realized that we had nothing tangible to offer them once they were inside. We weren't keeping them engaged.

So we made adjustments. Jared installed an email sign-up form on our home page so we could send out regular newsletters. Alana had us do the "What Connor Taught Me" videos. And now we're about to launch our most ambitious endeavor yet.

"There was one thing that Connor wished more than anything," I say. "He hoped that someday the apple orchard would be brought back to life."

"Which is where you come in."

Alana posts a digital rendering of a beautiful new orchard: bountiful trees and tranquil benches nestled inside an idyllic park. There's even a bird soaring across the sun. Jared introduced Alana to a free 3-D modeling program, and Alana managed to teach herself how to use it over a single weekend.

"Today we are announcing the start of a major online fundraising campaign," I say.

"One of the most ambitious crowdfunding initiatives since the internet was first created."

"We are looking to raise fifty thousand dollars in three weeks."

"It's a lot of money, I know. But it's also a lot of amazing."

"The money will go to restoring the orchard," I say. "It will be a space for everyone to enjoy."

When I told Cynthia we had decided to use all the attention the Connor Project was getting to raise money to restore the orchard, she hugged me tighter than I've ever been hugged before. And when I told her what I wanted to call it, I thought she might never let go.

"It's up to all you wonderful people out there to make the Connor Murphy Memorial Orchard not just a dream..." Alana says.

She waits, clears her throat, and repeats, "Not just a *dream*..."

Oops. That's my cue. "But a *reality*," I say.

We thank our viewers and end the video. Alana's face fills my entire screen.

"That went well," I tell her, relieved it's over and mildly impressed with myself.

"Yeah, next time we need to rehearse before we go live," Alana says.

Sometimes I feel more like a vice president than a co-president. But it's fine. It's all for a good cause.

"Okay," Alana says. "Now let's discuss local outreach."

I move my cursor over to reveal the time. It's already late in the morning. "You mean, like, right now?"

"There's no time like the present."

"Actually, I can't right now. I'm sorry. I have plans."

I used to marvel at the endurance of Alana's smile. I understand now that she has several other looks. In fact, she doesn't smile nearly as often as I once thought. The look she's giving me right this second, for example, is downright chilling.

"Very well," she says. "I'm going to print up postcards to promote the orchard campaign."

"That's a great idea," I say.

"What would really be great is if you could help me hand them out around town."

"Of course. Definitely. Just let me know when you want to do it."

"Okay. Great. Well, I have a lot of work to do, so you go have fun and I'll talk to you later."

She signs off, clearly annoyed with me. But I decide to take her advice. I will have fun. Now that I finally understand what the word means.

• • •

I look behind me. "No peeking."

"I'm not," Zoe says.

Her eyes seem closed, but a blindfold would have been a safer bet.

"We're almost there," I say. "Watch your step up here. The trail gets bumpy."

She holds on to the strap of my backpack while I guide us through Ellison Park.

A few more feet and I've found the perfect spot. Zoe obediently keeps her eyes shut while I unload supplies from my backpack.

"I'm nervous," she says.

"So am I."

I direct her where to sit (with words only; I still get nervous after all this time to actually make contact with her).

"Is this a blanket I feel?" Zoe says.

"You can open your eyes."

She looks down, and all around, and at me. "A picnic!"

I open the white paper bag that I've been carrying this whole time—the last thing I picked up before getting Zoe.

"You said you never tried the Korean taco truck, so..." I hand her a taco wrapped in aluminum foil. Our fingers brush lightly and we smile at each other.

"And for my last surprise." I raise my arm into the air, but she doesn't get it. I wiggle my arm and give her a hint: "It's not jazz hands."

She keeps looking until it finally sinks in. "Your cast is off! I totally forgot that was happening."

I lower my arm and pull my sleeve down. I don't want her

to inspect it too closely. It's not a pretty sight, ghostly pale with thick dark hair. I wanted the cast off for so long, but now that it's gone, I kind of miss it. I feel unbalanced and naked, like a part of me is missing.

"I have a weird question," Zoe says.

Every time she asks me something, I brace for the end of everything. "Okay."

"What did you do with the cast?"

Not such a weird question, actually. After the doctor sawed it off, he asked me what I wanted to do with it. My gut said trash it. It had spelled nothing but trouble for me from the start. Keeping it would only be a reminder of all the pain.

"I kept it," I say. "I don't know why."

It's the truth: I did keep it and I really *don't* know why.

My answer seems to satisfy her. Same for the taco. There's kimchi dropping everywhere. She searches for a napkin in the white paper bag. "So this is where you worked all summer?"

"Yeah. It feels weird to be back."

"I feel dumb asking, but what exactly does an apprentice park ranger do?"

"You're not dumb at all. Believe me, I didn't know what it was, either. I just assumed I'd be walking around a lot, you know, being surrounded by nature, but there's a lot more to it. You have to know everything about the park, its ecosystem, geography, natural resources, history, because if a visitor asks you a question, you need to have an answer. Then there's the maintenance duties: cleaning the restrooms, restocking maps, changing light bulbs. Also, you have to know basic first aid, just in case of an emergency. And then, on top of all that, you're sort of the police officer of the whole park, which means learning all these laws and making sure people follow them."

"Sounds like you really enjoyed it."

"I did, yeah."

Being at the park was such a welcome reprieve from my normal existence. Having someplace to go, something to do. Half the time I'd forget that I was here to work. I'd just stop and look around and feel, I don't know, calm, I guess.

"So when you and Connor were talking about trees in your emails, you were really talking about trees?" Zoe says.

"Of course. What did you think we were talking about?"

"Nothing."

Before I can inquire further, she asks me something else: "Have you always been so into nature?"

"I think so," I say, washing down my taco with water. "I probably get it from my dad."

That's why he moved to Colorado. He thought the East Coast was too crowded. My mom is convinced that my dad's whole thing about green space was an excuse, that he was really just following Theresa out there, but that's how I remember it. Then again, it was a long time ago, so maybe I have it all wrong.

"Before my parents got divorced, my dad took me fishing a few times, and once we all did a whole camping weekend here in the park."

As I chew my taco, the memory takes hold. I remember my

dad hanging a hammock between two trees so he could sleep under the stars. I asked him how he knew the trees would hold him up. *Trust me,* he said. *A hurricane could tear through here and these trees would still be standing.*

I believed him, but I couldn't stop worrying. I kept picturing the trees toppling over and my dad getting hurt. But he was right. When my mom and I came out of the tent the next morning, he was still hanging there. He said it was the best night's sleep of his life. Before we cleared out, he helped me carve my initials in one of the trees, so we could come back to it next time. But there was no next time.

The first thing I did when I started my apprenticeship at the park was try to find that tree. Every time I walked a new trail I looked for it, but I couldn't find it. Eventually I gave up. The park is way too big and it was such a long time ago.

"What did he say about your speech?" Zoe says.

Serves me right for bringing up my dad. He doesn't know about my speech, of course. The last time I tried to share news like that with him it didn't go well.

Zoe gleans enough from my silence. "Have you not shown it to him?"

"How's that taco? Delicious, right?"

"Evan."

I love it when she says my name. She sits patiently, waiting for me to trust her. I feel like I can.

"I plan to show him," I say, proceeding with caution. "I guess I'm just waiting for the right time. He's been really busy lately, with work, and Theresa being pregnant. Also, they've been looking for a new house, and I know they're really hoping to move in before the baby's born."

"Wait. You never said anything about a baby. Boy or girl?"

"Boy."

Zoe lights up. "No way. That's awesome. You're going to have a baby brother."

"I guess," is all I say. Because, while I trust her, and I do, I don't trust myself to talk about this.

As Zoe turns quiet, I realize something: she lost a brother and here I am about to gain one. Maybe I don't have a right to be bitter about it.

"It hasn't really sunk in yet, the whole brother thing," I say. What I don't say: I wish my dad kept track of my life without me having to always be the one to tell him about it.

"Well," Zoe says. "You're going to be the best big brother. And I'm sure your dad isn't too busy to be so proud of what you've done."

As much as I've told her, she doesn't know the half of it.

• • •

"All this used to be private property," I say, gesturing around us. "Back in the twenties, there was this guy who lived out here with his family. People assume his name was Ellison, but it was actually Hewitt. Ellison is a made-up name."

I turn around to check if Zoe is still with me. We've been walking the trail for a long time and I've been talking even longer. Now that Zoe switched me on, I can't switch myself off. "Sorry, I don't know why I'm telling you all this."

"No, I like it. Keep going."

"Okay, well, what happened was, there was a big fire at John Hewitt's house and it wiped out everything, including his wife and kids. He couldn't bear to live here anymore, so he made some sort of deal with the state to have the land turned into a park in his family's memory. He asked that it be called Ellison. It's a combination of his wife's name, Ellen, and his kids, Lila and Nelson."

"No way," Zoe says. "I just got the chills."

"I know, right? My boss told me that."

The most remarkable part of that story, to me, is that the guy could have gone with the family name, Hewitt, and that would have included all of them. But I guess he wanted to take himself out of it and make it about them only. It's unfortunate that more people don't know who made this place possible and how.

"Do you know where the house was?" Zoe asks. "Where the family lived before they . . ."

I shake my head, sorry to disappoint her. I should ask Ranger Gus if he knows.

Zoe stops in her tracks and takes a wide scan of the surroundings. "To be honest, I always forget this place exists. Even though it's right under my nose."

And a perfect nose it is. Her beauty easily trumps the park's. "So," I say, "while I was here all summer, where were you?"

"I worked at a camp over in Riverside during the day. And a few nights at that new yogurt shop on the boulevard."

I nod, pretending that I never once walked past that

yogurt shop this summer after hearing she was working there. "Sounds like you were busy."

"Guess so," Zoe says. "I try to be home as little as possible."

It's the opposite for me. Or, it was.

Zoe walks ahead. I advised her to wear sneakers today, but I wasn't picturing Converse. They're not exactly made for hiking. We're about to head down a steep slope.

"Careful on those stones," I say. "They can be slippery." I want to take her hand and guide her, but with her eyes open she doesn't need me to, and I'm not sure if she wants me to.

"When I was about twelve..."

"Yeah?"

"I tried to run away," Zoe says.

I pick up my pace so I can hear her better.

"My parents were so consumed with Connor, like twenty-four seven. I had this plan to sneak into the park with my sleeping bag and stay out here until they came and found me."

Ranger Gus says there are homeless people who sleep in the park and decamp by the time the rangers make their morning sweeps. The rangers only know this because of what the people leave behind.

"I packed a bag full of supplies," Zoe says. "You know that movie *Moonrise Kingdom*? It was like that. Except I didn't pack a record player."

She stops at a fork in the trail.

"Anyway, I never actually did it," Zoe says. "I came outside to the edge of the park and it was so dark in here I chickened out and went home. I slept under my bed, thinking my mom might come to wake me up in the morning and not know where I was. But...she never even noticed."

I can't imagine what it must have been like having to share a house with Connor. Like having a tornado for a roommate. It was hard enough for people who shared a classroom or bus or hallway with him. I guess living with that chaos every single day could make the woods seem pretty comfy.

I steer us left before Zoe has a chance to choose a direction. The path to the right leads to Clover Field and the oak tree.

"Hey," she says. "You know how I was telling you about that open mic night I did at Capitol? Well, I might be doing another one next weekend."

"You *might* be?"

"Yeah, I might be."

"Well, I *might* want to be there."

"I might like that."

A bird whips past us and ascends to the open air. That's me up there, soaring. I've never been this high.

We hear a chirp, but it's from Zoe's phone. "My mom," she says. "She wants me to ask if you have any more emails for her. Sorry, I know she's annoying."

"Oh. No. That's okay. Does she want them, like, now?"

"Not *now* now. Whenever you can."

Right. Whenever I can.

To the ground I fall. I can never stay aloft too long. Not when there's an ugly and heavy truth always dragging me back down.

CHAPTER 18

Today I'm passing by The Zone in the cafeteria and I hear my name. I'm not sure who dubbed it "The Zone," but it's the row of tables near the middle of the room where all the notable people in school sit. If an eighteen-wheeler happened to drop from the sky and land on this one spot, the entire upper crust of this school would be wiped out in one fell swoop. (I do happen to know, after reading *Macbeth* last year, where the phrase *one fell swoop* comes from.)

Sitting front and center in The Zone is the new powerhouse couple known as Roxanna. Roxanna is composed of Rox and his new girlfriend, Annabel. Poor Kristen Caballero has been banished to one of the outer tables. It's just natural selection, I suppose. As I pass Roxanna, Rox nods and says, "Hey, Hansen." Annabel looks me in the eye, which she's never done before in the three years we've been in school together.

All I do is stare back at them in dumbfounded silence. I'm still getting used to how this whole not-invisible thing works. A lot has changed since I made that speech. I've finally escaped the indifference of *meh*. I am now, exclusively, *eh*. I am Evan Hansen.

I make it through The Zone and proceed to Jared's table. He's chomping on a calculator-sized (and -shaped) hash brown. I squat down next to his chair.

"We need more emails," I say. "Can you meet me after school?"

"Not today," Jared says. "I have a dentist appointment."

"Okay. How about tomorrow?"

"Maybe."

I don't have time to screw around. As a budding capitalist, Jared knows that it's a fatal problem when you don't have enough supply to meet demand. "Unless you just want to show me how to do it," I say. "I've watched you enough. I bet I could figure it out."

"Oh really?" Jared scoffs. "You think so? Well, be my guest, brother." A wicked joy materializes on his face. "And don't forget to add the offset for GMT, or else all the time zone conversions are going to totally freak out."

Maybe not, then. "Well, can you meet me tomorrow or what?"

Jared straightens his posture. "Sir, yes, sir. Reporting at seventeen hundred GMT-minus-four."

"I don't know what you're saying."

Jared rolls his eyes. "Five o'clock."

"Let's make it four, actually. I have plans at night."

I leave Jared as he's savoring his last bite of hash brown and finally arrive at my new home base: Zoe's table. It's an eclectic mix of people here. A few musicians from jazz band. A kid from the golf team, which I wasn't even aware our school had. A mildly, sort of half-committed Goth girl. The backup goalie for the girls' soccer team. (Ms. Bortel was permanently replaced as varsity coach and gym teacher; apparently she had been caught on video savagely ridiculing, by name, a number of generously proportioned students.) And finally, Zoe's friend Bee, who as far as I can tell is her closest friend. I'm not positive about that, though, and I get the feeling that Bee isn't always sure, either, where she and Zoe stand. I've learned that Zoe's opaqueness isn't only directed at me.

Bee is the first one to acknowledge my arrival. "Are you dressing up, Evan?"

I check my clothing. I'm pretty sure, unless I'm missing something, that I'm dressed the way I'm always dressed.

"For Halloween," Bee clarifies.

Oh, right. I forgot that Halloween is coming up. "I haven't decided yet."

I never dress up. I don't have a reason to. I'm too old to trick-or-treat and the school has a strict no-costume policy.

Zoe leans over. "We should come up with something together. A famous pair. Bonnie and Clyde. Mario and Princess Peach."

I look down at her plate. "French fries and ketchup."

She smiles. I wonder which one of us would be the ketchup, and where we'd go in our costumes, and what it means when she refers to us as a *pair*. It doesn't matter what we dress as. We could be anything. SunButter and jelly. Netflix and chill. *American Gothic*. Whatever it is, for once, I'm in.

• • •

The following afternoon Jared and I are at Workout Heaven. As soon as we sat down, Jared tore into a candy bar and now he's really taking his time with it, as if purposely tempting the miserable, sweating bastards around us.

"How about this?" Jared says.

> Dear Evan Hansen,
>
> **They tried to make me go to rehab and I said no, no, no.**

"That's a song," I say.

"A *great* song."

"Change it."

> Dear Evan Hansen,
>
> **I don't want to go back to rehab. I don't mind the yoga, and the group meetings are all right. But people share some scary shit, like about sucking dick for meth.**

"Jared!"

"It happens. I saw it on TV."

"Take it out."

> Dear Evan Hansen,
>
> I have to find a way to kick this. I don't want to
> end up back in rehab. It's just no fun.

"That's fine," I say. "New paragraph."

"What's with your arm?" Jared says.

"I just got my cast taken off."

"I see that, genius. I mean, why do you keep squeezing it like that? It's creeping me out."

I look down. It's true. My right arm is clutching my left. "I don't know. Whatever. Can we just keep going?"

We fight our way to the end of one email and generate a response wherein I'm being the best friend everyone expects me to be—positive, supportive, generous. It's a role I'm committed to. When Connor needs a purpose, I give him one. When he's teetering, I straighten him out. When he's ragging on his family, I remind him that they love him and they're only trying to help.

We crank out ten emails. We're in such a flow that I almost don't catch one of Jared's inspired inventions.

> Dear Evan Hansen,
>
> You know that insanely cool guy from school
> Jared Kleinman? What am I saying? You
> obviously know who Jared Kleinman is.

**Everybody does. What do you think about
inviting him into our awesome friendship and
making this thing a trio?**

"No, Jared. Obviously not."

"Why? What's the problem?"

"You weren't friends with him. That's not part of the
story."

"Well, maybe it's time to expand the story," Jared says. "It's
getting kind of stale, don't you think?"

"No, I don't think that. Not at all. I was his only friend. You
know that. You can't just make things up."

Jared removes his glasses and cleans them with his shirt,
letting his pale stomach wave hello to all of the gym's patrons.
"You're totally right, Evan. I mean, what was I thinking, just
making things up in a completely fabricated email exchange
that never happened?"

It's like dealing with a child. "Just, please, don't change the
story, okay?"

He returns his glasses, businesslike, to his face. "Well, if
you want me to redo this email, you're going to have to wait
until next week, because I'm busy the rest of the week, and
this weekend I'm hanging out with my camp friends. Or, as I
like to call them, my *real* friends."

"Actually," I say, scrolling up the screen, "I think we're good
on emails for now. Let's call it a day."

We pack up our things and zigzag through the obstacle
course of workout machinery. On our way to the exit, Jared

urges me to look over at one of the moms running on a treadmill. I refuse, but he won't let up.

"Seriously," Jared says. "I think she's waving at us."

He's not lying. The woman is calling us over to her treadmill.

Against my better judgment, I follow Jared over to the woman. She lowers the speed on the treadmill so she can breathe enough to get the words out. "You're the guy from the video," she says. "The Connor Project guy. Evan, right?"

I nod.

"I knew I recognized you. I love your speech. So much. So do my kids."

It's crazy how many people the Connor Project has reached. I get emails and messages from people every day from all around the world telling me how their lives have been affected by this thing we've built. We started a movement. Touched a collective nerve. And now I'm seeing it in the flesh, beaming on this woman's face.

I thank her and we finally leave Workout Heaven. "Dude. You're a hit with the MILF crowd."

"Stop."

"Just saying. Honestly, though, I should be getting some of that screen time, too. It's only fair. How about I do a few man-on-the-street videos for the orchard campaign? I got a dope new camera for my birthday."

"I think Alana and I have the fundraising thing covered. I'll let you know if I think of anything, though, definitely."

"Got it," Jared says, looking down at the sidewalk. "Hey, I bet Zoe's happy that your cast is gone."

"I guess."

"I mean, talk about killing the mood, right? Having to see your brother's name written on your boyfriend's arm all the time?"

"I'm not her boyfriend. I don't know what we are." I mean, I've wondered about what we are, obviously, constantly, but right now all I have are just wild guesses.

"Don't even worry about it, bro," Jared says, removing his car key from his pocket. "The only thing you should be worrying about right now is building that orchard for Connor. Because if there was one thing about Connor, the guy loved trees. Or wait, *you* love trees. That's weird. Isn't that weird?"

By now I'm used to Jared's blunt humor, but this latest jab feels more brutal than normal. And that feeling only gets validated as he hurries off to his car without me. I guess he won't be giving me a ride home.

I walk away from Workout Heaven and toward the bus stop, trying not to think about what Jared said and how he said it, but failing miserably. In no time at all, that ugly heaviness returns, spreading through my body, making it difficult to drag my legs along the sidewalk.

And then, in this spiraling state, I feel a sudden chill—the sensation of being followed. I whip my head around and check behind me. But all I find is the empty night.

I've been watching him. I can't help it. What started as curiosity is something else now. In some crazy way, it almost feels like Evan and I really were friends. I've heard it said so much, I'm starting to actually believe it. Who knows? Maybe in some alternate universe we could've been.

Not that I have much experience in this area. I basically spent my whole life alone. Until I met Miguel. That was his name. Sometimes M. Never Mike.

(I keep wanting to see him, but I stop myself. What's the point of putting myself through that again?)

We met sophomore year at Hanover. An all-boys school. I thought I'd hate that, but it actually made life simpler. (I'd rate my experience with girls somewhere between Very Unsatisfactory and Not Applicable.) It was the fresh start I needed. In public school, I could never escape the vision everyone had of me. At Hanover, I was new again. Untainted.

No one made me believe that more than Miguel. My first week, we got paired together in biology. I muttered a joke that made him laugh. *How do you tell the sex of a chromosome? Pull down its genes.* It felt normal, our interaction. What I always imagined normal would be.

He knew a little about everything. Spoke about subjects I'd never considered: cryptocurrency and alkaline foods. Quoted people I'd never heard of: Nietzsche and David Sedaris. Listened to artists I'd missed: Perfume Genius and the War on Drugs. Asked questions I didn't know to ask: Did the government demolish Building 7 on 9/11? Will humans survive ocean acidification? Where are all the baby pigeons? He could sort out the exact right dosage of edibles to get you floating, as opposed to sinking.

He told me I was innocent. Which was the opposite of how I viewed myself, but something I felt was true in my heart. He saw me before I saw me.

He was the first person I'd known who was openly and proudly gay. (I was something in between. Fluid. The way I thought about both girls and guys. Back then I had only begun to put those thoughts into action.)

We hung out a little at school. But after school, we were a duo. We'd go downtown. Stay warm in the bookstore. Watch the skateboarders at Erwin Center. I'd be waiting outside the bakery when he got off work. I'd go with him to bring the unsold baguettes to his cousin. We'd end up on a bench, tossing bread to birds, regretting how much waste there was in the world. Sometimes these conversations happened on a bus. Other nights on his living room couch. His mom would come home and whip us up a feast. I'd leave at bedtime, my belly and head full. (Heart too.)

And then one day in second semester, he was in a panic. They found weed on him. For the first time, his swagger was missing. I tried to downplay it. *It's just a little weed. And so what if they do kick you out. You'd be lucky to get out of this place.*

You think it was easy for me to get in here? Maybe for you.

I started thinking the worst. What if he *did* get kicked out? Where would that leave me? What would I do without him? And then, another split-second decision.

I went to the dean, told him it was mine. I don't know what I thought would happen. I wasn't thinking it through, just following some gut thing. We all signed the same school contract—zero tolerance. Penalty: expulsion. My parents tried to fight it, but it was no use. Miguel's record stayed clean and I got sent to rehab. My father had threatened to send me the year before. My mother persuaded him to send me to a summer wilderness program instead, and then to Hanover. What's crazy, I was basically just smoking weed at the time. But it didn't matter. My track record didn't support my story. I had run out of chances. (The irony: it was rehab that introduced me to a new set of bad habits.)

Wilderness camp was a literal walk in the park compared with rehab. The kids I was with were hard addicts. Some of them didn't even resemble kids. Weathered skin, teeth, eyes. Almost not human, more like zombies. And that's how the staff treated them. Treated *us*. But I didn't belong there. I acted like I did. Pretended I was a bigger user than I ever really was. Just to blend in. Survival. But inside I was shaking. I missed home. (For once, I had something at home to miss.)

After rehab, we saw each other less. Different schools. He had a full schedule with work and Amnesty International. Also, his mom didn't want him hanging out with me. (I never met his dad and doubt that he ever knew I existed.) But we still texted a lot. I'd complain to him about public school, how I was being treated. People hear you went to rehab and they act like you're poison. You start to believe it, too. *Fuck 'em*, Miguel would say. Simple and resolute. *Fuck 'em*. It helped.

Whenever I stopped to think about my life, the turn it took, the anger would consume me. (I wonder now: What would've happened if I'd stayed at Hanover? Maybe life could've gone a different way.)

And then: one day, this past spring. Miguel came over. He made a big deal of it, too. *I feel like maybe I'm the first Mexican in your house who wasn't getting paid to be here.* I said no. What I didn't tell him: he was the first *anyone* in my house. The first person I'd ever invited over. (I'd hooked up with people by then. But it's not like I was bringing anyone home to meet the parents.)

The house was empty. We hung in my bedroom. He made fun of one of my books. *The Little Prince? Really? That actually explains a lot.* He said I was a boy in man's clothing. (He introduced me to a ton of books and authors. I never returned his copy of *The Mysteries of Pittsburgh*.)

There was a new energy between us. (We were older now. More experienced. Thoughts had become actions.)

We got high and lay on the floor. *Your hair's getting long,* he said. I wanted to find scissors immediately. But then he said, *I like it.*

He played me this one song. When it was over, I asked him to play it again. One line stood out: "Don't hold back. I want to break free." (I listened to that song every day for months. Until it became too painful to hear.)

Lying there, I noticed a birthmark on his neck. I had never noticed it before. I reached out and touched my finger to it. We locked eyes.

That birthmark: a magic button. Once pushed, the whole world suddenly lit up.

CHAPTER 19

Keeping up with fans has become part of my new daily routine. *Fans* is an obnoxious word, I know, but honestly, I'm not sure what else to call them. *Followers* is also weird. (Across all platforms, I've got at least a hundred new followers since I last checked.) I guess they're just fellow lonely people who have found hope in our little community, the one I happen to be the face of.

What I do know for sure is that these people all seem to have a desperate desire to connect with someone. They feel inspired to share their incredibly personal stories. When they couldn't live up to the expectations. When they borrowed money they couldn't repay. When they feared they'd never leave that foster home. When they lost a child. When they cheated on the only one who stood by them. When the job they needed went to someone else. When the person in power abused his privilege. When the purpose that drove them no longer seemed worth it. When they struggled to get out of bed, or go outside, or show up for work. When they didn't know where to aim their rage. Or how to endure their isolation. Or reverse their mistakes. Or not give up.

I recognize almost all of it and yet it's so much bigger than me.

And when these people write me, they don't just want to talk; they want to listen, too. They're interested in hearing what I think about things. At first, they wanted to know more about Connor, but now they also want to know about me and my life, and not just the big, dramatic stuff but also the mundane things, like what hair product I use and where I shop for clothes. (I don't tell them that my mother takes care of both of those things.)

Many people keep asking the same question: *How come you never post any pictures of yourself?* I've always been camera shy. From what I can tell, Connor was the same way. There aren't many pictures of him out there, either.

Surprisingly, Vivian Maier took hundreds of photos of herself. It's surprising because she was such a private person. She'd use aliases all around town and she'd never share information about her past. She seemed to enjoy being anonymous, and yet, she took tons of selfies—long before selfies were a thing. If someone as shy and awkward as Vivian Maier could take a selfie, I should be able to take one, too.

I smooth down my hair in the mirror, then sit on the bed and hold out my phone. I snap a few pictures and review the shots. I look like someone who's preparing to commit a sex crime. I reset and try again. This time I stand in front of the window and catch some natural light. I realize that my messy, unmade bed shows in the background. But my smile isn't egregious. I crop out the bed and make it a close-up. After messing around with some filters, I summon the strength to share it with the world.

I put away my phone and open my laptop. I should finish my homework before delivering the new emails to the Murphys. But first I click over to my uploaded photo and see if there's been a response. My photo already has a dozen hearts. I refresh my screen and the number of hearts jumps even higher. Someone already posted a comment:

So hot! 😎

Even though I'm completely alone, I blush and kind of laugh/gasp.

"What are you looking at?"

It's my mom. (Of course.)

"Nothing," I say, quickly closing my laptop.

"Nothing? You were just sitting there with a huge smile on your face."

"I was? I don't think so."

I slide my computer into my bag, next to the printed-out emails.

"I feel like every time I come into your room, you shut your computer," she says. "I don't know what you do on there that you don't want me to see."

I zip my bag shut. "I was doing homework, Mom."

"Do you have a minute?" Standing there in the doorway, she resembles a prison guard blocking escape.

"Actually, I was about to go to Jared's."

"I thought you already saw him this afternoon."

"I was supposed to, but he canceled, so we're meeting tonight. We have this Spanish project we have to finish." I have one sneaker on, but I can't find the other. "We'll probably be going pretty late, so don't worry about waiting up. He'll drive me home."

"You can't wait five minutes?" she says.

I pretend to consider it. "I really shouldn't."

"I saw the strangest thing on Facebook today."

"Oh really? Do you see my sneaker over there?"

"It was a video from something called the Connor Project. Have you heard of that?"

I freeze. I knew this moment was destined to come, and yet I somehow convinced myself that it never actually would.

She's not finished reporting what she's learned. "It says on their website that you're the president."

Co-president.

"I watched the video," she says.

Her and every other mother in town, apparently.

"It was you doing a speech. About that boy. Connor Murphy. How you climbed a tree together."

I'm done climbing. I don't have the energy for it anymore. I sit down on the bed.

"You told me you didn't know him. That boy?"

"I know. But…"

"But then in your speech, you said he was your best friend."

She comes close and bends down to see my face. "Evan. Look at me."

I can't run anymore. I've only got one shoe on.

"What's going on?" she pleads.

I test it out, what it feels like to let it all go. I tell her, "It wasn't true."

"What wasn't true?" she says.

I'm so tired of walking this tightrope. Sometimes it just requires too much. I've been longing for the safety of solid ground. I could end it—right here and now.

But then where will I be? Everything else will end, too. Everything I have with the Murphys will be gone. My mom will make me tell them the truth. They'll hate me. They won't understand what I was trying to do, that I was only trying to help.

No. That's not what I want.

"When I said I didn't know him," I answer finally.

She presses her palm to her forehead, massaging her brain, trying to understand. "So you broke your arm with Connor Murphy? At an orchard?"

I nod. It's the first thing Jared ever taught me.

"You told me you broke your arm at work," she says. "At the park."

I stand up. "Who do you think drove me to the hospital? Who do you think waited with me in the emergency room for three hours? You were in class, remember? You didn't answer your phone."

"You told me your boss took you to the hospital."

"Well?" I say, shrugging. "So, I lied, obviously."

"When were you planning on telling me any of this? Or you weren't?"

"When would I tell you, exactly? When are you even here?"

"I'm here right now."

"One night a week?" I resume the sneaker search. "Most parents try a little harder than that, just so you know."

"Isn't that lucky for them."

Where the hell is my shoe? "I have to go to Jared's."

"I'm not sure I want you going out right now, actually."

I'm down on all fours, checking under the bed. Sure enough, that's where I find it, hiding behind the curtain of my blanket. I also spot the plastic shopping bag that contains my cast. I didn't know where else to put it, so I shoved it down here. I never thought I'd have to see it. Or think about it.

I stand up and slip my sneaker on. After that, my backpack. "I told Jared I'd be there ten minutes ago."

"All right, listen. I'm missing class tonight so I can be here to talk to you, Evan. I would like you to please talk to me."

"Okay, well, am I supposed to just drop everything because it's convenient for you? I can't just not do my homework because you decided to skip class."

In the most deliberate manner possible, she inhales and exhales, trying to remain calm. "I don't understand what is going on with you."

"Nothing is going on with me."

"You're standing up in front of the school and giving

speeches? You're president of a group? I don't know who that person is."

"You're making a big deal out of something that isn't a big deal."

"Evan." She grabs my shoulders, forcing me to see her. "What is going on with you? You need to talk to me. You need to communicate with me."

"Nothing is going on with me. I told you—"

"I'm your mother!"

It shocks us both. She never yells at me.

"I'm your mother," she repeats, quieter, her lip trembling.

I look down, unable to endure the hurt in her eyes. There's plenty of it already in the sound of her struggling to catch her breath.

And then, lowering onto the bed, shrinking, she says, "I'm sorry."

No. I'm the one who's sorry. It's me.

"I'm happy for you," she says, eyes watery. "I'm happy you had a friend, sweetheart. I'm just... I'm so sorry he's gone."

My friend. I shoved our one real moment together into a plastic bag and hid it under my bed.

"I wish I had known him." She wipes away a tear. And then, she notices something. "Is your arm hurting?"

I realize I'm clutching it again and I let go. "No."

"Listen to me. If you ever want to talk. I mean, about *anything...*"

I wish I could. I wish I had. But that chance has passed.

There's no way out now but forward. Forward, right now, means getting out of this house.

"I should go," I say, my voice hollow.

"Oh." She moves away from the door. "Okay." She picks up a pill bottle on my dresser. "You okay on refills?"

"Actually, I'm not taking them anymore. I haven't needed them."

She studies my face. "Really? So, no anxiety? Even with everything that's happened?"

I shake my head. "I've been fine," I tell her. And it's true.

Now she's the one shrugging. Neither of us has the answers. "All right, then. That's great to hear. I'm proud of you."

It's the perfect time to leave, now, while she's got a buoy of good news to float on. But I don't get out fast enough.

"I guess those letters to yourself must have really helped, eh?"

I can't think of anything more painfully untrue.

Eh. She's the one who insisted I be Evan. The name I was born with didn't meet with her approval. Seventeen years later and she's still trying to tweak me just a little bit more to her liking.

"I have to go," I say, stepping around her.

I half expect her to follow me, but when I turn back to check, she hasn't moved. She's looking at me as if I'm a stranger. I guess maybe I am.

CHAPTER 20

The Murphys' garage is bigger than the entire bottom floor of my house. It's cleaner and more organized, too. In my experience, garages are where people store all the junk they don't want inside their home. But Larry Murphy seems like the sort of guy who doesn't tolerate junk. He just throws it away.

Zoe's father asked me to join him in here while the ladies cleared the dinner table. I usually help Cynthia, but tonight we're just two guys talking shop. The fight with my mom is only a shadow now. Larry doesn't want to interrogate me. He wants to help me.

He's showing me the contents of a plastic storage bin that he pulled off a high shelf. "Brooks Robinson," Larry says. "Jim Palmer."

I don't recognize these people as baseball players until he shows me their cards sheathed in protective plastic.

"Look at this," Larry says, probing deeper into his bin. "Here's the entire '96 team."

"Wow," I say, because I assume I'm supposed to.

"You get the right people to come to an auction, baseball fans, I bet you could raise a thousand bucks for the orchard, easy."

"It's a great idea. I'm definitely going to talk to Alana about it."

Larry didn't have much to say about our idea to rebuild the orchard when we first presented it. Cynthia was all in, but Larry just sat there quietly. Maybe that's his style. For all I know, that's the style of all dads.

He pulls out a baseball glove from the bin and sets it aside. "I swear I have a Cal Ripken in here somewhere."

"This is really generous of you," I say. "To donate all this stuff."

The door to the house opens and Zoe appears. "Mom says that your show is on and she doesn't want to DVR it again."

"Well, tell her we're busy."

"Dad, are you torturing him?"

"What?"

"Evan, is he torturing you?" Zoe says. "You can tell him he's being boring and you want to leave. He won't be upset."

"He can leave whenever he wants," Larry says.

"Evan, do you want to leave?"

In the first moments alone with Larry, I was praying Zoe would come rescue me. He and I have never really had a conversation, just the two of us. But I'm actually having a good time talking to him. "No. Really," I say, "it's cool."

"Fine," Zoe says. "Don't say I didn't warn you. And, Dad, don't let Evan take any more selfies for his groupies."

"I don't know what any of that means," Larry says.

"Ask Evan. He knows." Zoe smirks at me before shutting the door.

Larry looks to me for guidance. I shrug, trying to not let the fact that Zoe just exhibited what I'm pretty sure was jealousy cause me to unleash an embarrassing fist pump.

He's quiet a moment. Then he says, "So, you and Zoe...?"

My face turns what I can only assume is the reddest red a face can turn.

He keeps looking at me, not unkindly.

"This glove is really cool." I pick up a baseball mitt.

"Pretty nice, right?" Larry says, seeming just as happy to have switched topics. "You can have it if you want."

"Oh. No. I couldn't."

"Why not? It's never been used. I probably bought it for a birthday or something."

Only now does it sink in whose baseball glove this is. To hand it back wouldn't look right. Wouldn't feel right, either. A birthday gift. Connor will never get another one. Even worse, the gifts he did get are being given away.

"My dad and I, we used to throw the ball around in the backyard every Sunday afternoon," Larry says. "I thought Connor and I could do that. He used to complain that I was never around, I was working all the time, so I said, all right, let's set aside Sunday afternoons for just the two of us. And then, all of a sudden, he wasn't interested anymore." He laughs softly. "Nothing with Connor was ever easy."

He slides his hands into his pockets. "Take it," he says, like he's offering me nothing more than a breath mint. "It's just going to sit here, collecting dust."

I guess I have no choice.

"You'll have to break it in, though, first," Larry says. "You can't catch anything with it that stiff."

Great. The gift comes with responsibility, too. "How do you break it in?"

"Your dad never taught you how to break in a glove?"

I don't answer. I don't have to.

"Well, there's really only one right way to do it," Larry says, reaching into the bin. "You have to use shaving cream."

I figure it's a joke, but then he pulls out an actual can of shaving cream and starts to shake it.

"Here," he says. "It's full."

Now I've got a baseball glove in one hand and a can of shaving cream in the other. I don't play baseball or shave.

"What you do is, rub that in for about five minutes. Then you tie it all up with rubber bands, put it under your mattress, and sleep on it. The next day, you repeat the same thing. You do that for at least a week."

"A week? Really?"

"Every day. Consistent. There are no shortcuts."

Larry even has a bag of rubber bands. "Nowadays, with your generation, I hate to say it, but it's all about instant gratification. Who wants to take the time to read a book when you can read the Facebook instead? But there's no substitute for doing the work. None. It just takes a little patience."

He sprays the shaving cream onto the glove and begins to work it in.

"I didn't let Connor take shortcuts. Cynthia was the one with the second chances and the 'Try harder next time.' And I was the one who said no. I said, 'Connor, you keep taking shortcuts, you're going to lose the trail eventually, and pretty soon you're going to end up somewhere you don't want to be with no idea how to find your way home.'"

There's a slight crack in his voice. He clears his throat, composing himself, and stares down into his bin. It's all emptied out. We're not talking about sports or girls anymore.

"Connor was lucky," I hear myself saying. "To have a dad who cared so much."

Larry arranges the items on the table. "Well, your dad must feel pretty lucky to have a son like you."

"Yeah," I say. "He does."

Here I am, lying about things that don't even require lying.

Larry smiles. "Well, if you want to go catch up with Zoe..."

"Right. Yeah." I head for the door, my hands full—glove, shaving cream.

But something stops me. I turn back. "I don't know why I said that. About my dad. It's not true. My parents got divorced when I was seven. My dad moved to Colorado. He and my stepmom have a new family now. So, that's sort of his priority."

Larry studies me. Instant regret sets in. I'm not sure why I revealed all that. It's just, he was open and true with me, vulnerable, and I wanted to be the same way back to him. It seemed right and fair, and now . . .

He puts a hand on my shoulder. "Don't forget the rubber bands," he says, dropping the bag into my hands.

I nod, breathing out. "Thanks."

"You're good to go."

• • •

The light is still on in my mom's bedroom when Zoe pulls up to my house. But by the time I make it up the stairs, there's no longer a glow underneath her door.

The note I find in my bedroom reads: *Te amo hijo mio*. I'm baffled until I remember that I told her I was with Jared working on a Spanish project. I picture, for a moment, my mother having to Google how to write what she wanted to say.

It's past eleven. She was clearly waiting up for me. I told her not to, but I guess she couldn't help herself.

Cynthia suggested I spend the night at their house. *Zoe drives you to school anyway*, Cynthia said. *Call your mother and let her know. You can take Connor's bed*. It was a kind offer, but too much. I couldn't sleep in Connor's bed. As numb as I've become, I've still got a little sensitivity left.

Actually, scratch that. To call what I'm feeling *numb* isn't accurate. If anything, I'm feeling more now than ever. And not just because I stopped taking my medication. For the first time I'm actually experiencing life. I finally know what it means to kiss someone. Like, *really* kiss, for many seconds at a stretch. That happens all the time now. It's basically commonplace, although *never* boring. And tonight I learned how to break in a baseball glove. Something my own dad never bothered to teach me.

Zoe says I should send my dad a link to the speech. But I don't think he'd care about any of it—the Connor Project, the orchard. When he wrote one time on Facebook that he was having trouble keeping the shape of his new cowboy hat, I sent him an article that contained time-tested care instructions; he never responded. I used to mail him postcards, hoping we'd become pen pals, but the one time I received a response, it was in Theresa's handwriting. He enjoys hiking, so I suggested we walk the Appalachian Trail together. He seemed to like the idea, but when I reminded him about it this summer, he came up with an excuse about how he's already flying east for my graduation in the spring, and now with the baby coming, he can't afford to come twice. So what do I do next? I research a trail close to where he lives in Colorado and I pin all my hopes on that. (Pun *very* much intended.)

I walk over to my map. I'm tired of putting myself out there. For what? How long am I supposed to wait? Eighteen hundred miles between him and me. Maybe it's just too far. Pretty soon he'll have another kid, a baby pressed in his arms. You can't get any closer than that. How can I compete? Why do I even want to after all he's put me through? I just thought, on this one specific occasion not too long ago, I really thought he'd be proud, that he might appreciate the fact that I brought back to life that faded WELCOME sign outside Ellison Park, a place he used to love to visit, often with me by his side, the two of us together, the memories we had. I just thought that my accomplishment, the gesture of it, would reach him somehow, would connect, but then, of course, like always, that day when I told him, when I sent him that photo...

It doesn't matter. I'm done. I remove the pin and toss it in a cup. While I'm up, I fit my new baseball glove onto my hand. I use my free arm—the one that's no longer broken, the one I'm still learning how to live with—to throw a punch at the stiff leather. I punch again, a little harder this time, and then again, harder, and again, and again, until my fist shines the most satisfying red.

CHAPTER 21

The waitress asks if I'd like a refill, but I think I've had enough coffee for one day. If my foot drums against the floor any harder, the owners of Capitol Café might try to tack on building damages to my bill. I don't normally consume caffeine (Dr. Sherman told me to avoid it), but it was either a coffee beverage or complimentary water, and Zoe said it would be better for her if I spent money while I'm here. I can't afford dinner, so, yeah, pass the cream and sugar.

She's currently onstage, tuning her guitar. It's not technically a stage. It's just a section in the back with a microphone and two speakers.

I'm more nervous than Zoe and she's the one about to perform. I just want tonight to go well for her. The place is pretty empty. There's an old couple eating dinner, another performer waiting in the wings, and a few people with laptops occupying stools. But it's still early.

Her voice booms, "Hello," and everyone looks up. She pulls back from the mic. "Yikes, sorry."

Someone kills the soft music that's playing in the background. The stage, or whatever it is, is all Zoe's. She strikes a single chord, testing out the sound. I hold my knee still, concerned that my pounding will interfere with her set. Zoe takes a deep breath, shuts her eyes, and begins.

It's a different style than I'm used to from her. Normally her guitar accompanies dozens of other instruments to form a lush sound. Here, it's thin and bare. Just a soft and modest jangle.

And then she opens her mouth and my apprehension gives way to awe. She's not slick or even graceful. She's almost having a conversation with us, more than singing notes. It's rough and vulnerable and genuine. It's everything she is, but less guarded.

As I loosen in my chair, so does Zoe onstage. The timidity I sensed in her at the start retreats. Her voice becomes more musical, slipping into a higher, silkier tone on the bridge and going full out for the final chorus. I think it's a cover, what she's playing. I've heard the song before, but not like this. She's made it her own.

When she finishes, I slap my hands together. She peeks up, and now that she's stopped playing, she's shy again. I don't care that I'm the only one clapping. The old couple smiles, showing their appreciation. The rest of the room is oblivious. Zoe doesn't seem to notice or care. She's doing her thing up there. This is even better than seeing her perform in jazz band. Way better.

The next song is also a cover. My pocket vibrates. In between songs, I check to see who texted me. It's Alana, but I don't have time to read her message. Zoe is introducing another song.

"This next one I wrote," she announces. "It's brand-new and I'm probably going to screw it up, but whatever. It's called 'Only Us.'"

Again, I'm tense. It's like watching her dangle from some great height without a harness or safety net below. I remember the way I felt walking onto that stage to make my speech in front of the whole school. The memory speeds up my heart. I try to bat away the negative feelings. There's no intimidating crowd here. Zoe has this under control.

She begins with delicate strumming. The pattern she's building feels familiar but also new. It sounds hopeful, her song. I like it already. I like it even more when I hear the lyrics. By the time she reaches the last refrain, I almost know the words by heart.

> *What if it's us?*
> *What if it's us and only us?*
> *And what came before won't count anymore,*
>   *or matter*
> *Can we try that?*
> *What if it's you?*

And what if it's me?
And what if that's all that we need it to be?
And the rest of the world falls away
What do you say?

My ears are untrained, but I detect nothing unsound or unwanted. She's flawless.

• • •

"So when does your mom get off work?" Zoe says as we're walking up my driveway.

The last time Zoe was standing on my doorstep I was trying to get her to leave before my mother could spot her. Tonight, thankfully, I don't have to worry about that. "She has class Sunday nights," I say. "She won't be home for another few hours."

"So we have the whole house to ourselves?"

It's not fair that Zoe can just say things like that and send me into momentary paralysis. I didn't think I could be more entranced by her, and then I heard her sing. "For the next three hours," I confirm, inserting the key into the door.

"We should throw a kegger."

I laugh. "We should definitely throw a kegger. For sure."

"Until your mom comes home."

"In three hours." It's possible I've forgotten how to use words. "Thank you, for, you know, coming over."

"I've been asking to come to your house for *weeks*, and every time you've immediately said no."

"I know." I wanted to say no this time, too, but I can't keep her away forever. "Which is why I appreciate that you're here now."

We step inside and a downpour of shame befalls me. I tried to tidy up as much as I could, but there was only so much I could do. I can't run out and get a new couch that doesn't have faded fabric. I can't paint over the water spots in the ceiling or rub out stains in the carpet. And there isn't enough space in our closets to hide away all the clutter. I didn't even notice half of what was wrong with my house until I started spending so much time at Zoe's.

"Welcome," I say, trying to rush her upstairs to my room. Not in a pervy way. I would just feel more comfortable in my room.

Too late. She lingers in the hallway, pondering a photograph. "Is this you as a baby?"

"That fat guy there? Yeah. That's me."

"Don't say that. You're adorable."

Well, fine, if she's going to compliment me, I guess we can linger downstairs for a few seconds longer. The photograph she's currently admiring was taken in our old house. I don't remember much about it, except what I've seen in photo albums.

"Is this your dad holding you?" Zoe asks.

"No. My uncle Ben." Photographs of Mark are never to be displayed in the Heidi Hansen household. They belong in boxes and albums only.

I remember that the backyard of the old house connected

to the woods, sort of like Zoe's house. I have a memory of my dad shooting arrows into a tree, but I'm not sure whether that really happened or I made it up.

I start climbing the stairs, giving Zoe no choice but to follow. My phone vibrates again, reminding me that I still haven't checked Alana's message from before. Upstairs, I see a note from my mom stuck to my door. I try to take it down covertly, but Zoe catches it.

"My mom and I do a lot of message writing," I explain.

"Pen and paper," Zoe says. "Old-school."

"Oh, no, we do texts and emails, too. Pretty much anything but talking face-to-face."

"Face-to-face?" Zoe says. "Who would ever want to do that?"

"Not me. Not your face."

"And I appreciate that," she says, earning a smile from me and reminding me why I love—I mean, excessively like her.

"Are you ready to see the place where absolutely no magic happens?" I say.

"I cannot wait."

I open yet another door for her. The image she is now seeing of my bedroom is fake news. My bed is made. My closet and dresser drawers are closed. My desk is organized. My pill bottles are tucked away in a sock. The manufactured aroma of air freshener permeates.

But not everything is perfect. I didn't want her to think I was a maniac, so after cleaning diligently, I arranged a few things out of place. I hung a shirt over my chair, piled some papers on my dresser, and left my most cerebral book out on the night table.

While Zoe is surveying my room, I read my mom's note. *Eat please*, it says. It's rather curt for her. I guess she's still mad about the other night. Honestly, I don't feel great about it, either.

"I can totally see why no magic happens here," Zoe says, sitting down on my bed.

"Seriously?"

"No." She slides over and touches the bed. "But how do you sleep with this lump in your mattress?"

I knew I forgot something. I ask her to hop off the bed so I can reach under the mattress. I pull out the plastic bag with the shaving cream–slathered baseball glove inside.

"You're actually listening to my dad?" Zoe says. "Do you even like baseball?"

Every answer is precarious. "No, not really."

I figured I'd break in the glove just in case. Maybe the Connor Project will organize a charity baseball game someday. I'm also doing it so I can tell Mr. Murphy that I did it. I like him, and I want to give him something I think will make him happy.

Zoe scans the pile of papers on my dresser. "What are all these?"

"Oh. Those are just...my mom is obsessed with these college scholarship essay contests she found online. She keeps printing out more of them."

She lifts the pile off the dresser. "There are so many."

I didn't pay close enough attention to which papers I left

out on my dresser. "I know. I mean, I'd have to win probably a hundred of them to actually pay for college. When you add it all up. Tuition, housing, books."

I still haven't gotten around to starting those essays. I know my mom is trying to help us both, but college is tomorrow's problem and it's tough enough trying to solve today's. And it's not like I'd win any of these anyway.

"So your parents, they can't...?" She doesn't have to finish her sentence.

"Not really."

"I'm sorry."

And now I'm the sorry one, because she looks sad. I don't want to make her sad.

"Oh! I meant to tell you earlier. We had a Connor Project meeting a few days ago, and Alana came up with a really great strategy for raising more money for the orchard. Alana is truly destined to run a company or, like, the world someday." What I'm saying isn't working. I've somehow made Zoe's sad face sadder. "For now I guess we'll just start with the orchard."

She sighs and looks to the floor. "Can we talk?"

"Oh shit." I finally did it. I blew the only good thing in my pitiful life.

"What?" she asks, suddenly alarmed.

"No. Just. You're breaking up with me, right? *That's* why you came over today."

"Breaking up with you?"

"Not that we're dating. I wasn't trying to be presumptuous. I don't know what this is, if we're dating, officially, or if it's more like...never mind. Why am I even still talking right now? It's fine. Don't worry, you can tell me. I'm not going to *cry* or start breaking things...."

She stares at me, and I feel my hands start doing their thing. I preemptively wipe them. A useless tactic. I'm great at those.

"I'm not breaking up with you," she says.

I pause, making sure I heard her correctly. "Really? Okay. Thank you."

"Don't mention it." She laughs.

Wait. Does that mean that Zoe and I *are* dating? Because, you know, I sort of *felt* like we were, but I wasn't sure she felt the same way. When do people discuss that sort of thing? Or does it go unspoken until you both just know? Also, how do you know that you both just know?

"It's just, the Connor Project," Zoe says. "I mean, it's great. What you've accomplished is just beyond. Seriously."

There's a *but* coming.

"But, maybe we don't have to talk about my brother all the time. Maybe we can talk about...other things."

"Oh. Yeah. Of course. I just thought maybe you'd want to know what's going on with everything."

"No, I know you did, and I really do appreciate what you're doing." She sits down on the now lump-free bed. "But my whole life, everything has always been about Connor. And right now, I just need something for me. If this is going to be a..."

She pauses and I nearly fall over into the space of it.

"Relationship," she finally says, "I don't want it to be about my brother. Or the orchard. Or the emails."

I've stopped breathing. *Breathe, Evan, breathe.*

"I just want...you," she says.

"Really?"

She sighs, frustrated with me. "Did you hear the new song I sang tonight?"

"Of course," I say. "It was amazing."

"Did you hear the lyrics? 'You and me. That's all that we need it to be.'"

"Were you—was that about—"

She shrugs. "Who else?"

"Oh."

I wish I'd recorded her set so I could replay the song over and over. For now my memory has to fill in the space. A certain line comes to mind: "What came before won't count anymore, or matter. Can we try that?"

Yes, I answer inside. *Yes*, a hundred thousand times.

This time we were at his house. (Miguel would still have me over, but only when his mom was at work. I always liked his mom. Sharp tongue but soft heart. Amazing cook. Super welcoming. Until I got expelled. The sad twist that only M and I could appreciate: my trying to help her son was what led her to hate me.)

Ever since that day at my house, our friendship had bloomed into something else. Junior year was hell, but Miguel was my silver lining. The one worthwhile part of my life. I always looked forward to seeing him. But lately, that feeling was more like a compulsion. This gravitational force pulling me toward him. I didn't *want* to be near him. I had to.

That day at his house, he lay next to me. I studied his body, trying to memorize it before it became hidden again. The way his skin seemed to absorb the energy of the lamplight. His chest caving in, forming a shallow pool. I wondered who else in his life was granted this privilege. Who else got to push that birthmark button. My social life resembled a line connecting only two points. But Miguel's was a circle. He had other friends at Hanover. A big family with lots of cousins. And there was an ex he still spoke to. Where did I fit in? Near his center? Or toward an outer ring?

What is that? he asked, breaking the silence.

I followed his gaze, realizing too late where he'd been look-ing. I had forgotten that I'd removed my bracelets. Something I normally wouldn't do. Something his gravitational force per-suaded me to do.

I pulled my wrist away. *Nothing,* I said.

He stared into my eyes. It felt like a challenge.

I got out of bed, rolled my bracelets on. A few scars from a few idle nights. Passing time, really. A lighter, matches, candle wax. Fine, not nothing, but not totally something, either.

He sat up. *You always do that,* he said.

Do what? I said, putting on my shirt.

Anytime I get too close… His feet hit the floor.

I tried to laugh. *What are you talking about?*

We're always here at my house. You had me over one time. It's like you only give me these tiny glimpses.

I challenged him with a dead stare. *Why do you even care? It's not like we're…* I shrugged. *I don't even know what we're supposed to be.*

He shook his head and sighed, stood up. *How can we get there if you don't let me.*

(Spoken like a statement. An ultimatum. I had no choice, really.)

Miguel didn't know what the past year had been like. He'd heard, sure, but he wasn't actually there. He knew only the legend, not the reality. Day after day after day. Scratching and scraping. The damage done to me and by me. Every good thing turned bad. Lying in bed at night and imagining myself just...

You don't understand, I said.

He looked at me for a moment. And then, he came up to my face. Nose-to-nose. Eye-to-eye. Not as close as we were a moment ago and yet somehow more intimate than that. *So,* he said. *Tell me.*

I stood before him and I shook. I shook from his stare.

Be fucking real with me.

How? How could I do it? When underneath whatever he thought he saw in me was something so beyond repair?

I stepped back, clenched my jaw, locked myself up. Got dressed as fast as I could. He tried to stop me, called me back. But my split decision was already made: run for your life.

(Still running, I guess.)

There's this photo of me going around now. Short hair. Big, goofy smile on my face. I saw it everywhere at that assembly a few weeks back. My mother must have found it on my phone. I guess she had no way of knowing that I edited the photo. A selfie, taken by Miguel. In the original, he is by my side, his smile as wide as mine.

I was certain of one thing: how I felt when I was around him and when I wasn't. The first was exhilarating. The other unbearable. Being with him was like being hooked on a drug. When we stopped seeing each other, I went into withdrawal. It was a long, dark summer.

CHAPTER 22

In the hallway at school the next morning, Zoe gives me a kiss in front of everyone. "I have rehearsal after school so I can't drive you home," she says. "But don't forget, I'm picking you up at seven for dinner."

She kisses me again quickly, this time on the cheek, and heads off. I watch her walk away, and all I can do is think about the next time I get to see her.

"Where were you last night?"

I turn and find Alana.

"I texted you, like, fifty times," she says, shaking her head. "Don't worry, I handed out the postcards without you."

"Oh shit, I forgot. I'm really sorry," I say. "I must have put the wrong date in my phone."

"What is your deal, Evan?"

I look around. I'd prefer to have this conversation in private.

"The fundraising deadline is a week from now," Alana says, "and I feel like you are a thousand miles away. You haven't made any new videos. You haven't posted on the blog in, like, forever."

"Well, I've been busy."

"Busy with what?" Alana asks.

Living? Trying to?

"I was doing, you know, different things," I say. "How much do we have left to raise?"

"Oh. Not much. Just seventeen thousand dollars."

Seventeen. Thousand. Okay, that's a lot of dollars. "Look, I'm sure we'll get there. We just need to, you know, keep people engaged."

"Exactly," she says, relieved that I'm finally making sense. "That's why I'm putting the emails between you and Connor online."

"Wait. What? What do you mean?" Seawater rushes into my tank. "How do you know about the emails?"

"Mrs. Murphy sent them to me," Alana says. "Just a few, but she said there are a ton more. That you, like, keep bringing her new ones."

"You can't do that."

She throws her head back dramatically. "I can't?"

"It's just, those conversations, they're private."

"Um, not anymore. They belong to everyone now. I mean, that's the whole point. And the more private they are, the better. That's what people want to see. We have a responsibility to our community to show them everything, to tell them the truth."

The truth? Which truth? I answer all their emails and tell them about my life. I even uploaded a selfie. Haven't I shown enough? What more does "our community" want from me?

Her wristwatch beeps. "I have to run, but I'm going to be sending you a list of questions to answer. Some of the emails don't make sense."

"What? What do you mean?"

"Well, for example, you said that the first time you went to the orchard was the day you broke your arm. But then, in other emails, you talk about going there together since, like, last November."

That's easy to clear up. You see, I've never actually been to the orchard. I am not who you think I am, Alana.

"Those are probably just typos," I say. "I mean, they're just emails. I think you're reading into them, like, way too much."

Her old smile returns in full force. "You can explain it all when I send you the questions. You know how much the community loves hearing from you."

She walks away. I check my surroundings, trying to gauge what kind of scene we just made. Turns out, no one was paying attention. Everyone—walking, typing, locker-stuffing—is too consumed with their own lives to care about mine. They've got their own girlfriends and boyfriends and best friends and parents (two of them) and projects (without a capital *P*). Most of them have totally forgotten about Connor Murphy. They might have contributed a few dollars to our orchard campaign, but it's not because they ever cared about keeping Connor's memory alive. They were just doing what everyone else is doing. The same thing I'm trying to do: get through the day.

As I'm heading to homeroom, I text Jared.

Dude.

I was going to text you.
My parents are out of town this weekend.
The last time they used the liquor cabinet
was Rosh Hashanah '97.
We can drink whatever we want.

I can't this weekend.
I have seventeen thousand dollars to raise.
Remember the Connor Project?
You're supposed to be working on it?

Remember you told me
you didn't need my help?

I didn't tell you to do nothing.
I know you think this is a joke, but it isn't.
It's important.

For Connor.

Yes, for Connor.

"It's interesting you say that."

I look up from my phone. It's Jared, in the flesh.

"Because," Jared says, pocketing his phone, "when you really stop and think about it, Connor being dead is pretty much the best thing that's ever happened to you, isn't it?"

Even for Jared, that's a horrible thing to think, let alone speak aloud. "Why would you say that?"

"What's poppin', Evan?" says a passerby.

"Well, think about it," Jared says. "People at school actually talk to you now. You're almost popular, which is, like, miracle of miracles. If Connor hadn't died, you think that guy just now would've known your name? He wouldn't have. No one would."

That's true. I can't deny it. But that's not what this is about. It never has been. "I don't care if people at school know who I am. I don't care about any of that. All I ever wanted was to help the Murphys."

"Help the Murphys," Jared repeats, like it's a company slogan. "You keep saying that."

"Don't be an asshole."

"*You* don't be an asshole," he says, and storms off.

The bell rings, signaling the official start of the school day. It might as well be ending a boxing match. I feel like I've already gone twelve rounds.

CHAPTER 23

Zoe parks her Volvo in her driveway and shuts off the engine. She seals our arrival with a smile, and I smile back. She seems extra bubbly tonight and I can't quite figure out why. Car rides with Zoe usually involve more music than talking, but on the way here, she kept the stereo low so she could tell me all about band practice. Apparently, Jamison, the bassist, who's really nice, can't stand the drummer because the drummer is a total egomaniac, and without the two of them vibing with each other, the entire rhythm section is off. Drama in jazz band. Who knew?

We step inside the house, and Zoe deems it worthy of announcement. "We're here," she yells, leaving her shoes on the mat in her foyer.

I kick my shoes next to hers while she walks on ahead of me. "Sorry we're late," I hear her say.

"We're just in here having a glass of wine, getting to know each other," Cynthia says.

I catch up to Zoe and stop dead in my tracks.

My mother is here. My mother is here, holding a glass of wine, sitting with the Murphys.

"We invited your mom to come join us for dinner tonight," Larry says, clearly thinking this is something that will make me happy.

"Oh," I say, making eye contact with my mom. She is just as shocked as I am.

"I didn't realize Evan was joining us, too," she says.

"I'm sorry," Cynthia says, laughing away a silly mistake. "I didn't think to tell you."

Zoe's smile balloons to the size of a parade float. "Hi, I'm Zoe." She shakes my mom's hand. "It's so nice to finally meet you."

My mother returns the smile, hers a balloon with holes, and says nothing. She's never heard Zoe's name before, at least not from me. I can see the confusion in her eyes.

Larry stands. "Are we ready for another bottle?"

"Open the Portland," Cynthia tells Larry. Then, explaining to my mom, "It's completely one hundred percent sustainable, the entire production process. There was a whole feature on them in the *New York Times*. Incredible."

I whisper in Zoe's ear, "Did you know about this?"

She nods proudly. "It was my idea."

"Hey, you two," Larry says, muscling the cork from a bottle. His V-neck sweater outlines his imposing chest. "Why don't you sit down and join us?"

Zoe and I drop ourselves on a love seat, where absolutely no love will take place. The women sit side by side on the long sofa, Cynthia's refined style making my mother look like the college student she actually is. Her flowery top has endured too many cycles in the wash.

"I thought you had work tonight," I say to my mom.

"Well, this seemed important," she says. "So. I'm playing hooky."

This. What exactly is *this*? It feels a lot like when you wander into a courtyard in *Call of Duty* and there's thirty combatants waiting to rain bullets down on you. It's called an ambush.

"Your mother and I were just talking about how sneaky you and Connor were," Cynthia says, tapping my knee.

I force a closed-mouth grin, teeth grinding in terror.

Larry returns with the new bottle, which he's poured into a fancy glass container. "No one had any idea how close you two were," he says.

I search desperately for a distraction. "Something smells really good."

Cynthia gazes in the direction of the kitchen. "Chicken Milanese."

I feel my mom staring at me. "I didn't realize you were spending so much time here." She can barely squeeze the words through her tight smile. Clearly, they'd been talking before we arrived. But what exactly was said? What does she know?

"You've been working a lot," I say.

"Why did I think you were at Jared's?"

I look away. "I don't know." I've left my body, watching this scene unfold from a distance. Or maybe that's just what I wish.

"You can rest assured we take very good care of him," Larry says, refilling my mother's glass. "He always eats a good meal when he's with us."

"How nice." My mom takes a long sip.

"Evan was showing me all those scholarship contests you found," Zoe says. "That was really impressive. There are, like, a million."

Finally, a statement my mom can get behind. "Well, Evan is a great writer."

"I don't find that hard to believe at all," Larry says.

If they're going to talk about me like I'm not here, then maybe I can just go ahead and leave? Because I'm certain I can't stay.

"His teacher last year for English said he wrote one of the best papers she'd ever read about *Sulu*," my mom says.

"How about that," Cynthia says, equaling my mother's pride.

"It's *Sula*." I didn't mean to say it out loud.

"*Sula*? What did I say?"

" 'Sulu.' " I look down at the floor. The floor is the only safe place to look.

"I believe Sulu is a character on *Star Trek*," Larry says, "if I'm remembering correctly." He laughs innocently, and Zoe joins him. She goes to grab my hand, and without thinking I pull away. I don't want anyone to touch me right now.

My mom stares into her wine. "My mistake."

I shouldn't have done that. Now her embarrassment is my shame. An unbearable silence grips the room.

Zoe changes the subject. "Speaking of scholarships..."

"I guess now is as good a time as any," Larry says. "Cynthia, do you want to...?"

"Well," Cynthia says, letting the word make a dramatic dent on our brains. She places her wine on the coffee table. Whatever is happening right now, I can't stop it.

"Zoe happened to mention to us the other day that Evan was having some difficulty," Cynthia says. "That is, in terms of the financial burdens of college. And Larry and I started thinking about it. We were very fortunate to have been able to set aside some money for our son."

The mention of Connor trips her up. Larry holds her hand. I hold myself.

"I'm okay," she says, pausing for a breath. "I called you this morning to invite you to dinner, Heidi, because, well, first of all, because we want to thank you for allowing your son to have come into our lives. He was a dear, dear friend to our Connor, and we have come to just love him to pieces."

Larry and Zoe laugh again. My mom manages a small smile, not wanting to be left out, but, of course, it's too late for that. And she's only now starting to grapple with that fact.

"And with your blessing, we—Larry and I and, of course, Zoe—we would like to give Evan the money we put away for our son so that he can use it to fulfill his dreams, just like he helped Connor"—deep breath—"fulfill his."

I feel my hand being squeezed. I smell chicken in the oven. I see a sculpture of an unknown animal behind Cynthia's head. I might puke.

"What do you think?" Larry asks.

I *think* that this is the kindest, most compassionate, most generous gesture I could ever imagine someone making. It's also the most obscenely undeserved.

I can almost see my mother's competing emotions duking it out inside her. Ultimately, there's no clear winner. She responds with only this: "Wow, I'm . . . I don't know what to say."

I don't know, either.

"It would be such a gift to us if we could do this for Evan," Larry says.

Cynthia agrees. "It would be a tremendous gift, Heidi."

I see my mother's emotions pick a side. Her face has hardened.

"Well," my mom says. "Thank you so much, but we're going to be fine. I may not have a lot of money, but I do have some."

"Oh no," Cynthia says, "we didn't mean to—"

"No, no, I understand." My mom relinquishes her wineglass, as if suddenly realizing it's full of poison. "I'm just . . . we have money. So I'm sorry that you were under the impression that we didn't. And whatever money we don't have, Evan will either get a scholarship or take out loans or he'll go to a community college. There's nothing wrong with that."

"Not at all," Larry says.

"I think that's the best thing for us to do. I don't want Evan to get the idea that it's okay to rely on other people for favors."

"It's not a favor," Larry says.

"Well, but, as his mother, I need to set that example for him. That you can't expect things from strangers."

"We are not strangers," Cynthia says.

Everyone turns to her, all her former joy replaced with hurt. I wonder if I'm the only one who can see the dagger sticking out of her heart.

"Of course not," my mom says, rising from the sofa. "Thank you for the wine. It was delicious."

"Wait," Cynthia says. "You're not staying for dinner?"

"I think I'd better go to work after all."

"Oh no," Cynthia says.

"Yes," my mom says, staring one of her daggers at me. "If I'd known Evan was so concerned about our finances, I would never have taken the night off in the first place."

She grabs her purse and her phone falls out, forcing her to get on her knees to retrieve it from under the coffee table. Everyone watches silently, not knowing what to do or say. It's excruciating, every long second that it takes for her to get back up on her feet, straighten out her faded shirt, and finally turn and walk out of the house.

Then she's gone. And everyone turns to me.

• • •

Later that night, I open the front door to our house. The lamp is on in the living room. I find my mom sitting on the couch, still in her clothes from dinner. She's not reading. Not watching TV. Not drinking. Not preparing to go to work. Just waiting.

The Murphys felt terrible for offending her. Cynthia offered to call her and apologize. I told her it wasn't necessary. I tried to explain how stressed she's been lately, with work and classes and everything, just really tired and overwhelmed (and whatever other adjective I could think of to describe her that sounded vaguely plausible). I sat at their table, forced the chicken Milanese into my unhungry stomach and did my best just to get through the rest of the dinner, moment by aching moment.

"He basically guaranteed me a paralegal job after I graduate," my mom says, pulling at a loose thread in her shirt. "He gave me his business card."

I tried to remind myself on the ride home to remain calm. But already, I'm annoyed.

"So? What's wrong with that? You make it sound like it's a bad thing."

My mom finally looks at me. "Do you have any idea how *mortifying* it is? To find out that your son has been spending all this time with another family and you didn't even *know* it? You told me you were at Jared's."

I shrug. "If you're not here, then why does it matter where I am?"

"They think you're their son. These people."

Remaining calm is no longer possible. "They're not 'these people,' okay? They're my..."

"What? What are they?"

I don't even know.

"Because they act like they've adopted you, like I don't even exist."

"They take care of me," I say.

She's up off the couch now. "They're not your parents, Evan. That is not your family."

"They're nice to me."

"Oh, they're lovely, lovely people."

"Yup."

"They don't know you."

"And you do?"

"I thought I did."

The disappointment in her voice. It sounds like my own voice, the one inside my head, the one only I can hear. The one that reminds me every morning when I wake up and at night when I go to bed what I am. A liar.

But if I'm full of shit, then so is she.

"What do you know about me, Mom? You don't know anything about me. You never even see me."

"I am trying my best."

"They like me. I know how hard that is to believe. They don't think that there's something wrong with me. That I need to be fixed, like you do."

She comes closer. "When have I *ever* said that?"

Is she serious? Where do I even begin? "I have to go to therapy. I have to take drugs...."

"I'm your mother," she says unapologetically. "My job is to take care of you."

"I know. I'm such a burden. I'm the worst thing that ever happened to you. I ruined your life."

"Look at me," she says, grabbing my face hard. "You are the only...the one good thing that has *ever* happened to me, Evan."

Her eyes weaken. I'm supposed to ease up now. Let her off the hook. But I'm so tired of curbing my emotions just to make room for hers.

"I'm sorry I can't give you anything more than that," she says, losing it.

I pull away from her. "It's not my fault that other people can."

CHAPTER 24

Like they've seen a ghost. That's what these kids look like when I arrive at the bus stop. Is it possible that I actually appear to them as hollow and immaterial as I feel inside? Or maybe it's just the fact that I haven't stood out here with them for a few weeks and they're surprised that I'm back. So am I. But also, I'm really not.

I lied to Zoe and told her that I didn't need a ride to school this morning because my mother was going to take me. After what happened last night, it was easy for her to believe it.

I didn't sleep. I couldn't. Morning came. I thought about skipping school, staying under the covers. I forced myself up. My mom had left for work. I found no notes waiting for me on the bathroom mirror or kitchen counter or on the front door on my way out.

• • •

I stare at the ceiling through English and make good progress on boring a hole through my desk in calculus.

I just want to be alone, the way I've always been. I don't want to be bothered or noticed or questioned. But that's just wishful thinking.

When I'm heading to lunch, out of nowhere, Alana seizes me. She's clearly been staked out here in front of the cafeteria, waiting for my arrival.

"Why did Connor kill himself?" she asks.

Alana is all business all the time, but today she's got an extra intensity, and I just wish for once she could muster a simple hello before laying into me about...

"Wait, what?" I say.

"He was doing better," she says, a stack of papers in her hands. "That's what he told you in every single email. And then a month later, he kills himself? Why do so many things in these emails just not make sense?"

"Because sometimes things don't make sense, okay? Things are messy and complicated."

"Like you dating Zoe?" She looks around and adds, "Do you know what people are saying about you?"

What are people saying? It never occurred to me that people could be talking about me. For so long, going unnoticed was my default. Suddenly, I view my situation the way an outsider might: *Evan Hansen is dating his best friend's sister just a few weeks after his death.*

Fuck, that looks bad.

I try to wipe the thought from my mind and address Alana.

"Why are you so obsessed with this? I mean, you didn't even know Connor."

"Because it's important."

"Important because you were lab partners? Or because, I don't know, maybe because it gives you another extracurricular for your college applications?"

Alana's expression changes into something I've never seen on her: defeat.

"Important," she says, trembling, "because I know what it's like to feel invisible. Just like Connor. Invisible and alone and like nobody would even notice if I vanished into thin air. I bet you used to know what that felt like, too."

She waits for me to say something. When I don't, she shakes her head at me and walks away.

I no longer feel hollow. My chest is pounding, sweat on my brow. Alana awoke a primal reflex in me. Fight or flight. For once, I'm ready for the former.

I scan the cafeteria for Jared and spot him in the food line. We haven't spoken since our whatever-that-was the other day. It seems to take him forever to emerge on the other side of the line and settle up at the register.

"We need more emails," I tell him. "Emails showing that Connor was getting worse."

Jared rolls his eyes and laughs.

"This isn't funny," I say.

"Oh, I think it's hilarious," Jared says. "I think everyone would probably think it's hilarious."

"What is that supposed to mean?"

"It *means*, you should remember who your friends are."

I practically had to beg Jared to be my friend, and now he tries to stand here and threaten me and pretend like his feelings are hurt? He's even more manipulative than I thought. "You told me the only reason you talk to me is because of your car insurance."

He shrugs.

"It's very interesting," I say.

"What is?"

"Your 'Israeli girlfriend'"—I make the air quotes so he doesn't miss my point—"and your 'buddies' from camp? I've never heard you once mention any of their names."

"I can if you want," Jared says. "What's your point?"

I step closer. "Maybe the only reason you talk to me is because you don't have any other friends."

He smiles, but with no confidence. "I could tell everyone everything."

He's bluffing. If I go down, he goes down, too. I lower my voice. "Go ahead, Jared. Do it." He doesn't react, so I keep going. "Tell everyone how you helped write emails pretending to be a kid who killed himself."

Once the words are out, I want to go back in time and unsay them. I've imagined in the past what it would take to render Jared speechless. I'm sorry I stumbled on the answer.

"You're a fucking asshole, Evan," he says finally. There's more bite in the words than in the delivery.

For once, I gave him a taste of his own medicine. I thought it might feel better to be the one dishing it, but it's almost as bad as receiving it. I watch him walk away in the shoes I've worn.

At the same time, I remember to smile. I want to assure anyone who was watching us that whatever they think they just saw was nothing more than harmless joking between friends. One of the people who happens to be watching from across the room is Zoe. It seems that flight is now the only real option.

Somehow, I place one foot in front of the other, and I turn away from her and walk right out the door.

● ● ●

But I can't hide from Zoe for long. That night, after I've avoided her all day, she sends me a text: *I'm outside your house.*

Hiding in my bedroom used to be a cinch. Not too long ago there was maybe one person in the entire world who might look for me, and on many days even that person—the one who'd given birth to me—would lose track and the number would fall to zero. But lately, I feel like a wanted man.

I get out of bed and look out my window. I see Zoe, in the glow of the streetlamp, sitting on the trunk of her blue Volvo.

After some hesitation, I type a response: *Be right there!*

The exclamation is only for show. I'm always excited to see Zoe, but right now I've got layers upon layers of dread telling me to stay in seclusion.

I open my drawer and find my Ativan. Strangely, the sight of my medicine makes me feel sick. I'm not that person anymore. And I don't want to go back. I drop the bottle and shut the drawer.

I cast aside my doubt, and moments later I'm walking out of my house and joining Zoe on the street. "Hey," I say, unsure whether to invite her inside or get in her car or what.

She makes no move to embrace me. She just sits there. I remain standing, acknowledging the distance between us. How can there not be distance after what happened last night? It's one thing to assume there'd be distance and another thing to have it confirmed. Now that I'm witnessing it, I can't stand it.

"What's going on?" she says. "I just want to know."

I check her face for some hint of intention, anything, but find it blank. "I'm not sure what you mean. Nothing's going on."

"Nothing? Really?" she says, a sudden edge to her voice.

I feel the ground beneath me start to wobble. "Is something wrong?"

She forces a laugh. "Uh, yeah? You've been ignoring me all day? I don't get it. I tried to do this nice thing for you, and then, I don't know, your mom freaked out, and..."

"Yeah," I say, breathing out. "I know."

"It's just kind of..."

"What?"

"Weird. Don't you think?"

Yes? No? Maybe? I really don't know what to think anymore.

She sees my confusion. "We've been dating awhile now,

and I just thought everything was going, that we were..." She pauses, looks down. "Your mom had no idea who I was. How's that possible? Did you not mention me even once?"

It's complicated. So complicated. "My mom and I...we're not...it's not like that."

"Not like what, Evan? I kept telling you that I wanted to meet her, and you'd always just change the subject. What is that? First you have this secret friendship with my brother and now I'm your secret girlfriend? I'm tired of it. Of just being ignored all the time."

I want to go to her.

"I'm sorry," I say.

"Stop..."

"Really, I am, I didn't mean—"

"Stop it! Will you? Stop being sorry!"

Her words echo through the neighborhood. I want to follow them into the air and just disappear.

She drops her head and turns mute. If she wanted to leave, she could get in her car right now and go. But she's not doing that. She's still here.

I join her on the trunk, facing forward. A gust of wind rattles the leaves of a black oak. That kind of tree, at that height, is probably older than my house. And yet, as mighty and proud as it looks, it still shakes in the wind.

"It's just been hard," she says. "These past few weeks."

I know what she means. It has been hard. I want her to tell me everything she's been feeling—about our relationship, about what's been going on with us. I can do better, I swear. We can get past this.

"I just..." she starts.

"You can tell me."

"I just miss him," Zoe says. "It's not the same without him. He could be a jerk sometimes. But I still miss him."

Him. *Him.* What the fuck is wrong with me?

She looks me in the eye. "Don't you miss him?"

I was his best friend. "Of course," I say. "Of course I miss him."

She drops her head on my shoulder. "Don't go."

Fighting for air, I tell her, "I won't."

"No. I mean, ever."

I look ahead into the black night.

CHAPTER 25

Last night walloped me. Sitting there, watching Zoe come undone. Not being able to be truthful with her. It was pure agony.

And yet, I'm willing to endure the agony to keep her. She means that much to me. She's kind and quirky and funny and bright and passionate and insecure and ambitious and volatile and talented. She has a voice and something to say, and she's also interested in what I have to say, even if I'm babbling on about birds and trees. She finds my idiosyncrasies endearing. She thinks the dorky way I dress is cute. She says my bedroom has a "boyish charm." She doesn't mind holding my sweaty hands. She challenges me. She makes me think twice about saying sorry. She forces me to try other sushi rolls besides my standard California. She wants us to coordinate Halloween costumes. (We've settled on Bonnie and Clyde; I already bought my fedora.) She fills me with the kind of confidence that makes me want to start driving again. She wants to know every part of me, where I live, what I looked like as a baby, who my mom is. She even cares about my future. She tried to get her parents to pay for my education. Zoe and I could end up going to the same college. There's no reason we couldn't stay together for a long time. I used to think that the idea of a soul mate was the most ludicrous drivel I'd ever heard, but maybe not. Maybe it's something beyond our understanding and maybe Zoe is my one true match. She could be my wife. I would cast aside all my misgivings about marriage, disregard all those bleak divorce statistics and the example of my own parents for her. There's nothing I wouldn't do for her.

And not just her. The Murphys, too. They've given me so much. They've invited me into their home and into their lives with open arms. Their generosity and support and acceptance overwhelm me. Larry's guidance and trust. Cynthia's love. Her embrace. Zoe told me herself how much her mother likes having me around. How "obsessed" she is with what I've done. How I bring with me ... Connor.

The lies. No matter what I tell myself, I can never escape the lies. If only I could find a way to explain it all. Maybe the Murphys would understand. Maybe everyone would understand.

But I've already played it out in my head, over and over, the act of totally coming clean, leaving nothing unsaid, and each time I do, I reach the same terrifying conclusion: it'll all be gone. I'll be back where I started. No Murphys. No Zoe. No friends. Nobody. Nothing. Alone.

And they'll be left alone again, too. Left with the same nothingness. No comfort. No hope. They'll be robbed of all the solace they've gained these last few weeks. It'll leave them devastated once again. The way they were when I first met them. Before we built this community of alienated souls. Before everything changed for the better. For all of us.

It's time to refocus.

Sitting up in bed, I send Alana a message asking her to video chat. Lucky for me, she's always on call. It's unclear whether she requires sleep.

"Good morning," I say when her face appears on my screen.

"Yes?" she says, not even bothering to look up from her desk.

"Alana, I've been a bad co-president and I'm sorry. You were absolutely right. But I'm back now. I'm rededicating myself to doing everything I can do to make this thing a success." Because the alternative is too terrifying.

"Too late," Alana says. "I've already moved on."

This was not the reaction I was prepared for. It takes a moment to recover. "You've 'moved on'? What does that mean?"

She slaps down her pen. "You've made it abundantly clear to me that you're not interested in being a part of the Connor Project."

"But I am. I swear. I can make more videos. I can write stuff for the blog."

"I can do all that myself."

"It's not the same if you do it, Alana. People want to hear what I have to say. I was his best friend."

"You know what, Evan? I'm starting to wonder if that's even true. You keep saying you were best friends. You're like a broken freaking record about it. But nobody ever saw you together. Nobody knew you were friends."

I feel faint. "That's because it was a secret. He didn't want us to talk at school."

"I know the story, Evan," she says, returning to the work on her desk. "We all know the story. We've heard it a bazillion times."

"But... you've seen the emails."

Alana almost laughs. "Do you know how easy it is to create a fake email account and backdate emails? Because I do."

My chest squeezes, making it hard to breathe. I try to pull in air, but I can't get enough of it.

Whatever Alana is seeing on my face triggers a morsel of pity. "Look, Evan, the Connor Project appreciates your contributions, but unfortunately it's time to part ways. I'm the *president* of an organization that currently needs to raise, oh, fourteen thousand dollars, and I'm afraid I have no more time to waste. Goodbye."

"Alana! Wait! I can prove we were friends."

Her finger freezes over the keyboard, her curiosity overruling. "How?"

I minimize the chat window and locate the file on my computer.

"Here," I say, sending it through.

I watch her eyes as she opens it and recognizes what it is.

"If we weren't friends," I say, "then why did he write his suicide note to me?"

"Oh my god."

"Do you believe me now?"

She reads it aloud: "'Dear Evan Hansen, It turns out, this wasn't an amazing day after all. This isn't going to be an amazing week or an amazing year.'"

Those words never go down easy. Right now, I can't even swallow them. They're choking me. "You can't show that letter to anyone, okay? Nobody else needs to see it."

"This is *exactly* what people need to see," Alana says, a wildness in her eyes. "We need something to create new interest."

I'm up out of bed, walking around with my laptop, my whole body shaking. "Can you please delete it?"

She's busy typing, barely listening. "Don't you care about building the orchard? This is the best way to make Connor's dream come true."

"No, Alana, it isn't. Please."

A message appears, and my breath catches. At the top of my screen is a notification informing me that Alana Beck just posted to the Connor Project Community. My finger quivering, I click the link, and instantly, I enter into a brand-new reality—a giant asteroid has struck Earth.

"You put it online!"

I pray with all my being that what I'm seeing right now

on-screen is just a private message and is not actually visible to the public. But, to my extreme horror, it's visible to all. Irreversibly so.

Alana wrote a preface to the letter: *Connor's note is a message to all of us. Share it with as many people as you can. Post it everywhere. If you've ever felt alone like Connor, then please consider making a donation to the Connor Murphy Memorial Orchard. No amount is too small.*

"Alana, you don't understand," I say, gasping for air. "You need to take it down. Please, *please*, take it down."

She can't hear me.

"Alana!"

She vanishes into thin air.

I sit down. The bed isn't solid beneath me. There's nothing strong enough to catch my fall.

I refresh my screen. I can't help myself. The responses are flooding in, an angry tide. They don't stop.

Have people seen this? Connor Murphy's suicide note.

This is the actual, authentic

Forward

The whole world needs to see this

Share it with everyone you know

This is why the orchard is so important, guys

I just gave fifty dollars for the orchard
and I think everyone else should give as
much as they can

Repost

He wrote his suicide note to Evan Hansen,
because he knew his family didn't give a shit

His parents, by the way, are insanely rich

Forward

Share

Like

Five

Twenty

Here's a hundred

Maybe they should have spent
their money on helping their
son instead of

Please retweet

Evan Hansen was the only one who was paying any attention

Favorite

Share

Forward

"And all my hope is pinned on Zoe"

Zoe's a stuck-up bitch. Trust me, I go to school with her

Share

Forward

Ten bucks

Just contributed another fifty

Gave forty-one. The age my daughter would be if she hadn't taken her life

Almost there

Keep spreading

Larry Murphy is a corporate lawyer who only cares about money

Cynthia Murphy is one of these disgusting women

A hundred and sixty more dollars and the orchard
will be fully funded

Fuck the Murphys

Make them feel what Connor felt

I love you guys

Oh my god, we are two hundred dollars
over our goal

Their house is at the end of the cul-de-sac with the red door

Zoe's bedroom window is on the right.
The gate to the back is completely unlocked.

Zoe's cell phone number, if my sources are correct

I gave twenty

I'm not saying to do anything illegal

All hours, day and night

A thousand

Ring the doorbell

Keep calling until they answer

How long have I been sitting here, holding my breath?

I shut my laptop and search for my mom. She's not home. Big surprise.

I sink to the ground. The weight of everything, the whole world, closes in on me. There's nowhere to go. Nowhere to hide. The ground below rumbles. Perfect timing for an earthquake. I deserve to be swallowed by the earth.

I sit up and identify the true source of the rumble. It's Zoe calling. Hand trembling, I answer.

"Can you come over?" she says. "I'm really scared."

I don't know how I'm going to get up, brush myself off, and go over to the Murphys'. I don't think I have it in me.

But. Zoe needs me.

"Of course," I say. "Of course I will. I'll be right there."

• • •

"I don't understand," Cynthia says, scrolling through the endless comments on her tablet. "Where did they get Connor's note?"

Larry, pacing the kitchen slowly, shakes his head, back and forth, back and forth. "I don't know."

I'm seated across from Zoe and her mother at the table, my foot jackhammering the tiles. It's dark out, although I'm sure it was still afternoon when I got here. Until now I've sat silently and watched the Murphys struggle to make sense of the narrative unfolding online and the onslaught of negativity now directed at them. I've offered moral support not through words, but simply by being here. By holding Zoe's hand. By nodding when spoken to. But it's time now for me to say something, even though I don't trust my voice to function.

"I tried to call Alana. She's not answering."

"Some of these are adults," Cynthia says, ignoring me and showing the tablet to her husband. "Do you see their pictures? These are adults."

Zoe is also reading comments on her laptop. Her eyes are all out of tears. It seemed obvious when I got here that she had been crying, but her cheeks are dry now, as if she's turned numb to the avalanche of anger befalling her.

Alana's post has spread everywhere and seemingly to everyone. I keep searching for an exit. I can't find one.

A phone rings and no one moves.

"Let it ring," Larry says.

Zoe ignores her father and answers it. "Hello?"

We all stand by.

"Zoe?" Larry says. "Who is it?"

"Have fun with your miserable life," Zoe says, and ends the call.

Larry demands the phone. "Let me see the number."

"It's blocked, Dad. Leave it alone."

Cynthia's cheek is twitching. "What did they say to you?"

"It doesn't matter," Zoe says.

"Did they threaten you?" Larry says.

"It doesn't matter," Zoe repeats.

Last night, I observed in her a deep and straightforward sadness. This is something far murkier. A mixture of fear and fatigue and despair and, yes, sadness that seems to leave her feeling absolutely nothing.

"That's it," Cynthia says, shutting her tablet. "I'm calling the police." She stands up and starts digging through her purse.

"Let's take a second here," Larry says. "I'm sure this will blow over."

"That's always your solution, isn't it? Do nothing."

"Is that what I said, Cynthia?"

Zoe begs them to stop, but they can't hear her, or else they simply can't help themselves.

"Wait and see," Cynthia says, locating her phone. "Let's just wait and see, right, Larry?"

"What do you expect the police to do? It's the internet. Should they arrest the internet?"

"I had to beg you, every step of the way."

"Now hold on," Larry says, raising his hands in protest.

"I had to *plead* with you," Cynthia says. "For therapy, for rehab..."

"You went lurching from one miracle cure to the next."

Cynthia laughs with scorn. "Miracle cure? Really? Is that what you call it?"

"Because all he needed was another twenty-thousand-dollar weekend yoga retreat."

"What was your alternative, Larry? Other than picking apart everything I did?"

"Putting him on a program and *sticking* to it," Larry says, walking away.

Zoe speaks up. "No, Dad, you wanted to punish him."

"Listen to your daughter, Larry."

"You treated him like a criminal," Zoe says.

Larry stands at the bar and pours himself a drink.

"Are you listening to her?" Cynthia says.

"You think you were any better, Mom?" Zoe says. "You let Connor do whatever he wanted."

"Thank you," Larry says from across the room.

This house is burning. I did this. I set it on fire. I never meant to. I only wanted to help them. This was my refuge. Improbable, but true. A place where I could come and feel safe and accepted and wanted. Now it's crumbling before my eyes. Engulfed in anguish and anxiety and unrest. It has become *me*.

Cynthia is in her husband's face. "When he threatened to kill himself the first time, do you remember what you said?"

"Oh for Christ's sake," Larry says.

"'He just wants attention.'"

"I'm not going to stand here and defend myself," Larry says, retreating to the window.

Cynthia won't give up. "He was getting better. Ask Evan. Tell him, Evan."

Me? My foot stops pounding. I try to speak, to say something. *Try, try, try*: my broken record.

"Evan did everything in his power to help him," Cynthia says. "That's how much *he* cared."

She paints me like a hero, but underneath this mask is a monster.

"Evan was in denial of what was happening right in front of him," Larry says.

"Don't put him in the middle of this," Zoe says.

"You don't think I cared?" Larry says, facing the window. "It might be hard for you to believe, but I loved him just as much as you did."

It moves *me*, but not Cynthia. "What about the note, Larry?" she says, retrieving it from a drawer. She places the letter on the table. "It's right here. 'I wish that everything was different.' He wanted to be different. He wanted to be better."

Larry turns back. "I did the best I could. I tried to help him the only way I knew how, and if that's not good enough..."

I stare ahead. Listening. Not listening. In my daze, I barely register the object at the center of the table, the table I've been sitting at now for over an hour, the table I've somehow, against all odds and sense, been invited to eat at night after night for weeks. I don't see the object and then I do. It's the source of everything. The thing that made me the liar that I am: an apple.

The apples rest in the same copper bowl where I first spotted them. They're different from the ones I initially pondered those many weeks ago, and their meaning has changed. They were once the lucky origin of a lie. Now they're the harshest reminder of the truth.

Next to the bowl of apples is my letter. My eyes land on the last paragraph: *I wish that everything was different.*

I turn away. I can't bear to look at it. At myself. At what I've done. *What have I done?*

"He was trying to be better," Cynthia says. "He was trying."

A buzzing, starting at my core.

"And he was *failing*," Larry says.

Buzzing through my bones and blood and skin.

Cynthia pounds the table. "*We* failed *him*."

"No."

The sound of my voice startles us all.

Everyone falls silent.

Eyes flickering, making it hard to see. There's only one failure here. One colossal failure. Not them. Never them. They don't deserve this.

"You didn't fail him."

It comes as a whisper. I'd shout it if I had the strength.

I only ever wanted to bring them peace. The same peace I found in them. The feeling that I belonged somewhere. That I meant something. They gave that to me. To *me*.

Cynthia lifts the letter. That damn letter. "Look at what he wrote."

No. Not anymore, this feeling in my chest, this giant mass of hurt, building and building and building. I can't hold it in any longer, this guilt and pain and angst, climbing down my throat, strangling my gut, seizing my entire being totally and completely.

The buzzing is now all-out shaking, my whole body in a kinetic frenzy.

I can't go on with this inside of me.

Try, fail, *try*. I shut my eyes and I just...

"He didn't write it," I say.

I hold my breath, try to freeze time, thinking if I can just keep the air inside my lungs forever, maybe I'll never have to face what comes next. But I breathe, because I'm weak and I must, and I open my eyes, and everyone is looking at me, and I know it's only begun: the end of everything. But there's no way out now.

I speak it out loud: "I wrote it."

A hand on my cowering back, Cynthia's. I shrink from her, ashamed, and yet also wishing she'd never let go. How can a mother's touch do that? Help and hurt all at once?

"You didn't write Connor's suicide note, Evan."

The unthinkable. Who could believe it? Who could *do* it? This poor woman, her trust in me. The thought of it stings my eyes. One drop. And then another. The mass inside leaking out.

I breathe. I try to breathe. "It wasn't a... it was an assignment, from my therapist." I gasp for air. "Write a letter to yourself. A pep talk. 'Dear Evan Hansen, Today is going to be an amazing day and here's why.'"

Larry leans over the table, eyes searching. "I don't think... I don't understand."

I try to control my shuddering, *try* to find the fortitude to answer him, this man who once placed his gentle hand on my shoulder. "I was supposed to bring it to my appointment. Connor took it from me. He must have had it with him when he... when you found him."

Larry sits down, sinking in his chair. His mind can't process it.

"What are you talking about?" Zoe says.

Zoe. Her voice hurts the most. Strikes at my deepest center. I wipe my nose, my eyes. Streaks on my shirt. "Connor and I . . . we weren't friends."

"No," Cynthia says, unwilling to believe. "No."

I'm a sickness. A sobbing, shaking sickness. Infecting these innocent, good people.

"There were emails," Cynthia says. "You showed us the emails."

A fairy-tale friendship. A sad invention.

"You knew about the orchard," Larry says. "He took you to the orchard."

"That's where you broke your arm," Cynthia says.

A web of lies, weaved bit by bit, now tangled around me. Because the truth hurt too much. Not a funny story at all. No, what really happened is: "I broke my arm at Ellison Park. By myself."

Alone and feeling alone and not able to . . .

Cynthia stands. "No, that day at the orchard, you and Connor at the orchard . . ."

She looks at me, really looks at me, and that's all it takes.

"Oh god," she says.

I watch her crumble.

Zoe: "But you told me that he . . . that you two would talk about me, and that he would . . ."

It breaks me anew and I'm already shattered.

"How could you do this?"

The torture in her. I watch the final piece of the house I love reduce to ashes.

Zoe jumps up from the table. Cynthia goes after her.

There's only Larry now. I wait for him to crush me, the way I deserve. I want it to happen. I yearn for it. I wait, but after a moment, he has only one thing to say.

"Please leave."

It's the *please* that destroys me.

I follow him out. He shuffles down the driveway and into the street. Stands there, right in the middle, circling, pacing, talking to himself, rambling. I can't hear what he's saying. Not until I get closer:

What have you done? What the fuck have you done?

I know it so well. The moment of reckoning after the worst mistake. The crossfire of regret, helplessness, hopelessness, hatred, on and on and on. A tsunami of self-torment.

He pulls at his hair, grabbing whole chunks, striking blows to his own skull.

No. No. No. No. No.

A rabid animal.

What the fuck is wrong with me?

I've asked all the same questions. Still asking them now.

I turn back to the house. He let it all out. What he'd been carrying. Everything. But he's still not free. Still has himself to deal with. Always the hardest one to face.

He lowers onto the pavement, sits down in the street, right in the middle. Eerie the way it looks. Familiar. Staged like a sacrifice.

I turn around, checking for cars. It's dark here, no streetlights. We're hidden in the shadows. I feel compelled to try.

Get up, I say.

He shakes his head, keeps shaking it. He can try to wish the pain away. Not going to make it stop. Trust me, I tried.

A distant headlight. Evan sees it, too. But doesn't move.

I try again. *Hey. Get up.*

If the pain is in you, it's in you. It follows you everywhere. Can't outrun it. Can't erase it. Can't push it away; it only comes back. The way I've been thinking, after all that's happened, maybe there's only one way to survive it. You have to let it in. Let it hurt you. And don't wait. It'll reach you eventually. Might as well be now.

I bend down, get right in his face. I try to reach him. The way someone once tried to reach me.

It's the last instinct we have. And the most difficult. Nearly impossible. But still, it's our only choice:

Own it, I say.

I wasn't able to.

You hear me? Evan? That's what you do. You get up. And you own it.

CHAPTER 26

A vision. Staring into a mix of light and night, I see a vision. It's the same vision I've had before, a story I've told, one that became real to me and everyone, and somehow still feels real now, even though it's not. I'm on the ground, again, waiting for help, needing it, alone and helpless and empty, and the person who arrives in my mind once again—him.

He's come to get me.

I blink, remembering where I am, in the middle of the street. I register the nearing headlight. It would be so easy to sit here and do nothing. To remain hidden in the dark and let the next moment take me. All the torment: over.

I'm drained of every ounce of energy, but I force myself up. The last thing I want is the Murphys to wake up to a gory accident in front of their house. Another tragedy on their hands, after all the suffering and heartache and misery I've caused. I just want them to have some semblance of calm, if not tonight, then soon. Very, very soon.

For me, there's only war inside, a raging battle with no end in sight. And fine. I know I deserve every harrowing minute of it.

I step onto the curb as the car passes. I lean back against a roadside tree. A tree. Another fucking tree. They're everywhere, these soaring reminders.

I am alone, the way I deserve to be. The way I'm meant to be. A fucking nothing. Unworthy to the core. How could I fool myself into thinking I could be deserving of anything close to happiness? To acceptance? And then fool others into thinking it, too? How disgusting and pathetic to want something so badly, so desperately, that I could be willing to do the most heinous things. I am broken. A defective piece that has no match and can never fit into the whole. I tried to pass as something more, but now they see me for what I am. What I've always been.

My phone vibrates in my pocket. It's my mom. She keeps texting me, begging me to call her.

I turn around and dig my claws into the trunk of the tree, pressing my forehead into the bark, hoping to scrape my skin raw. Unlike that day, my impulse now is to try to pull the tree down and let it topple over me. I'm done climbing. I'd only end up falling anyway.

Falling. Amazing. I'm still doing it. Telling stories. Even now, standing alone on a dark street, not a soul around, and I can't even be honest with *myself*. When will that finally happen? Because there aren't different versions of the story. There's only one version. One story. The truth.

I look up at the tree, follow its branches skyward into the starry heavens.

"The truth."

Saying it aloud—I thought I was all out of tears. The stars start to blur and swirl in wet puddles.

It's not a good story.

Own it.

I fixed up that sign. That dumb sign. WELCOME TO ELLISON STATE PARK. EST. 1927. I put so much into it. I thought he'd like it, my dad, that he'd be proud, something. I texted him a picture of what I'd done. His response? He had something he wanted to share with me. Something special. His own accomplishment. He sent a picture back. One of those ultrasounds. And a message: *Say hello to your brother.*

Everything I'd done. Everything I was. It didn't mean anything.

I saw this incredibly tall oak tree and I started climbing. I wanted to see what the world looked like from up there. I got close to the top and I gazed out in every direction. I could see over the tops of trees, past Clover Field. I could see buildings downtown. A cell phone tower. I could see all that, more than I ever saw before, so much space, but I felt the same way I did back on the ground, closed in, by everything. That's when I looked down. I realized how high up I was. I hadn't even reached the top of the tree. There was still more to go. But I had seen enough. I saw the ground below, all the way down. I looked up once more, at the whole world; it was beautiful, I knew it was, but I wasn't a part of it. I was never going to be a part of it. In that moment—it was quick—I just loosened my grip, unlocked my legs, and...

I woke up on the ground. I thought I was dead. Then I felt the pain. My arm was numb. I couldn't move. I guess I was in shock that I'd actually done it, that I'd *tried* to do it, and that I'd failed so miserably. Half relief, half disgust, and still all alone. I wanted someone to find me. To be there for me. To help me. I waited. Any second now. *Any second now.*

I waited so long. The park wasn't open yet. There was no one....

I got up and walked back to headquarters. I couldn't tell Ranger Gus what happened. What I tried to do. People like that, who do that, they don't become rangers. Everything would've been over. And then there was my mom. I couldn't face her. I didn't know how.

It won't be any easier now.

But where else am I supposed to go?

I move away from the road and the tree. I step onto the sidewalk. I start walking.

• • •

"I'm looking for my mother," I tell the woman at the front desk.

"What's the patient's name?" she asks, placing her fingers on the keyboard.

"Actually, she works here. Her name is Heidi Hansen. I'm her son."

The woman looks up.

"Can you please ask her to come down here?" I say.

She sizes me up. "Sure."

I step off to the side.

There's a chance my mom has already left the hospital to go to her night class. I could have texted or called before coming, but that would have required too much explanation and I'm all out of words. The last few I spoke to the Murphys left me with barely enough energy to make it to the hospital.

I hear my mom's panicked voice. "Where is he?"

The woman at the front desk points me out. My mom's jittery eyes rest upon finding me in one piece. Seeing her has the opposite effect on me: I finally lose it.

"Oh, honey," she says, reaching me.

She guides us outside to a courtyard and onto a bench. I try to pull myself together. Besides a janitor inserting a new bag into a trash can, we're alone out here. I watch the janitor stretch the bag over the edges of the can. He wheels his rickety cart over the concrete and back inside the hospital.

She rubs my back and encourages me to breathe.

Long minutes pass.

"Talk to me," she says.

It's not a command. It's a welcome mat. All I have to do is step to her.

"I saw the note online," she says. "The note that Connor Murphy..."

I nod.

"It's all over everyone's Facebook. 'Dear Evan Hansen,'" she recites. "Did you...you wrote it? The note?"

I feel shame, of course, but also relief. If she hadn't found out on her own about Connor's note, I'd have to be the one to tell her.

"I didn't know," she says.

And now the shame really kicks in. The last person I want her to blame is herself. There's only one of us at fault here. "No one did."

"No, honey, that's not what I mean. I mean...I didn't know that you...I didn't know you were hurting like that. That you felt so...how did I not know?"

I finally realize what she's talking about. "Because I never told you." I couldn't even tell myself. It's taken me the longest time to find my way back to the truth.

She presses her hand into mine. "You shouldn't have had to."

"I lied. About so many things. Not just Connor. Last summer, when I..."

I lose my wind.

"I just felt so alone...."

I reach for the hardest words.

"You can tell me," she says.

I shake my head. "I can't. You'll hate me."

"Oh, Evan. I won't."

"You should. If you knew what I tried to do. If you knew who I am. How broken I am."

"I already know you. I know you better than anyone else does. And I love you."

How can she know me when *I* don't even know me? What I

say, what I think, I can't decide which parts are real and which are made-up. I try, over and over, to reach myself. How is that even possible when I'm already here, walking in my own skin? Sometimes I wonder if I'm still lying under that oak tree and I've been sleeping this whole time and everything that's happened is a dream.

"I'm so sorry."

I'm not even sure what I'm apologizing for. For all the things I said and couldn't say. For all the things I did and couldn't do. For everything. For every single thing.

She absorbs my silence, seeming to understand the scope of it. "I can promise you that someday all of this will feel like a very long time ago."

A mother has to say that kind of thing. She doesn't realize: this will haunt me for the rest of my life.

"Do you remember the day your dad drove by to get his things?" she asks.

Okay, if she's talking about my dad, then I know things truly are dire.

"It was a few weeks after he moved out. 'Temporarily,' we said. Your father and I were both nervous about how you'd handle it, watching all his stuff get taken from the house. But you were so excited when you saw that big moving truck in the driveway you barely seemed to notice. We stuck you in the driver's seat and you wouldn't let us take you out. You were having a blast up there."

It's hard to imagine.

"And then, a few hours later, your father was gone, and the

truck was gone, and it finally sank in. It was just you and me, all alone in that big house. You were upset, obviously, and I understood that, of course, completely. And then, later that night, I was tucking you into bed and you asked me something."

"What?"

"You wanted to know, 'Is there another truck coming? A truck to take Mommy away?' And it crushed me. And I knew that no matter how hard I tried or how badly I wanted it, I wouldn't always be able to be there for you. I knew I'd come up short—and I did. And I do. But the answer I gave you that day is the same one I'll give you now and every day after." She looks into my eyes and lifts my chin. "Your mom is staying right here. You're stuck with me, kid."

And *she's* stuck with me: the mess I am.

Although, I guess, technically, being here with me is a choice. My father made a different choice. My mom could leave if she wanted. Maybe I forget that sometimes.

When I showed her the sign I painted at the park, she literally screamed, she was so impressed. My dumb sign. She still brags about it to people.

"Let's go somewhere," she says. "You're overdue for the ride of your life."

This strange sentence can only be a horoscope. "Don't you have a class?"

She waves her hand at the air, swatting away the ridiculous notion. There may be class tonight, but not for my mom. We stand and begin to walk.

She keeps pushing forward, putting on a brave face. I don't know how she does it.

"You hungry?" she says.

"No."

"Not even for pancakes?"

"Not even for pancakes."

I will never eat again.

"Where do you want to go?" she says. "I'll take you anywhere."

I open the door for us. "I just want to go home."

· · ·

I hover like a ghost in the passenger seat of my mom's car. I can barely feel the seat beneath me, or see the road ahead, or draw air into my lungs. But life goes on. How else can I explain getting from the hospital to my driveway?

My mom puts the car in park, but I'm not ready to go inside yet.

"I think I'll sit here for a minute," I say.

"Okay."

"Leave the keys. I'll lock up."

She looks over. I don't know what she's searching for, but I let her see whatever she needs to see. My eyes make some sort of promise.

She hands me the keys and gathers her things. I watch her walk up the path and into the house. *Our* house. We came here, many years ago, looking for a new start.

The driver's seat is empty now. It's been a long time since I tried it. I crawl into the seat and take my mom's place.

I touch the wheel, run my fingers along the smooth arc. I place my hands at ten and two, gripping tightly.

I adjust the seat for comfort. I stretch out my leg, test the pedal. I press delicately at first, then with force.

Ten years ago, I sat in another driveway, in another driver's seat. What if he'd taken me with him? Where would I be now?

A shadow moves in the master bedroom. The next room over is where I begin and end all my days. Those many nights ago, I thought I saw Connor standing on the street, looking into my window. Sometimes his presence feels so real, so close, I can't convince myself that it wasn't him that night, or on the nights after. Even though I know it can't be.

But tonight I'm the one looking up. The camera of my mind zooms in, traveling up to the second story of my house and into the bedroom I know so well. Every inch of it. What's hidden inside and under. On the wall, there's a map. It used to be marked with destinations. Places to go. Dreams. Now it's bare. A great, blank canvas.

The house is quiet. Same as it was on that day. Except my family wasn't upstairs like they are now. That day, my last day, I was here all alone.

Miguel and I hadn't spoken since the day I left his house. He had sent me a few messages right after. I never responded, and he stopped sending them.

It was the longest summer of my life. I couldn't eat. Couldn't read. Couldn't sit still. Couldn't even sleep without plenty of help. At night, I'd go into the park behind my house, get high, stare up at the stars. Searching for answers. For why I was the way I was—so broken. And so alone, again.

I couldn't shake Miguel or what we'd had. All these emotions, hurt and hate and more hurt. I would draw him in my sketch pad, that birthmark on his neck, then trash the page. I had replayed our last day together so many times. He wanted to see me. But there were parts too dark to show. Parts he wouldn't like. Parts that would send him running. If anything I was only avoiding the inevitable. He would have left me if I didn't leave first.

Then: after so many days spent alone, suddenly I'm at school. Something about being back in that space. On a whim, I decided to reach out to him. I sent a text:

First days blow. Hope you're steering clear of Mr. Nielson's morning breath.

I waited for an answer. Mrs. Coughlin caught me using my phone. Gave me shit. But next time I had a chance to check, I had a message from him: a thumbs-up emoji. *Huh?* I tried to interpret. It left me with a strange feeling. Like he almost couldn't be bothered.

Then: that day happened like it did. The thing with Evan at lunch. Then later with his letter. I felt swallowed by the swarm. Surrounded by all these people and somehow lonelier than ever. None of them saw me or knew me. The only one who ever did I'd pushed away.

I left school, feeling myself falling. Fast. But then I saw it, on my phone: that thumbs-up. Suddenly, it looked different to me. Took on a new light. Like a beacon of hope. A bridge to him. To what I'd given up. Maybe it wasn't such a shitty reply after all. It's not like I gave him much to respond to. I didn't exactly put myself out there. I never once did. Never once showed him the rawest me. Not when there was so much risk involved. And now, out of the blue, he receives a message from me, the first in months. Can't blame him for being lukewarm.

I was the one who'd created the silence in the first place. And now, I could just as quickly end it. If only...

Standing on a street corner, I sent Miguel another message. This one was agonizing to write. Even more agonizing to feel. But the words alone were the simplest I knew:

I miss you.

I laid myself bare. No room for misinterpretation. What I felt. The rawest me.

I waited. Soon, on my screen, three wiggling dots in a white thought bubble. A response forming. My nerves at attention. Anticipation. My broken soul being patched up. And then, just as suddenly, the dots left.

I waited for his message. I waited. But it never came.

All the fear I'd lived with...

Fuck 'em, he'd always say. Maybe I misunderstood him all those times before. Maybe he wasn't taking my side against the world. Maybe that was just his motto with everyone. Everyone but himself. *Fuck 'em*. Yeah. OK. Fuck him.

I cried. So much. I had no one. Nothing. I *was* nothing. I vowed to make it stop. The hurt.

The rest is a blur. . . .

I called a guy from rehab. He gave me what I needed.

I wiped Miguel from my past. Erased the photos in my phone.
(The ones I hadn't already cut him out of.) Deleted his text
messages. Removed his name from my contacts.

I entered the house. I went to my room. I locked the door.

(I couldn't own it.)

(I tried to numb myself, to deflect the pain, not realizing that
it always returns.)

(It always returns.)

(Let it in.)

Now, in this same house, I hear laughter. I can make it out
clearly, coming from above.

I follow the sound. Up our winding stairs. Down the hall.
Toward a light. An open door. My bedroom.

My mother sits on my bed. A fading smile. Spread open on her
lap is my sketch pad.

My father arrives. He steps inside the room, looks over her shoulder.

He's funny, she says. *He always had a sharp sense of humor. He used to love jokes. When he was a little boy. Do you remember?*

Of course, he says.

Why did the chicken cross the road? He had a million different answers to that one. One day he said to me, Mom, why did the duck cross the road? Because he wanted to prove he wasn't chicken.

My mother stares at the sketch pad. *I used to sneak in here, search everywhere. For a clue, something. I flipped through this book, I can't tell you how many times. But I never actually looked at what was in here. I mean, really looked. I never saw it.*

You did what you could.

It wasn't enough.

No one blames you.

But I do.

But I don't.

It's no one's fault. And it's everyone's.

(That day, in his bedroom, he stood in front of me. Maybe if I'd…)

I leave them clinging to each other. It's time to go. I take one last walk through the house. Everywhere, memories.

In the kitchen: Cynthia and her rules. No pots or pans allowed in the dishwasher. Same for serving bowls, ladles, spatulas. *It's all dishwasher safe*, I'd tell her. She only wanted certain things inside: glasses, plates, utensils. Everything else was piled on the counter. She'd stand at the sink. Hands in thick gloves. Scrubbing away. One by one. Scrubbing.

In the living room: two dots in the ceiling. We said they were nipples, Zoe and I. The joke was someone fell upstairs and imprinted their chest. Made no sense.

In the bathroom: the doorframe is two shades of white. The left side had to be replaced. I took a hammer to it. I can't remember why. (After that, my father started locking up his tools.)

In the garage: a second fridge where Larry keeps his craft beers and frozen sweets. Labeled bins on shelves. The whole place spotless. Except for that paint splash on the floor. Shaped like a creature. Larry was livid when it appeared. He tried every cleaning product. The paint creature matched a color Zoe had in her art supplies. She swore it wasn't her. Wasn't me, either, although everyone assumed it was. Still, to this day, one of those family mysteries.

In Larry's office: paperwork on the desk. Contracts. An illustration with my name on it: *The Connor Murphy Memorial Orchard*. My father's notes in the margins. I study his handwriting. He doesn't close his *g* or *d*. I do the same.

In the backyard: our pool is sealed for the winter. *Drain his energy*, one of the docs said. And so they signed me up for swim team. Zoe would time my laps. I asked her to yell at me with a German accent. She did it, too. All that training and I quit before the first meet.

I step into the grass. There's this one memory. From our old house. We had a yard much smaller than this. A neighborhood kid was over. I picked up a rock. Big one, like a potato. I pretended to throw it. My hand was wet. The rock slipped out. I followed it in the air, dreading its arc. *Crack*. Right to the face. He writhed around. I didn't help him. I was frozen. So scared. He ran home, hacking, coughing. I sank into the grass. I couldn't move.

Later, his mother tore into mine, making her believe: *There's something wrong with your son.*

I turn my attention to the sky. A clear night. Stars visible. Where are they, exactly, those stars? They're gone, but still here. Extinguished, but burning bright. A contradiction. How can that be? Maybe I'm like those stars now. I have a place in the universe, just not here anymore. How does it end up this way? I try to follow how it happens, all of it. Still, I can't begin to understand.

I make my exit.

EPILOGUE

Seated on a bench, I start a new letter:

Dear Evan Hansen,

That's how all my letters begin. There's comfort in routine.

Today is going to be a good day, and here's why.

After all this time, well over a year now, no matter how many letters I write, I always have trouble with this next part. Even on a normal day, when I've got nothing going on, it's hard enough. Today, though, is not normal. Today requires the most delicate kind of answer.

> **Because today, no matter what else, you're you. No hiding. No lying. Just you. And that's enough.**

The me I am is not the me I was. Just like the me I am is not the me I will be. Those versions of myself I can't change or predict. I'm not even sure I have much influence over the present me. But it's all I've got. I probably shouldn't fight it.

It reminds me of that saying: "The apple doesn't fall far from the tree." I guess that means we're just products of whoever made us and we don't have much control. The thing is, when people use that phrase, they ignore the most critical part: the falling. Within the logic of that saying, the apple falls every single time. *Not* falling isn't an option. So, if the apple *has* to fall, the most important question in my mind is what happens to it upon hitting the ground? Does it touch down with barely a scratch? Or does it smash on impact? Two vastly different fates. When you think about it, who cares about its proximity to the tree or what type of tree spawned it? What really makes all the difference, then, is how we land.

• • •

One day of school. That's all my mother let me skip. I showed up at the bus stop the next day, and to my surprise, I heard no whispers. No long stares on the ride to school. No weird looks in the hallway. Someone offered me a "Congratulations." I didn't understand what the person meant until later on, when I ran into Alana.

She threw her arms around me. "We did it," she said on the brink of tears.

"We?" I said.

"Yes, *we*. Come on, don't hold a grudge. I know I threatened to kick you off the Connor Project, but I had to send a strong message. Without that tough love, you never would have sent me Connor's note and the orchard wouldn't have been funded."

The fundraiser. I had totally forgotten about it.

"Alana. We have to talk."

"Definitely. We have a ton of work to do. Moving forward, you and I have to be on the same page about everything. True co-presidents, okay? Seriously, Evan, I need you. Connor needs you."

The truth wasn't out yet. I figured I should be the one to tell Alana while I still had the chance. It was only a matter of time before the Murphys would pass along my confession. "Are you free today after school?"

"Now, *that's* the passion I've been missing," Alana said. "Absolutely. I'll text you later."

As the day went on, I lost my nerve. Part of my hesitation was about Jared; he was wrapped up in this, too. Also, Alana seemed happier than I'd seen her in weeks, all because of the success of our crowdfunding campaign. We raised close to sixty grand. When the truth came out, would people want their money back? Would they demand *more* than a refund? Would they press charges against me? After all, my lies are what convinced them to donate in the first place.

That afternoon, on video chat, Alana laid out all the work we needed to do. The orchard would have to be purchased. There was talk of us becoming a nonprofit organization to achieve tax-exempt status. We'd need help from all sorts of experts: brokers, accountants, architects, farmers, contractors, lawyers. On second thought, we didn't need a lawyer. Larry had agreed to handle all our legal matters free of charge, but that was before.

"And we can't forget our backers," Alana said, reaching the end of her long list. "We've got hundreds of rewards to fulfill and mail out, not to mention the in-person prizes. Speaking of which, you promised to go out to lunch with someone. Send me your schedule when you can."

Alana had put countless hours into making our dream a reality. Now, because of me, chances were it would all amount to wasted effort. "Alana, I have something to say."

"Of course. I'm open to any suggestions you have. I know I can be a control freak, but I've learned my lesson. We're stronger *together* than we are apart."

Maybe at one point that was true, but not anymore. If the Connor Project had any chance of carrying on, it would have to be without me. I couldn't find the courage to spill my guts. But there was something else I *could* do.

"I don't want to be a part of the Connor Project anymore," I said. "I'm over it."

She waited for a punch line that never came. "What are you talking about?"

"I'm sorry."

"Wait, you're serious?"

She was so far away from me, just an image on a screen, but I still couldn't look her in the eye.

"You're quitting?" Alana said. "I just finished going over everything, and what, it's too much for you? You're just going to bail on me? What kind of person does that?"

"A terrible person."

"Yes, a terrible person. A weak and...and...passive person." I couldn't argue with any of it.

"I knew it," Alana said, her glasses fogging up. "I should

have cut you out long ago. Admit it, your heart was never in this. You used me, that's what you did. You used me and the Connor Project. You got everything you wanted out of it and you don't care who gets hurt along the way. I can't even believe you. That is so..."

"Monstrous."

I watched the realization sink in. For as long as I'd known Alana, she was always so calculated and polished. At times even robotic. But her reaction now was genuinely human.

"I think you should announce that the Connor Project is cutting ties with me," I said.

"Oh, believe me, I will," Alana said.

"Right away," I suggested. "It's really important news, don't you think?" I hated everything about what I was forcing myself to say.

"You're sick, Evan. You know that?"

Within the hour, the announcement was made. She kept it civil, claiming we were merely *parting ways*. I wanted her to throw me under the bus and drive over my body until I was good and flat, but she was probably worried that villainizing me would hurt the project. She didn't know what I knew, that I would soon be public enemy number one anyway. My hope was that the Connor Project might survive the storm because they had done the right thing and let me go when they did.

Unfortunately, the orchard campaign marked the Connor Project's apex. It never again commanded widespread attention. People moved on to the next thing: homecoming,

Mid-Coast basketball tournament, Rox's new hairstyle. Alana was too busy finishing what she started to launch any new initiatives. To her credit, she never quit. You give that girl a task, and you better believe she's not stopping until it's complete.

If you asked Alana Beck right now if she ever knew Evan Hansen, she might say that we were nothing more than acquaintances. She ignored me for the rest of senior year. Walked right past me in the halls. Left any room I entered. Pretended I didn't exist. She wasn't the only one.

• • •

I called Jared the day after facing the Murphys, and predictably, he was furious. "Are you a fucking moron? Seriously, do you know *anything*? Please tell me Zoe's dad wasn't there."

"Of course he was," I said. "Why?"

"Because you just confessed a crime to a lawyer. And not just any lawyer. The lawyer you committed the crime *against*."

I knew I was in unthinkable trouble, but I was still in the process of appreciating how serious it truly was. Jared felt that we should speak to his uncle, an attorney, and get our stories straight. Instead, I suggested I approach the Murphys directly and beg for mercy.

"Evan, please, listen to me. Do *not* do that."

It was the most earnest I'd ever heard Jared Kleinman.

"Really, Evan, when you think about it, this whole thing is on you," Jared said. "It was your idea."

That's not the way I remembered it, but I was done arguing. "Look," I said. "I'm not trying to point fingers here. I know what I did, okay? I'm not blaming you or anyone else. I never mentioned your name. They don't know anything about you."

I could hear his fingers tapping a keyboard. I imagined him in his room, hurrying to wipe any incriminating evidence from his hard drive.

"Don't talk to your uncle, please. Let's just hold off a minute and see what happens. Maybe the Murphys won't even say anything."

It was an absurd conceit, but that's all I had to go on.

"If you fuck me…" Jared said.

"I won't. I swear."

He hung up.

When the dust settled, I tried to reach out to him in a series of texts:

> Hey, man.
> I just want to say I'm sorry.
> For everything.
>
> I know I was a dick.
> I am a dick.
> I'm trying not to be.
>
> Are we good?
>
> If you ever want to hang or whatever…
>
> All right. Talk soon.

But we never did talk. Not in a real way. We said hello when it was unavoidable. He acknowledged me, but only in the most professional manner. You would have thought we were ex-lovers the way we tiptoed around each other. My biggest fear was that he had already gone to his uncle, setting the wheels of justice in motion, and I wouldn't find out about it until the authorities arrived to whisk me away.

The following December, months after graduation, I was walking to catch a bus. An SUV pulled up. It looked like Jared's truck, but it wasn't Jared behind the wheel. Or was it?

This new Jared was slimmer than the old one, and he wasn't wearing glasses. Then he spoke: "Still walking around town like a weirdo, eh?"

He told me to hop in and drove me to work. I kept glancing over at him. Maybe he finally started using that gym membership. How does a guy motivate himself? How does he take that next step and make a real change? My money was on a girlfriend.

"You look good, man," I said.

"I know we haven't seen each other in a while, but I'm still not into guys," Jared said.

"I thought you were at Michigan. What are you doing home?"

"I quit and joined the army."

"You're kidding."

"Obviously. I'm home for winter break, genius."

It took a second to remember the way we were, but after

that initial calibration, the rest of the trip was a breeze. The more time I spent with Jared in that car, and it wasn't more than ten minutes, the more I realized how much I missed my old (family) friend. He had always tried, in his crude way, to save me from myself.

And my role was to be our moral compass. I had neglected my responsibilities in a catastrophic manner, but it wasn't too late to redeem myself. I wasn't about to let Jared go without addressing the elephant in the back seat.

"I never told anyone," I said.

I wanted him to respond in kind, to clear my conscience, but he kept his eyes on the road and simply said, "Forget about it."

Sure thing. No problem.

We said goodbye and I thanked him. Jared and I weren't the soldiering types, but in a way, we'd been to battle together, and there was no one else besides the two of us who knew the true depths of what we had done.

Perhaps the cold shoulder Jared showed me through senior year was about more than simply hurt feelings (or a lawyer's directive). Maybe he just couldn't stand to be reminded of our past. Either way, the takeaway for me was the same: miracle of all miracles, Jared Kleinman had a heart.

• • •

That first week after my confession was the worst of my life. Even with the aid of medication, which I had started taking again, I could barely function. My stomach was swirling acid. My left eye twitched uncontrollably. That Friday, I went to the nurse and missed half my classes.

I once saw a documentary about a shipwrecked man who survived out on the open sea for sixteen days. After they saved him, it was a long and deliberate process to return him to good health before he could resume normal life.

I, too, had survived a wreck, albeit a self-inflicted one. In my case, though, I was thrown right back into society. I left school for the weekend with everything and returned the following week with nothing. I was confused. I literally couldn't perceive what was reality and what was fantasy. I'd hear someone talking, only to find there was no one else in the room. I attached a story to every stare I received. One time I did a homework assignment twice because I had forgotten I'd done it the first time. I began to question whether I ever fell from that oak tree and broke my arm; I'd crawl under my bed in the middle of the night just to confirm that my cast was not imagined.

Unlike the man from the documentary, I received no help or sympathy, because no one knew what I was going through. And anyway, did I deserve anyone's sympathy? My mom and Dr. Sherman were the only ones in my life who had even the slightest clue, and neither of them was aware of the full extent of what had happened. The details were known only to me, and as time went on, those details began to haunt me daily.

I had to stay off social media. People kept grilling me about why I wasn't with the Connor Project anymore, and they continued to say nasty things about the Murphys and Zoe. My grades slipped. My attendance became unpredictable. I missed school after breaking into hives and again for an unexplained fever and again for shingles (which I'm told is a disease that typically only old people get). I went from a homebody to a practical agoraphobe.

It was all because the Murphys were taking their time revealing my secret. I waited and waited, wondering how and when it would happen. I waited: for my name to be announced over the loudspeaker; to be confronted by another student; to receive a letter in the mail informing me that I was being sued; for an email from a stranger; for the police to arrive at my house. Every sound made me flinch: ringing phone, school bell, door knock, car horn, voices.

I waited to be punished like I knew I deserved. At times, I'd bury my head in my hands and plead for it to be over already. It was the same feeling I'd had when I was waiting to see what Connor would do with my letter, except this was infinitely worse. The stakes were so much greater.

I wanted so badly to reach out to Cynthia and Larry. I thought about leaving a letter in their mailbox, letting them know how I felt about them, how I appreciated all they had done for me, and how sorry I was. I wanted them to know how much I missed them. But I decided not to. When it comes to the Murphys, what I want doesn't matter.

By Thanksgiving, the truth still wasn't out. My mom and I drove upstate to spend the holiday with her parents and her sister's family. When my grandmother opened the door, she was wearing a Connor Project T-shirt. She had just received it in the mail as a reward for her donation to our campaign. Later, while saying grace, my grandfather singled me out: "I'm thankful to have a grandson who understands humility and service, and who gives me hope for humanity's future." I pictured the Murphys seated around their own dinner table, trying to summon the strength to be thankful after all they had lost. I didn't eat a thing.

On the ride home, I made up my mind: I would give myself up. It was probably what the Murphys had been waiting for all along, for me to do the right thing and confess on my own.

But when we got home, my mom opened the mail and I caught a glimpse of a small card left out on the table. Inside, it read: *Thank you for the flowers and your letter. Your words meant a lot. Happy Thanksgiving, Cynthia.*

"What is this?" I asked.

My mom shrugged, and not because she was clueless. "I didn't like how things left off with us, and knowing all she's been through, I thought it would be nice to reach out."

"Mom, what exactly did you say to her?"

"Nothing. I just said hello, I'm thinking about you, thanks for everything, and..."

"And *what*?"

"Honey, come on, I know you've made some mistakes, but you're not a bad person."

"You have no idea how many mistakes I've made."

"Of course I don't. No parent knows what their kid is really up to. Ask Cynthia. None of us are saints. We're all just doing the best we can."

My mom's words bounced around my head all night. I took Cynthia's thank-you note up to my bedroom and read it several more times. Maybe Mrs. Murphy didn't *want* the truth to be known. Maybe those fake emails were just as shameful to her as they were to me.

As the calendar year ended, I began to wonder if my secret was destined to remain a secret. Fall became winter, and the inferno of my nerves reduced to a smolder. I wasn't any less worried about the future. I just adapted to a new kind of normal. There wasn't a day that went by when I didn't think about the hurt I'd inflicted. I didn't deserve to be able to forget. Even if I had deemed myself worthy, it still wouldn't have been possible. There were too many daily reminders. One, in particular.

• • •

When it came to Zoe, my goal, at first, was to become invisible. I tried to remove myself from existence so she wouldn't have to see me, and therefore would never feel any added pain or discomfort because of me. I avoided eye contact, took roundabout hallway routes, kept my head low and my body small. It was the opposite of what my heart wanted.

My heart wanted to go to her, to talk to her. As time passed, I slowly came out of hiding, permitting myself to be seen and to see her. I waited for a sign, some hint that she wanted me to come to her, the subtlest invitation, but I never received one, and so I kept my distance.

Even when Zoe wasn't actually present, I'd see her. When a blue car passed that looked like her Volvo. When I heard certain songs. When I walked by my baby photo in our hallway. When I saw a worn-out pair of Converse. When I caught an interview with the famous actress who shares her name.

That was one of the hardest parts about my new life. I wasn't sure who knew what and I could never ask. It was too risky. When my peers looked at me, did they see a liar and a phony? Or did they see a typical high school rise-and-fall story? Or did they not see me at all? Was I back to being *meh*? I felt more out of the loop than when I started the school year. And I felt more alone than I'd ever been in my life. Halloween came and went, and instead of dressing up with Zoe, I was home by myself (as myself), like I'd been every Halloween since I was a kid. It was much easier to be a loner when I was naive, when I didn't understand what it meant to belong, to love and be loved. Now I knew too much.

I could only watch Zoe from the sidelines. I'd catch her laughing with Bee at lunch. I'd see her texting with a smile on her face. I'd pass by a flyer for an upcoming jazz concert, knowing I couldn't attend.

One morning, in February, as if by destiny, we passed each other in an otherwise empty hall. We both looked up at the same moment, meeting eyes, and instead of turning away in disgust, she smiled. I hadn't received that smile in so long and it flattened me but also lifted me. I allowed myself to read into it and I ended up buying her a gift for Valentine's Day. A journal. I wanted to hand it to her in person, but fearing rejection, I mailed it. There was a message written inside: *May you always have the courage to tell your truth.* I never heard back from her.

Whether she used the journal or not, I'm pretty sure she kept writing songs. In the spring, I found myself near Capitol Café and perused the upcoming show calendar in the window. I saw the weekly listing for open mic night. Then, in a different box, I saw the name *Zoe Murphy*, with no other performer listed. She had earned her own night at the venue. I marked down the date, but never went.

$$\bullet \; \bullet \; \bullet$$

The night I confessed to the Murphys, when I was sitting all alone in my mother's car in the driveway, I never actually drove anywhere. The following spring, after I'd turned eighteen, I was finally able to get behind the wheel and move.

Credit to Dr. Sherman. He encouraged me to set new goals for myself, and driving was at the top of my list. It took about six months, but I finally experienced what it feels like for a senior to drive himself to school, and I did it just before graduating. At our ceremony, before handing out our diplomas, Principal Howard mentioned Connor. I didn't see the Murphys in the crowd. Or Zoe. But I was there and I heard his name clearly.

At home that day, I reached underneath my bed and

removed my cast. Connor's name was severed down the middle, but the cast was still in one piece on the other side. I wrapped it around my arm, and briefly, the two halves of the cast appeared as one, the six letters reconnected, **CONNOR** restored. When I removed the cast, it was as if I could still see his name on my skin. I realized then: I can never wash him away.

I found an old yearbook from eighth grade. Everyone had been given their own page to decorate. Most people made collages of family photos, or drew the logos of their favorite sports teams, or wrote out inspirational quotes they'd found through Google searches. Connor had listed his ten favorite books. I decided to try to read all of them.

I went back and studied every post he ever made online. Every now and then, I'd make an anonymous donation to the Connor Project for whatever amount I could manage.

Then, one day, I stumbled into a small fundraising event in a supermarket parking lot. As soon as I heard Alana's voice in the mix and realized where I was, I turned right around with my mother's shopping list. But before I could get away, someone called out my name.

I looked back, expecting to find a classmate from school, but the kid in front of me was a complete stranger.

"Can we talk a minute?" he said.

He started in the direction of my car. I didn't have much choice but to follow.

"I was hoping you'd be here," he said, smiling.

I had avoided public events for exactly this reason. I didn't want to be the Evan Hansen that "the world" thought they knew. I didn't want to have to lie anymore.

"It's funny," the kid said, gazing ahead. "At first, I was actually happy to hear that Connor had made a new friend."

My blood froze. I stopped walking.

"The more I looked into it, the way people were describing him, I knew something wasn't right."

"I'm sorry, but who..."

"Relax," he said, still with that easy smile. "I'm not going to say anything. I *was* going to...I really wanted to, but..." He paused and turned toward the crowd. "I mean, look at this. He's finally getting the attention he deserved."

I took a closer look at him. He had bright, arresting eyes against a dark complexion. Hair that fell in a sort of effortlessness mine has never known. A smile that I imagined could please both a girlfriend and her parents, too. "So, you and Connor were...?"

"Friends," he said.

He told me how their friendship started, and then faded, and then abruptly ended. "That afternoon, after school, he texted me. I was trying to respond, but I was at work, and I didn't want to just...I called him later that night, and it went straight to voice mail. It was a few days before I found out what he did."

He grew quiet, his head down. "If I knew he was...I just... I didn't know." He struggled to put the words together. "I keep thinking, if I'd been able to talk to him..."

A long silence followed, and in that silence I finally understood the reason he came to speak to me that day. Not to call *me* out, but rather himself. I knew something about the kind of guilt he must've been carrying around. And the fear. Behind his smile was a heavy burden.

But of all the things he told me that day, one thing stands out: "Connor, he was just...I've never met someone like that. That innocent. That pure. Sometimes I think maybe he was too pure...for all this."

The Connor he described was nothing like the one I'd known or heard about. I felt this renewed sense of regret. But at the same time, at least I was finally getting a chance to learn. I spent the next few months trying to figure out what to do with the new knowledge I'd gained.

• • •

The summer after graduation, I wanted to return to my job at Ellison Park, but the place held too many distressing memories and it was too close to the Murphys' home. My WELCOME sign was still there at the entrance. Driving past the sign one morning, I got an idea. I started researching more about the history of the park. I turned my notes into an essay—about John Hewitt and his family, and about the sacrifices made by those who come before us—and submitted it to a few scholarship contests.

The essay didn't win, but after that, I started taking the essay writing more seriously, and over the course of the next year, I submitted to nearly every contest my mother collected. I only managed to win one award for a grand total of $1,500 for tuition, but I still counted it as a victory. Really, I just wanted to write. I *needed* to write. I think it's what Dr. Sherman was hoping for me all along. I guess I had to take the long way to get there.

And so, here I am now, on a bench, writing. These letters have finally become a proper outlet for me, but only when I'm honest, and that's still hard. Even after all this practice. It's been about twenty months since my confession. Sometimes it feels like twenty minutes.

Maybe someday everything will feel like a distant memory. Maybe I'll find a way to carry around the past without it weighing me down. Maybe, one day, I can look in the mirror and see something less ugly.

I pocket my phone and soak up the majestic view. Before me, a green field stretches out for ages. Wooden stakes rise from the grass in orderly rows. Tied to each stake is a small, spindly tree. It's an orchard. *The* orchard.

I never doubted that Alana would make it happen. Still, it's shocking to see. The Connor Murphy Memorial Orchard has been in existence for a year now, but this is the first time I've visited. I guess I was waiting for an invitation.

In a few more years—anywhere from two to ten, depending on the tree type—these saplings will reach maturity and bear fruit. Gala and Cortland and Honeycrisp. McIntosh and Golden Delicious. Something new, maybe. But the trees are still babies. Just starting life. They have a long way to go.

An engine disrupts the calm. Over in the lot, a car comes to rest alongside my mother's. The driver emerges. I rub my moistening palms uselessly against my jeans. Zoe starts up the path, the size of her growing.

Sometimes you keep wishing for something to happen, and then, after so many times not getting the thing you wished for, you stop wishing, and that's when it suddenly happens.

I stand up to greet her, my legs shaky. "Hey."

A smile. "Hey."

Zoe belongs in an apple orchard. Nature understands that it's only serving as background when she's around. The wind lifts up her auburn hair. The sun directs dramatic lighting. Where are the cameras? Where is Vivian Maier when you need her?

I wait for Zoe to sit down, but she's more comfortable standing. It's been so long I don't know where to start. "How are you?"

"Good," Zoe says. "Pretty good."

A new old pair of Converse. A jean jacket that I've never seen her wear. I wonder if the girl underneath is the same. "You graduate soon, right?"

"Yeah. In two weeks."

She had a whole school year that I never witnessed. In a way, it was easier not having to see what I was missing. It's hard to see it now. "How's being a senior?"

"Busy," Zoe says.

I nod like I know what she's talking about. Busy how? Busy preparing for college? Or busy socializing with, say, a boyfriend? Or both? It's not my business, I know. But seeing her in the flesh awakens something that's been sleeping.

"How's being a freshman?" Zoe asks.

Anytime I run into someone from high school, I have to explain why I'm still hanging around town. "Actually, I decided to take a year off."

"Oh," Zoe says with the same half surprise, half pity everyone shows.

"I just figured I'd get a job and try to save some money. I've been taking classes at the community college, so I'll have some credits to transfer in the fall."

"That's smart."

Also necessary. In the state I was in, I never would have survived going away to college. This time I took Dr. Sherman's advice and got a job where I'd be forced to interact with people. "In the meantime, though, I can get you a friends and family discount at Pottery Barn. If you're looking for overpriced home decor."

"You know, not at the moment."

"Okay, well, if you change your mind, I'm only working there for a few more months, so the window of opportunity is closing fast."

A silent laugh and then she turns to the open field and gathers her hair so it all falls over one shoulder.

"I always imagine you and Connor here," Zoe says. "Even though, obviously..."

After some digging, we've finally made it to the core. It's unbearable to go this deep, but also necessary. "This is my first time. I mean, I've probably driven by it a thousand times. I think about stopping and getting out of the car, but, I don't know, I feel like I don't deserve to."

We both stare off into the distance.

"It's nice," I say. "Peaceful."

"My parents, they're here all the time. We do picnics, like, every weekend. It's helped them. A lot, actually. Having this."

The relief I feel, that they're doing okay, it tickles the corners of my eyes. They spared me, gave me a fighting chance. I still have a hard time believing it. "Your parents. They could have told everyone. What I did."

Zoe breathes in the country air. "Everybody needed it for something."

"That doesn't mean it was okay."

"Evan," she says, forcing me to look at her. "It saved them."

I look down. A stone by my sneaker is loose, ready to be kicked. Some days, when my self-hatred overwhelms everything, I regret that the truth never came out.

"How's your mom? Your whole family?" Zoe says, sensing immediately that *family* doesn't quite sound right, but not having a better word for it.

"She's good. She took some time off, too, so it's taken her a little longer to get her degree. But she's almost there. And my dad, well, he's got the baby now."

"You're a big brother."

Technically, yes, but I haven't gotten around to acting the part. It's on my list, though. Most of my attention, lately, has been paid to a different brother. I used to think the Murphys let me go free. I'm sure it wasn't their intention, but they actually did the opposite. They left me with a burden that I carry everywhere. A burden that has become a responsibility. I'm only now learning how to fulfill it.

"I have something for you," I say.

Her jean jacket tightens around her. I have no idea if she received the journal I sent her, but this is a different sort of gift.

She waits with apprehension as I take out my phone. I find what I need and show her my screen. Her eyes widen and she takes the phone.

"I've seen this photo, but who is *this*?" she asks.

It's the same photo of Connor that's been passed around a thousand times. Except this is the uncropped version, showing not just Connor, but also . . .

"Miguel," I say. "He was Connor's friend."

She looks up, searching my eyes. "Really?"

I nod.

When Miguel showed me the unedited photo that day outside the supermarket, I stared at it in the same dumbfounded way Zoe is staring at it now. And then Miguel showed me more photos. And then he showed me messages that Connor had sent him. Not imaginary, made-up messages, but words that Connor had actually written. I felt sickened and healed all at once. Sickened because I was a pretender meeting the real thing. Healed because there was suddenly no need to pretend anymore. Connor *did* have a friend.

"They look so happy together," she says.

"They do." I reach into my pocket and hand her a folded piece of paper. "I'll send you the photo. And this is Miguel's number. In case you want to ask him anything."

I struggled with this decision for a long time. Why would I willingly draw attention to the very thing I've been struggling to leave behind? Because, well, when I look at that photo of Connor and I see him smiling, I'm left with this feeling that maybe, for a while there, despite what happened afterward, Connor experienced some brief happiness. I thought Zoe and her parents would want to know that. And so, for once, I decided to be brave.

Zoe stands still, biting her lip. "Thank you," she says quietly, slipping the paper into her pocket. She looks down. "It's been a hard year."

"I know." I want to commiserate, but I have no right to. "I've been wanting to call you for a long time. I didn't really know what I would say, but then I just...I decided to call anyway."

"I'm happy you did."

My pills correct the chemicals, but Zoe is medicine for the soul. Her words mend my mangled world. "I wish we could have met now. Today. For the first time."

Her eyes, bluer than the sky. "Me too."

Maybe we *are* meeting for the first time. This is the truest me I can be. I'm just sorry I got here so late.

"I should probably go," Zoe says.

The letdown. "Of course."

"It's just, exams are this week."

"No, totally."

She smiles and turns to go. I still have so many questions. I choose one.

"Can I ask you?" I say. "Why did you want to meet here?"

She pauses and gazes out over the land, absorbing it all. "I wanted to be sure you saw this."

I stare out, making sure I really see it, the immensity. It's all there: the past, present, future.

As Zoe drives off, I fight the emptiness with words. I finish my letter.

> Maybe, someday, some other kid is going to be standing here, staring out at the trees, feeling alone, wondering if maybe the world might look different from all the way up there. Better. Maybe he'll start climbing, one branch at a time, and he'll keep going, even when it seems like he can't find another foothold. Even when it feels hopeless. Like everything is telling him to let go. Maybe this time he won't let go. This time he'll hold on. He'll keep going.

I pocket my phone and return to the view. To sit back and watch is no longer possible. It never was, it turned out.

I step onto the pristine grass. It feels like an invasion, but a voice inside reminds me to loosen up. I don't pretend that I knew him before, but he's always with me now.

We're weaving in between trees, careful not to disturb, on a mission. We mean no trouble. There are so many of us, the lonely souls. All of us who helped build this. Those who will watch it grow. Those we've lost. We march on together. Climbing, falling, soaring. Trying to get closer to the center of everything. Closer to ourselves. Closer to each other. Closer to something true.

A NOTE FROM THE AUTHORS

According to the American Foundation for Suicide Prevention, a staggering 123 suicides occur every day on average in the United States. This story is a work of fiction, but the reality is that anyone anywhere can feel as if they have nobody to reach out to. No one should ever feel they have to suffer in silence. We need to keep talking about mental health and continue to reach out to those who might be suffering. If you or a loved one are in need of help, please know: you are not alone.

The following organizations are good resources:

Child Mind Institute

https://childmind.org

Dedicated to transforming the lives of children struggling with mental health disorders and learning disorders.

Crisis Text Line

https://www.crisistextline.org

Crisis Text Line is free, 24/7 support for those in crisis. Text 741741 from anywhere in the US to text with a trained Crisis Counselor.

The Trevor Project

https://www.thetrevorproject.org

The leading national organization providing crisis intervention and suicide prevention services to LGBTQ youth.

ACKNOWLEDGMENTS

From Val

Thank you to "the guys"—Steven, Benj, and Justin—for your trust, encouragement, wit, and humor; I admire your dedication to this story, and I'm a better writer for how hard you pushed me to honor it. My editor, Farrin Jacobs, granted me this opportunity and kept me going with praise, prowess, pity, and pasta; I've got nothing but love and respect for how you made sure this many-tentacled beast didn't choke all of us. My agent, Jeff Kleinman, knocked sense into me at the outset. As did Matt Schuman. I received valuable personal and technical information from Christina Gagliardo, Sanford Kinney, Dan Coughlin, Justin and Megan Kiczek, my nieces and nephews (especially Samantha Baker and Gavin Caterina), and Mike Emmich. To those battling anxiety and depression—hang in there. To Harper and Lennon—I hang in there for you. To Jill—now that I'm finished, want to hang out?

From Steven, Benj, and Justin

We would like to thank:

Lynn Ahrens, David Berlin, Laura Bonner, John Buzzetti, Jordan Carroll, Drew Cohen, Stephen Flaherty, Freddie Gershon, Michael Greif, Cait Hoyt, Joe Machota, Erin Malone, Jeff Marx, Whitney May, Stacey Mindich, Asher Paul, Marc Platt, Adam Siegel, Matt Steinberg, Jack Viertel, and the original Broadway cast of *Dear Evan Hansen*. We owe a special debt of gratitude to Farrin Jacobs for shepherding this book from the very beginning, and to Val Emmich for his artistry, his craft, and the incredible care he took of these characters and this story. Finally, we would like to thank the fans of the musical—your words, your music, and the stories you have shared with us are what inspired the creation of this book in the first place.

From all of us

We'd all like to thank the team at Hachette Book Group/ Little, Brown Books for Young Readers for working hard every step of the way to help us get this story into the hands of readers, including but not limited to the following people: David Caplan, Jackie Engel, Shawn Foster, Jen Graham, Stef Hoffman, Sasha Illingworth, Virginia Lawther, Michael Pietsch, Kristina Pisciotta, Emilie Polster, Anna Prendella, Jessica Shoffel, Angela Taldone, and Megan Tingley.

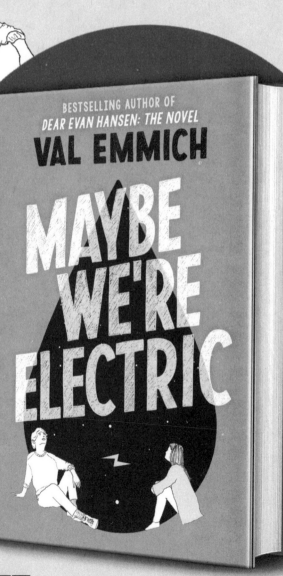